THE LETTER

To

Marcia

Best wishes.

Sylvia Atkinson

25-07-2012

SYLVIA ATKINSON

authorHOUSE®

AuthorHouse™
1663 Liberty Drive
Bloomington, IN 47403
www.authorhouse.com
Phone: 1-800-839-8640

Published by AuthorHouse   02/08/2012

ISBN: 978-1-4678-8082-4 (sc)

Library of Congress Control Number: 2011963073

This book is printed on acid-free paper.

Acknowledgements

Credit goes to Hilary Shields for introducing me to Tickhill Writers, and for painstakingly editing countless drafts of *The Letter*. I will forever remember her unstinting help and encouragement.

Nigel Wagstaff of Flight Line Graphics, who provided expert technical advice throughout, designed the map of India and saved the first draft when the computer and research materials were destroyed by floods.

I am honoured that Peter Archer, the war artist, has given permission for an extract from his painting, *Go To It*, to be incorporated into the book's cover. I am delighted that his son, Ben Archer, designed it.

Peter Archer's original work, depicting my father Corporal Thomas Waters M.M. laying the land line across Pegasus Bridge on D-Day 1944, hangs in the officers' mess of the Royal Corps of Signals regiment at Blandford Forum, Dorset.

Many thanks go to the Royal Corps of Signals Museum at Blandford Forum Dorset for housing my father's medals, archive and an exhibition of his action on Pegasus Bridge.

Also to Colonel Robin Pickering (retired), for the research on Thomas Waters M.M.

I owe the deepest thanks to my wonderful parents whose dignified courage has inspired my life. Also to my Indian family and everyone at home who have helped me to write this book, especially my husband. Without his love and unwavering support I would have given up long ago. It is to them that this book is dedicated.

Author's Note

The Letter is based on the fictionalized lives of my parents, who overcame disadvantage, race, war and disability. The historical events in India, Burma, China and France during World War Two are intended to be accurate. It is worth stressing that I have changed some names, imagined characters, compressed action and invented places in line with my story.

MAP

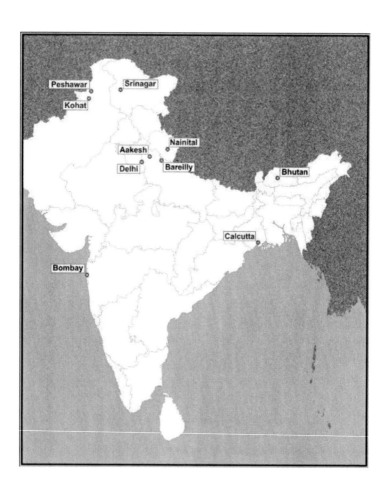

THE FAMILIES

The Scots

Margaret Riley (Maggie/ Charuni)

Mr and Mrs Riley	Margaret's parents
Nan	Margaret's eldest sister
Jean	Margaret's favourite sister
Mary	Margaret's youngest sister
Con	Margaret's brother
John (Johnny)	Margaret's brother
Willie	Mary's husband
David (Davey)	Nan's husband
Sheila	Nan's daughter

The Indians

Ben Atrey (Vidyaaranya)	Margaret's first husband
Pavia	Margaret and Ben's daughter
Saurabh	Margaret and Ben's eldest son
Rajeev	Margaret and Ben's youngest son
Dadi	Ben's mother
Vartika	Ben's eldest sister
Suleka	Ben's youngest sister
Hiten	Vartika's husband
Anil	Pavia's son
Muni	Margaret's maid

The English

Tommy Waters	Margaret's second husband
Elizabeth (Lizzie)	Tommy and Margaret's daughter
James	Elizabeth's husband
Albert Waters	Tommy's father
Shirley Waters	Tommy's stepmother, Albert's wife
Alice	Tommy's eldest sister
Florrie	Tommy's youngest sister
Matt	Florrie's husband

CHAPTER 1

Yorkshire 1985

Margaret's small fireside table was covered with the usual clutter of books, writing materials and the buff envelopes of bills, but the blue airmail letter tucked in among them threatened to cause havoc. A long forgotten nightmare returned disturbing her sound sleep. She was in an unfamiliar house. Corridors lengthened, changing shape while she frantically raced down them; open doors of countless rooms slammed in her face. Suddenly she was spinning, falling headlong down a black tunnel periodically lit by crashing lightning. Illuminated figures of children beckoned, urging her to come to them. She reached this way and that, frenziedly trying to catch them but they vanished whenever she drew near. Last night was the worst. The three elusive sprites danced closer and closer . . . She saw their eyeless faces . . .

Jolted awake, she got up and made a cup of tea. If only she had someone to talk to. For years her daughter Elizabeth had tried to persuade her to have a telephone installed so they could be in touch every day, especially in an emergency, but this wasn't an emergency. Not like the time she fell and was found by Peggy, a neighbour. The dizzy turn resulted in a trip to hospital and three stitches where Margaret's head hit the kitchen table. A subsequent appointment was arranged. She went with Elizabeth. The consultant said the fall was caused by the vagaries of old age, possibly a minor stroke, and recommended wearing a surgical collar, taking aspirin daily and regular check ups. Elizabeth insisted she wore the contraption. Margaret felt trussed up like a dead chicken.

The phone was different. Elizabeth and her husband James offered to pay for everything including future bills. Some of Margaret's friends chatted for hours but it always seemed so impersonal. A convenient phone call was no substitute for a sit down visit, and besides she didn't want to be instantly accessible. She liked things the way they were but was hurt when Elizabeth said she was unreasonable. Anyway it wouldn't be any use. How could she talk to anyone about the letter . . . especially on the phone? Yet Elizabeth would have to know . . . What would she think?

If Margaret didn't get a move on she'd be late for mass, but she was in such a muddle scrabbling through drawers and bags to find her purse. Thoroughly cross, she pushed a few coins in the Offertory envelope, threw a shovel of slack on the fire, checked she'd locked the front door three times, pulled the handle upwards on the back door to catch the lock and turned the key.

In the Sunday spring sunshine bold daffodils triumphed beneath the straggling privet hedge bordering the untidy lawn. The flash of yellow lifted her mood while she waited on the pavement for the customary late church bus to lumber round the corner. The patient driver banished the Sunday scrubbed boys from her reserved front seat, sending them down the bus. It was the same every Sunday but this one was potentially like no other and she wanted to get it over.

The smell of burning candles, heady incense, hymn singing children and the soft Irish brogue of the priest saying mass went some way to restoring Margaret's equilibrium. Reluctant to leave the church, she knelt and lit an extra candle in the side chapel by the serene flower-ringed statue of the Blessed Virgin. Although she went to mass on the bus one of the family always collected her. She could picture James, her son-in-law, reading his paper in the car. He wouldn't come in, said it wasn't his thing. Her daughter Elizabeth came at Christmas but the three of them spent most Sundays together.

James shrugged off Margaret's nod of an apology for keeping him waiting, resigned to her greeting people for as long as it took. He noticed she looked tired, her quick smile a little forced. He'd mention it to Lizzie.

At lunch the food stuck in Margaret's throat. She drank copious glasses of water to swill it down. Elizabeth asked if she was all right. "It's nothing. I slept badly. I think it's the start of a cold." James advised putting more whiskey in her cocoa, expecting a witty reply, but she hardly dared look at him across the table. She wanted to shout, "Stop! I've something important to say," but the words dried in her mouth.

She usually dozed in the lounge to the comforting scraping of plates, rattle of glasses and muffled voices of her daughter and son-in-law drifting in from the kitchen. Today she couldn't settle. Her stiff fingers fumbled with the Velcro fastening of the blasted surgical collar. Released, she threw the offending article on the floor and sank back in the cushioned armchair snapping her eyes shut. It was no good. She simply couldn't carry on like this. Fidgeting with the corner of her pretty blue cardigan she opened her eyes at the crunching of feet on the gravel drive. Through the tall window she caught sight of James going out, being pulled along by Rory, his boisterous setter. This was the chance to end weeks of indecision. She called, "Come, Elizabeth, take the weight off your feet for a few minutes."

Elizabeth carried on methodically filling the dishwasher. She thought it remarkable that her mother's cultured Edinburgh accent was as strong as ever, even though she hadn't lived there for more than fifty years. The call came again, this time louder, and more insistent. A rare occurrence, but the tone was a command, with possibly a reprimand at the end of it. Elizabeth dried her hands muttering, "I'm not a child . . . It had better be important."

Margaret's frail figure housed an iron will, but tense and uncertain where to begin, she imperiously indicated the matching sofas. Elizabeth obediently sat on the edge of the nearest, "Mum, you know I always finish in the kitchen before I sit down."

"Elizabeth, some things are more important than a tidy kitchen! Besides I want to talk to you without James."

"Without James . . . ?"

Allowing no further opportunity to query the unusual request Margaret continued, "I want you to know that I was married before . . . I mean before I met your father."

Relieved that the intensity in her mother's blue eyes was not the forerunner of bad news, Elizabeth said lightly, "Oh is that all? I know you were."

Astonished, Margaret exclaimed, "Who told you?"

"You did . . . years ago when I was nine."

One dark winter afternoon, leaving her mother reading and shivering by the fire, Elizabeth had crept upstairs and sneakily opened the fitted cupboard in the spare bedroom. It was crammed with feather pillows, sheets, blankets, bed spreads, towels, and other just-in-case household commodities. There were at least two of everything, nothing was thrown away. She was foraging through when she came across some unfamiliar khaki cloth and cardboard suitcases.

Getting them out quietly without something falling and alerting her mother had not been easy. She surreptitiously dragged them to the window to read the remnants of their glued and tattered labels. The spidery handwriting held snippets of names and destinations, a world of grown up secrets waiting to be solved.

When Elizabeth opened the cases there was a strange smell, not unpleasant but different, rich and earthy, evocative of strawberries and warm summers spent out of doors. She warmed her hands by running them over the stored deep velvet, green, gold and blue silk. Some of the fabric was embroidered with gold dragons, blue and pink birds. She draped this over the big double bed to catch the fleeting half-light but her favourite treasure was a creamy silk kimono. The front was plain but the back was covered with red chrysanthemums, intertwined with delicate green leaves, flowing down to the hem, contrasting with the dull-brown linoleum floor. Queen of the Orient, she preened in front of the three mirrored dressing table.

" . . . It was the day you caught me emptying the old suitcases. I thought you'd be cross because I was dressed in your kimono trying to fathom out the engraving on some discoloured bracelet."

"I do remember. It was my identity bracelet?"

"Yes, you said it was from the war. It read *Margaret Riley Atrey.* I knew grandpa's name was Riley but I didn't recognise the other name so I asked you. You told me Atrey was the name of your first husband. The only thing that bothered me was who my father was. You said that he was the man I'd always known. I was so relieved because for ages I'd been thinking I was adopted."

"You were a funny little thing, always wanting to know more than was good for you. My first husband was Indian so he couldn't have been your father." Margaret's chest tightened. She hadn't meant it to come out like that. She glanced fearfully at her daughter, " . . . you don't seem surprised?"

"That you were married to an Indian? India has been part of my life for as long as I can remember. You told me the kind of things you can only know if you've lived among the people. Other children's mothers got flu. You got malaria. Me and dad piled eiderdowns and blankets on top of you and gave you lots of drinks out of a special cup with a spout. When I kissed you goodnight you were all clammy. I asked dad if you'd die but he said you'd get better. So that made it okay. What really scared me were the Indian hawkers. You know the ones with legs like matchsticks who came to the back door selling cardigans out of suitcases. They spoke loudly waving their arms and nodding. You nodded back, speaking louder in some funny language. I hid under the kitchen table 'til they'd gone."

"Oh Elizabeth, we were only talking."

"But Mum you'd told me stories about brave warriors who didn't cut their hair and wore it rolled up under a turban. They carried curved daggers which, once drawn, couldn't be sheathed unless they spilt blood. I was convinced I'd be murdered and had awful dreams about being kidnapped and squashed in one of their suitcases." Elizabeth melodramatically embellished her tale, "Trapped, blinded by the colour of sweaters and cardigans, suffocated by the smell of wool . . ."

"My word Elizabeth, I had no idea! You always had a vivid imagination. I can't believe all that went on in your head."

"I liked it really, so no, I'm not surprised."

Margaret was tempted to leave it there, secure in Elizabeth's childhood memories, but she couldn't deny the past that roared in her ears. "Do you remember the photograph album in the green cover that I kept in the top of my wardrobe?"

"You mean the India album. The pages were separated with tissue paper and there were pictures of your friends, menus and birthday cards decorated with lace and tiny ribbons."

"Yes and a small black and white photograph of a little girl in the snow."

"Mmm . . . a man was standing near holding the reins of two black horses. I didn't know it snowed in India until I saw that."

"You remember so much."

"Of course I do. The girl was your friend's daughter and . . ."

"She was mine . . . Is mine . . . Her name is Pavia." Margaret repeated the name, savouring the shape of the tumbling letters, fighting back the tears. "I also had two sons, Saurabh and Rajeev."

Elizabeth took hold of her mother's hands, "Why are you telling me this now?"

Margaret started to explain, "Because I've had a letter . . ."

"A letter . . . ?"

Gripping her daughter's hands like lifelines Margaret said, "Yes, from India and . . ."

The dog barked. James was coming up the drive. "Elizabeth, please don't say anything about it to James now. It's getting late. Tell him in your own way when he comes back from taking me home."

CHAPTER 2

Elizabeth cuddled into James's back. In the busy week sometimes the only chance they had to talk to each other was in bed. Snuggling at weekends led to other things. James said sleepily, "You do know it's Sunday?"

Elizabeth nuzzled his ear. "Did you know mum was married before she met my dad?"

"God Lizzie you picked a fine time to tell me."

"To tell you the truth I sort of forgot about it." She divulged her mother's secret. Instantly wide awake James said, "Didn't you suspect there were children?"

"No I didn't give it a thought."

"How did they contact her?"

"Through a letter . . ."

"And . . ."

"I don't know the details."

"Didn't you ask?"

"You came back, and Mum didn't want to talk about it in front of you."

"Why not?"

"I think she was frightened."

"Frightened of me! I've always been there for her." Lizzie leant towards him. "It's no use kissing your way out of it."

"I'm just saying sorry, I didn't put it very well. I meant she was afraid you'd disapprove."

James lay back and stretched his arms over his head, "I thought she wasn't herself today, too quiet by far."

"It's the quickest Sunday lunch we've had without you two arguing. Politics and religion, you'll not change her views."

"Scottie and I don't argue. We discuss." Early in his marriage to Elizabeth, mellowed with whiskey, James tried to get Margaret to decide what he should call her. 'Mother-in-law' was too formal. He wanted something more affectionate. She thought about it and said he could call her Scottie. It was a nickname from when she was young. James thought it must have been at a time when she was happy because she had a far away look when she suggested it.

* * * * *

Margaret spent the week worrying. She thought she knew James but she'd been the victim of prejudice from the most unlikely quarters. The following Sunday she was relieved to see his silver Mercedes outside church. She was expecting some reference to last week's conversation but he was his good-natured self. Maybe he didn't know? What if she had to tell him?

The journey took an age: every traffic light on red; a police car on the straight stretch where there was an accident. James put his foot down on the motorway but lunch was already on the table when they arrived. Elizabeth filled any gaps in the conversation, offering to drive her mother home so James could have an extra glass of wine. Margaret was becoming more agitated by the minute. Knife and fork in hand James said, "Well you're a dark horse, Scottie. There's certainly more to you than meets the eye."

Elizabeth glared at her husband. Trust him. She thought they'd agreed to wait until her mother brought the subject up. Margaret was glad of the opening. She had a speech prepared, the bones of which she had rehearsed again and again during the sleepless nights of the previous week.

"James, I assume from that remark you are referring to my previous marriage . . ."

"But," James interrupted, "how on earth did they find you after all these years?"

"One of my grandchildren traced me. His name is Anil. He is the youngest son of Pavia, Elizabeth's Indian sister."

James wasn't interested in who was related to whom. He wanted to know the big picture.

Margaret began easily enough, "My first husband, Ben, was staying with our daughter Pavia at her home in Lucknow. During his visit Anil asked his grandfather questions about the family. Ben revealed that I had not died as the children believed but had been forced to return to Scotland. He produced a letter that I had written to him when we were university students. Apparently it was his habit to carry this, as a kind of good luck charm. Anil traced me from the address."

"It's absolutely incredible Scottie! Who on earth would keep a letter for over . . ."

"Fifty three years . . . The address was that of my parents' house but luckily the local postman recognised the surname and took it to my brother John, who still lives nearby. He forwarded the letter to me unopened."

"Why didn't you tell me?" Elizabeth said, upset by her mother's lack of trust.

"I wasn't certain whether to reply. I didn't know if I could stand the disruption."

"What do you mean disruption? Mum if there's any disruption it'll be caused by your secrecy."

"Elizabeth, you don't know what you're talking about. Custom dictated that I wrote to Ben asking for his permission to contact our eldest son Saurabh. I couldn't do it so I sent a short note to Anil, thanking him for writing and giving him my correct address. Saurabh's first letter arrived before I had made up my mind whether or not to write to his father."

"Oh I see." Elizabeth said.

"But you're not angry?"

"Far from it . . . I'm thrilled. I've got a million questions." A million answers Margaret didn't want to give. "How old are they? Obviously older than me . . ."

"Yes, Saurabh is ten years older and a high ranking Indian Army officer. He recently organised an *All India Hockey Tournament* in honour of his dead mother, and here I am alive and kicking!" But Margaret's humorous remark was at odds with the sorrow and anger stirring inside her and she couldn't go on to give the birthdays of her other children.

As early as Elizabeth could remember, what ever the cause, her mother insisted that family business was not discussed outside the home. How would she deal with this? If the Indian children were to be reunited with their mother it would have to be handled sensitively.

James had no such qualms, "You know the old saying, 'Only the good die young.' Well you've got no chance, Scottie! You'll last forever. Joking apart, if you want to go to India, we'll take you."

"James!"

"Don't be cross, Elizabeth." Margaret said in his defence. "I know James means well but I'm in my seventies. My health won't allow me to make the journey. I don't want to die in India."

"You won't die. India gets thousand of tourists every year. We'd be with you . . . It's not as if you'd be among strangers."

Margaret declared forcefully, "I mean it. It's out of the question." James wisely backed off from any more discussion on the topic.

Elizabeth had always wanted a brother and now she'd got two. An older sister was different, that would take more getting used to. What could her mother possibly be afraid of? Disappointed there'd be no trip to India she sought some kind of compromise. "Mum, will you let me write to Saurabh?"

Margaret didn't want to hang her life out to be scrutinised, especially by her children. She had almost dropped her guard last year, while watching *Jewel in the Crown* on television. The programme, screened on Sundays, was set in India during the time she lived there. It went on for weeks and was compulsive viewing for Elizabeth. Margaret pretended to enjoy it, and in a way she did, but it brought back bitter sweet memories that she couldn't share with her daughter.

"Scottie . . ." James said, fired up with the whole idea of an Indian connection, "letters would be a way of introducing your children to each other. You never know they might get on."

Margaret hadn't thought of it like that and before James drove her home she agreed that Elizabeth would write to Saurabh.

CHAPTER 3

Margaret switched on the radio, habitually tuned to radio four, ate her breakfast, washed the dishes and tidied the kitchen, but avoided picking up the airmail letter lying stranded on the sisal mat by the front door. It was absurd. She'd have to open it some time. Where was the scissor gadget James had bought to pick up the post and minimise the chance of her toppling over? Elizabeth said to put it in the same place each time she used it, but doing as she was told was not Margaret's strong point. She found the contraption disguised by the jumble of coats hanging in the hall, expertly flipped over the envelope and retrieved it from the mat.

Clearly printed on the back in a flamboyant hand was *Colonel Saurabh Atrey, V.C., V.S.M., India.* Sitting safely in her fireside chair Margaret's hand trembled as she tore open the envelope and removed two letters.

My Dearest Mama

My father was with me when your reply came. He is seventy-eight years old now. I wish you could have seen the glow on his face when he heard that you are alive and fine. After adjusting his spectacles he read it again and again. He asked me to wish you to come to India to be with all of us. We were helpless to find the truth as children. We accepted what the adults said, but I used to weep alone for Mama. A warrior who's not afraid of death I used to weep like a child at night over a pillow. This letter of yours is my most precious possession. I read it again and again. Long stories we will tell when we meet as surely we must.

She read the letter over and over memorizing every word; crying for the tousled headed boy grown into a brave soldier who could so easily have been killed without her knowing.

What could Saurabh mean by writing that his father requested her come to India? It was inconceivable that she would return to where once, naively happy, she had been plunged into desperation and despair. Yet she was disconcerted by faint murmurings of disappointment that there was no letter from Ben. She could scarcely believe he was seventy-eight years old but Margaret often forgot that she was seventy-two. Their love was a lifetime away. Pavia's enclosed letter drew more tears and self-recrimination.

. . . Papa said you had gone back to your father in Scotland. We couldn't believe that you would leave without kissing us and clung to each other. Your jewels and clothes were in your room waiting for your return. For a long time Saurabh pestered my father until he told us that the ship on which you were travelling had been torpedoed. Then it was useless to ask.

As a child the days sped past but when I was being married and having my own children I felt the loss of you most keenly. Of course my aunts, brothers and father were with me when I married Kailash. He has turned out to be a devoted husband and I am very fortunate to be married to such a good, kind man. He continued educating me, encouraging me to take my degree before we had our family but it is at those special times when you need your own mother. I had so many memories of you. I wanted you beside me at the most important times of my life.

To tell you the truth mama I am not as beautiful as I was as a child. I have put on a lot of weight since becoming a mother and grandmother . . .

The fair skinned, slender girl with eyes that would melt any heart was a grandmother. They had both learned to live with an emptiness that the years couldn't take away. Happy family photographs confirmed how much Margaret had missed. Her daughter was blessed with three children, two of them married with families. Margaret was not only a grandmother but a great grandmother. Saurabh had four unmarried children. The years had gone and there was no way she could recapture them.

She had news of her youngest son Rajeev from Pavia and Saurabh. His promotion to Brigadier, happy marriage and two sons was more than she could hope for. She wouldn't blame him if he didn't contact her. He had been such a sickly crying little one. How could she have left him, left them all? Things happened in such a hurry but that had been an excuse; acknowledging it made her feel worse.

The afternoon post arrived and with it came Rajeev's poignant letter, breaking through Margaret's remaining defences.

> *Dearest darling Mama,*
>
> *I got your letter sent to me through Saurabh. You do not know how thrilled I was first on knowing about your being there in England. It is a miracle for me. I had never thought of knowing your existence. No one had spoken about you to me. All these years and I was made to understand that you are no more. No body was able to explain about your absence except when someone did speak it was such a hush hush affair.*
>
> *You can imagine how one feels on knowing the mother who has given birth to you has suddenly gone from your life to reappear again . . .*

It is as if we have found a lost treasure. I think I cannot explain the feeling. We all want you to come and stay with us. You do not know what a void your absence from our life has created.

Do write or phone so we can speak

The longing to be with her children, so long submerged in the business of everyday living, was brought dangerously to life. They shared loneliness at the core of their being. Could they really forgive her? Could she forgive herself?

Margaret thought of her own loving mother and the happy family home in Queensferry where she was born and spent her earliest days. Their house was tall with a slate roof, hemmed in by other buildings, a higgledy-piggledy grey row overlooking the water. Standing on tiptoe, balanced against the window ledge she could see the gulls wheeling and cawing above the waves and the trains thundering across the Forth Bridge where her father worked on the railway. Where had the trains come from; filled with imagined people, where were they going? Margaret was slow to forgive her parents for leaving the sea when her father's work forced them to move.

Gorebridge, inland with its narrow twisting main road and linear sprawl of houses dripping into the valley, was a disappointment. Margaret's eldest sister Nan was away in service but the house was crowded with her parents, two older brothers, and two younger sisters. There was less than a year between herself and her sister Jean making them more like twins. Always together, they escaped from the confines of the house onto the hills; scrambling up the rough grassy slopes, avoiding prickly green and yellow gorse, flattening the tall bracken until, hot and panting, they reached the top.

It was forever summer. High above the village the subtle green shades of patterned flat fields sprawled out below them. On a clear day, in the distance, Margaret could see her beloved Firth of Forth and way beyond the water the blue-grey shadows of far away hills. One day she'd travel to those distant sights and discover the fascinating places in her school books.

Racing Jean down the hill with her arms flung wide, the wind billowing up through her cardigan Margaret soared high in the sky, riding on thermal currents like an eagle looking down at the world only to crash to earth. The sand paper grit of the hillside gouged red channels in her bare legs. Scarlet cheeked and bleeding she limped home to be cleaned up by her mother who scolded with every wipe that Maggie would be the death of her.

Margaret stirred the coals of the late afternoon fire, spinning flames in the black grate, reminiscent of the lights of halls where she sang and recited the works of Robert Burns, basking in the audience's applause, winning prize after prize. She was the first person in her family, and from the village, to win a bursary to study at Edinburgh University. She wondered what her parents would have given for such an opportunity. Through her their future held so much promise. Cursed with a restless search for transitory excitement and adventure she hadn't given them a thought.

She vacuumed the downstairs rooms and made a pan of mince and onion. No one came to visit, and she didn't feel like going out. By evening she couldn't be bothered to cook potatoes to go with the mince. She had a tin of tomato soup and soft white bread on a tray by the television while she watched the news, clearing away before *Coronation Street.* There was nothing else worth watching so she switched it off. She'd begun a letter to Jean but couldn't get on with it so read for a while, filling in time, trying to put aside her guilt and heavy heart.

At ten she drank her bed-time cocoa, wound the clock and pulled the metal spark guard round the hearth. She was ready for the succour of a hot water bottled bed and the smooth black rosary beads ever present under the pillow.

SCOTLAND
1931-1935

CHAPTER 4

Scotland 1931

Ghosts from the past crowded Margaret's dreams transporting her to their former world where youth was reborn. University life was hectic and she was already making a reputation with the fashionable Edinburgh literary set. Every topic was up for debate and a dozen people ready to discuss it, often well into to the night. She was glad to be able to dash home to the backwater of Gorebridge for the occasional weekend. There she could sleep late and didn't have to argue the finer points of anything. She left it to the last minute to leave, for there was Mass to go to, dinner to eat and the company of her brothers and youngest sister Mary.

One Sunday evening the Edinburgh train was already standing in the station when Margaret reached the booking hall. Ticket in hand, she ran along the platform peering into crowded compartments. She had reached the last before finding the possibility of a seat. Pulling open the tightly closed door, she clambered over the occupants, apologising in all directions, ignoring the shuffling of newspapers and squeezed in amidst irritated tutting.

The young man sitting opposite smiled as if the scene he had witnessed was a huge joke. Margaret automatically smiled back. For a while they silently shared their amusement grinning at each other. His thick ebony hair fell onto his forehead and his black-brown eyes danced invitingly. She was making eyes at a foreigner, in a carriage filled with pale Scots and she couldn't stop. He spoke formally, introducing himself, "My name is Vidyaaranya Atrey. I am a medical student at the university."

He epitomised sophistication, handsome in a tweed jacket and stylish plus fours. Margaret felt shy and awkward beside him. He didn't notice, shutting out the disapproving fellow travellers with a cavalier smile. She was bedazzled and talking too much. All too soon the train pulled into Edinburgh and they went their separate ways but not before arranging to meet later the same week.

Jean, who was a scholarship girl at school in Edinburgh and boarding in the city, was waiting by the ticket barrier. In a whirl, before her sister had chance to speak, Margaret gabbled, "You'll never guess . . . I've met a medical student on the train. He's in his final year . . ."

"Trust you to get into a conversation with a complete stranger! "For all you know he might not even be at the university."

"You worry too much. Besides he's the most handsome man in the world."

"Maggie you are the limit!"

"I know, but Jean, he spoke to me . . . to me!"

"Sometimes I think you're positively mad."

"I've arranged to meet him on Wednesday."

"You can't possibly go!"

"I am. Anyway he probably won't turn up,"

"Don't you want to hear my news?" asked her long suffering sister.

Margaret replied contritely that she did.

"I've won a bursary to study mathematics at Edinburgh next autumn. That's if I pass my *Highers* . . ."

"Of course you will! I'll help you. Let's celebrate with iced buns," Margaret said extravagantly. Jean took no persuading and the girls went in search of the nearest café.

* * * * *

Wednesday was cold, with drizzle in the air. A wicked wind whipped round the corner of the post office building on Princes Street where Margaret stood waiting. She had almost given him up when there he was picking his way across the tram-railed road in her direction. She tried to look blasé but the wind caught her full blast, blowing her red curls into a tangle around her face, taking her breath away. He pulled the collar of his overcoat higher and, by way of greeting, tucked her arm in his. The weather kept them on the move so they made for the shelter of the Princes Street gardens; two of her strides equalling his one. Out of the wind, matching his pace to hers, he said "You told me many things on the train but failed to tell me your name."

Blushing she stammered, "It's Margaret . . . Margaret Riley but my friends call me Maggie."

"Well my lovely Margaret, I mean to find out all about you."

Embarrassed by the words and the mischievous way he looked at her Margaret's blushes grew crimson. No one had ever said such things to her. She didn't care what she looked like. There was one mirror in the house and that was for her father and the boys to shave. Everyone was too busy working to gaze into mirrors.

She tried to say his name, "Vid . . . yaa . . . ranya." He encouraged her to repeat it but after several hilarious attempts they both gave up. "I'll call you Ben," she said, "It's an ancient name and at least I can pronounce it. What's more it suits you."

"I like it. I am the only son and the most important member of my family. I think Margaret was the name of one of your famous queens. I also deserve a name with a noble lineage. "

Something indefinable in Ben's manner made Margaret uneasy but she was too bewitched to let it bother her. He checked his watch. He'd be late for his lecture. They retraced their steps but she couldn't keep up. He raced over Waverley Bridge disappearing in a hiss of steam from a train passing below.

* * * * *

They met whenever they could. Ben's wealth was a passport to the moneyed crowd. Margaret quickly fell in with the lifestyle but tea at Jenners was beyond her wildest expectations. The swish restaurant with starched linen, polished silver and high prices was way beyond her reach. Her homemade dresses and cardigans were at odds with the slick outfits worn by most of her wealthy contemporaries. She made excuses not to go but Ben was persuasive, "Margaret, it's just a place to eat."

"I know but . . . Jenners!"

"So? You'll be the prettiest there!" She pulled a face. "Oh maybe not . . . Anyway you're going with me and I'm the richest!"

They went and were served last by a vinegar-faced waitress who oversaw Ben paying the bill.

Margaret borrowed a dress and coat from a friend to wear to her first classical concert at the Usher Hall. Captivated by the music she whispered spontaneously, "I want to dance and dance." The glowers of fellow concertgoers made her cringe and slide lower in the seat. Ben took her by the elbow and raised her up. How she loved him! On their way home it rained. They hummed the *Blue Danube* twirling round and round on the slippery cobbles until she was dizzy.

Ben was enjoying himself. In India he was adored by his mother and sisters who indulged his every whim. Everything was there for the taking and he wanted Margaret. The snatched hours in his attic room when they made love, her fair skin with its dusting of golden freckles; the brush of her wild hair across his chest increased his desire. He bought posies of flowers to put on the pillow, fed her sweets; the sugary taste of her lips dissolved in his kisses but some nights were his own.

Every breathe Margaret took belonged to Ben. Merely repeating his name thrilled her. He opened up a whole new world haughtily overriding anything that displeased him. Besotted with her and already an experienced lover Ben wooed away any inhibitions, teaching Margaret the delights of her body and how to fulfil him.

If only she hadn't discovered that sex was so enjoyable! The first time they made love it seemed so natural. The exciting sensations of passion overruled common sense or shame.

* * * * *

Jean shared lodgings with Margaret and was frequently invited to meet her sister's university friends; engrossed in revision she didn't notice them gradually dwindle. The 'Highers' meant everything to Jean. She was relying on her sister to steady her nerves, "Maggie my exams are first. I'm alright with the Maths but the French . . . You're so good at it . . . If I'm to pass I need your help. Then I'll help you."

"Jean there's a month to go. I don't need your help. I'm working in the university library during the day and in the evening Ben is helping me. Don't worry you'll sail through."

Surprised by the uncharacteristic rebuff Jean decided to ask some of her sister's friends about this so-called Ben. She discovered that they rarely saw Margaret, who was in danger of falling behind with her studies. What's more he was seeing other girls from wealthy influential families.

Jean was at a loss as to what to do, having sworn not to say anything to their parents about Ben. Forced into deceiving them she used the impending exams to make fewer visits home and tried to reason with her love-struck sister.

"Where is he when he's not with you?"

"Busy catching up on his work, like me . . ."

"Busy with other girls. That's where."

Margaret staunchly refused to believe it.

"At least ask him."

"I won't because I know he loves me. What would he want from anyone else?"

"He's different, not like our brothers or the other boys we know."

"That's part of why I love him."

"What if you fail your exams?"

"I won't."

"But you don't care if I fail mine!"

"That's not so. I do care!"

"Not enough to give up an hour with this Ben!"

Margaret slammed the door on her way out.

The exams came and went. Jean won the gold medal for mathematics with high scores in all the other subjects. Margaret scraped through slightly miffed. It was the first time she hadn't been top.

* * * * *

Margaret pretended to be asleep but she needn't have bothered. Jean was up and away organising the last requirements for admission to university before they went home for the summer.

She dragged herself out of bed but as soon as her feet touched the floor she was sick. It was the same every day. Their landlady asked if she was unwell. Ben tetchily asked why she was meeting him later and later in the morning. She described the symptoms. He said smugly "You're not ill. It sounds as if you're having a baby."

She couldn't be! Babies were something that happened after you were married and nothing to do with their lovemaking. What would she do if he was right?

CHAPTER 5

Margaret and Jean arrived in Gorebridge late on Friday night. The tiny bedroom shared with Mary, generally became alive with talk and merriment. Throughout their growing up Margaret and Jean had told each other everything but that was before Ben. Jean was convinced he was stealing her sister away and said so. Margaret said it was none of *her* business, accusing Jean of spying. Perhaps she was spying? She hadn't meant to but Margaret had changed and there was something terribly wrong. Jean tried to resolve the uneasy quiet between them.

"Maggie . . . you know I promised not to tell . . ."

"Have you?"

"No but don't think I haven't wanted to."

"I didn't mean to make it awkward for you."

"Awkward . . . says you, who never thinks of anyone except herself!"

"Jean, that's not true!"

Jean made to go downstairs. Margaret grabbed her arm.

"Maggie!"

"Sit down a minute . . . please!" Jean didn't want to create a fuss so sat on the bed. "I'm going to have a baby."

It took a minute for Margaret's words to sink in; unable to conceal her dismay Jean asked, "Are you certain?"

"Of course I am. Ben's a doctor. He should know."

Jean expected her sister to cry, to do something; anything but stand there as if such a thing was an everyday event like having tea.

"Maggie, surely you're sorry?"

"What have I got to be sorry for?"

"You can't bring a baby into this world without a father?"

"It's got a father, Ben."

"Oh and he'll put everything right?"

"Yes, he's coming tomorrow to ask father's permission for us to marry."

Jean's eyes grew wider and wider, "Aren't you afraid?"

"Of father!"

"Yes, of hurting him and mother."

"I don't mean to . . . once they meet Ben and get over the shock . . ."

"Over the shock . . . I can't believe you could be so selfish! . . . I'll never be able to look father and mother in the face. How could you?"

Peacemaker Jean challenging her was the last thing Margaret expected but her sister rounded on her again,

"Surely you're going to tell them tonight before he comes?"

"I don't know. I'll see how it goes. Ben will sort it out."

Jean mockingly retorted, "Ben will sort it out . . . Huh! You'll be a long time waiting for that!" She flounced downstairs and listened with disbelief to Margaret's account of the young man, who was to call on them the following morning, without hinting at the reason for his visit.

Their father was not certain about having a stranger thrust into their midst, "Maggie I hope you're not neglecting your studies."

"I passed my exams."

"So you did . . . So you did." Then looking keenly at her he asked, "Are you going to Mass?"

"Yes father" Jean replied.

"Not you Jean, you Maggie. Are you receiving the sacrament when you're not at home?"

Margaret squirmed, "Well . . . I . . ."

"What's all this faither?" interjected her mother, "The girls havni been here two minutes and you're at them already."

"Mother, I have a duty to God to make sure there's no slacking where He's concerned."

Steering her husband away from the sensitive area of religion she continued, "Maggie, did you say the young man was called Ben?"

"Yes, he's to qualify as a doctor and work at The Infirmary."

"A doctor . . ." repeated her father. "Grand friends you're keeping, Maggie."

Who would believe it? His Maggie and a doctor! He could count on the fingers of one hand the number of words he'd exchanged with a doctor. But having one as a visitor in the house . . . Well his daughter was worth ten doctors. He nodded to his wife who commented, "Maggie, you've not mentioned this young man before . . ." Margaret said that there was no need. "But there is now?" her mother said, raising her eyebrows. "And you Jean . . . what do you make of him?"

Jean was almost choking with shame. Faithful to her promise she muttered something about being at school and not meeting all of her sister's friends. Why didn't Margaret come out with it? Didn't she care that she was making a fool and a liar out of her . . . and what of their parents? Her father put on his coat. He'd chew this over with his pals over a dram or two. Jean flashed Margaret a look hoping to put an end to the charade. Her sister carried on sorting out the welcome with their mother; reassuring her that soup would be fine and the guest wouldn't stay long.

* * * * *

Jean lay at the edge of the bed. Neither girl slept, divided by the hostile space between them. They were up at daylight scrubbing and polishing until not a speck of dust remained, or appeared likely to land on anything in sight. Changed from their working clothes there was nothing left for them to do except wait. Jean restlessly flicked through the pages of a book while her younger sister Mary, practised scales on the piano. Their father looked at his pocket watch, lit his pipe and settling back in his chair by the fire said, "Maggie, come away from the window. I don't want the young man to think you've nothing better to do than watch out for him."

The wall clock with its whirring weights and chains struck eleven. Ben's train would be in the station. Jean buried her head further in the book. The atmosphere stifled Margaret. He must come, and soon, she couldn't keep up this light-hearted pretence much longer.

Inviting smells of broth and fresh baked bread drifted in from the kitchen making everyone hungry. Her mother, pinafore tied tightly protecting her Sunday dress, stirred, seasoned and left off tasting to call, "Are you a deef Maggie? Away you go and answer the door."

The watery winter sunshine filtering through the twigs of leafless trees melted the hoar frost's bridal coating on spiders' webs. Ben stood framed against the silver light. His breath rose into the air intermingling with Margaret's, banishing her fears. She led him into the house.

"I am delighted to meet you, Sir" Ben said, holding out his hand, "I'm sure Margaret has told you all about me. I have come to ask if you will do me the honour of giving me her hand in marriage."

Margaret's mother, her best apron hanging loosely in her hand, was transfixed by this young man and his unbelievable request. "Maggie, he's col . . ."

"Indian! . . . Ma . . . Ben's Indian . . ."

Her husband was the first to move, pushing past the outstretched hand. The silence in the room magnified the dull click of a key in the lobby cupboard. The door crashed against the wall rocking the foundations of the row of houses. In an explosion of rage Margaret's father took out his shotgun, expertly loaded and cocked it and, pointing the barrel at Ben mercilessly backed him down the hall roaring, "You heathen bastard! Out . . . out of my sight!"

A few inquisitive neighbours who had seen Ben arrive remained gossiping by the gate. The gun was swung in their direction and fired in the air. Closed windows and doors flew open. Heads poked out witnessing the family's shame. Gripped by a boundless fury Margaret's father bellowed, "There'll be no wedding from this hoose."

Her eyes blazing Margaret recklessly shouted, "Then I'll marry without!"

"Maggie, think what you're saying . . . You canny mean it," entreated her mother.

Margaret stonily replied, "But I do."

In a voice that matched the winter's day her father declared, "Then go, but if you do, you'll not enter this hoose again."

Oblivious to everyone's distress except her own, Margaret left with Ben for the station.

CHAPTER 6

Edinburgh 1932

Estranged from her family, and denied the privileges and protection, which, in the same circumstances, had long been the prerogative of the rich, Margaret quickly married Ben in an Edinburgh register office. He gave his occupation as landowner and two passing strangers acted as witnesses.

The tram rattled down Princes Street. Margaret twiddled with the narrow gold band on her finger. Maybe one day her father would realise that Ben's intentions were honourable but instead of celebrating with those dearest they were on their way to Patrick Thompson's department store. She knew they would have a lovely tea while listening to the string quartet, and watching glamorous models demonstrate the latest fashions to the store's discerning customers. Confident in her expensive clothes Margaret was looking forward to showing off the outfit and her husband. It was taking an age to get there, "Ben this must be the wrong direction?"

"Don't worry . . . we get off at the next stop. I have a surprise for you."

They strolled casually into the reception area of the exclusive hotel overlooking Princes Street gardens and the towering castle. Ben spoke to the tight lipped desk clerk, "I have a reservation, Mr and Mrs Atrey."

The clerk said, "You must be mistaken. The hotel is full.

"But our overnight bag was delivered yesterday," Ben protested.

The intimidating manager was summoned who pompously informed Ben that there were no vacancies. A porter escorted them to the door, unceremoniously depositing the lovingly packed luggage on the busy street.

"In India I could buy and sell him and hundreds like him" Ben said through clenched teeth, "snap my fingers and he would be no more." He snatched up the leather bag. They didn't go to Patrick Thompson's.

* * * * *

Ben had qualified and Margaret spent her days keeping the room in their lodgings neat and tidy, counting the hours until he returned from the Infirmary. They read together, went to concerts, shared their dreams and talked for hours while they wandered through the parks and streets of the enchanting city. She wished she'd taken her final exams but didn't miss the intellectual stimulation of the University. Ben was a dedicated doctor and with Margaret's help, aimed to rise to the top of his profession.

The baby's first movements fluttered lightly like butterfly wings. Ben was convinced it was a boy, heir to the Atrey estates accrued over hundreds of years. He sought out more suitable accommodation for the birth of his son.

The night before the move the temperature plummeted. In the morning the sky was heavy with the threat of snow. A steaming carthorse stood patiently on the cobbled street, which overnight had become a slippery death trap for man and beast. Margaret traipsed up and down the tenement's twisting stone steps assisting Ben and the carter to load their books into the wooden cart. They made steady progress but it was too slow for Margaret who rushed ahead to light a fire in their new home. Christmas was coming, their first as man and wife. Next year they would be a family.

The frosty ringed moon cast shadows through the curtain-less window. They crawled into a hastily made bed and gently made love. Margaret fell asleep in Ben's arms. She was woken by snow light and a wave of pain rippling through her stomach. She gasped automatically drawing her knees up; then it was gone. Untangling from Ben's long arms Margaret gingerly stretched out her legs, only to be forced to draw them back as the spasm returned.

Somehow she got out of bed, found the matches and lit the gas mantle on the nearby wall. It fizzed and hissed into life. She pulled the bucket from beneath the bed and squatted over it. Margaret hated doing this when Ben was in the room but the shared toilet was in the yard below and the cramping pains were unrelenting. She gripped the iron bedstead crouching over the bucket, calling out for her mother and waking Ben. Her frightened eyes searched his, "The baby's coming . . ." he said carefully lifting her onto the bed.

Margaret moaned . . . "It can't be . . . it's too early . . . Do something . . ." but there was nothing to be done. Ben left her with the hastily summoned midwife who restored order chiding, "Dinne take on so lassie. There's plenty of time to have lots more bairns."

But it was this baby Margaret ached for, cruelly gone before she had chance to hold it. Locked in disappointment Ben didn't speak of it and she couldn't bear to. Alone, months later, she broke down crying for her own mother who she missed so much.

CHAPTER 7

At weekends, as frequently as his work at the Infirmary allowed, Ben went to Waverly station to try to catch sight of Jean returning home to Gorebridge. He hoped to persuade her to visit them, for nothing he tried restored the lively girl he'd married. A familiar slender figure was in the crowd ahead of him; leaping down the station steps, taking two or three in one stride, he shouted, "Jean! Jean!" Heads turned but Jean carried on walking, acting as if she hadn't heard. Ben put on a sprint and caught her by the shoulder.

"Leave off laddie! She's not for the likes of you!" a man said protecting what he assumed to be a young woman pestered by the unwanted attentions of a foreigner.

"I'm her brother-in-law," Ben panted, squaring up to him. Jean confirmed it was true. The man muttered something which she didn't catch, and spat deliberately on the ground by Ben's feet. Mortified by the insult they took refuge in the station buffet. Ben sorrowfully told Jean of Margaret's miscarriage, begging her to visit. She refused to commit to anything and caught the train leaving him in the smoke filled room with his head in his hands.

Safe inside the railway carriage Jean tugged the wide leather strap slamming the widow shut. It wasn't fair. No sooner had she gained the university place than the bursary was withdrawn on the tenuous grounds of her sister's behaviour. Unable to deceive her parents, or trust herself where Margaret was concerned, Jean told her mother of the meeting with Ben. She was doubly annoyed by the reaction. A few parcels were got together 'to tide poor Maggie over'. Jean knew she would be expected to take them but counted on her father to put a stop to the nonsense. He chose not to; for a moment she hated all three of them.

* * * * *

Jean knocked on the door of Margaret and Ben's flat, waiting reluctantly on the doorstep wishing she was somewhere else. At the sight of her sister she burst into tears dropping the cumbersome basket, strewing home made cakes, bread, butter and jam down the stone steps. Dark rings of unhappiness highlighted Margaret's eyes, clothes hung from her boney frame, "Now Jean, don't take on so. I'm fine, just a little tired."

Trying to stop crying, Jean began to repack the basket. Margaret bent to help but every movement confirmed the weak state of her health.

Margaret asked about everyone, especially her father. Jean told her that he was much the same, reminding her sister of their father's habit of filling his pipe and relaxing in his chair by the fire before bed. On this occasion he placed two identical kitchen chairs opposite his and asked their brothers Johnny and Con to join him. The brothers did as they were told. Their father slowly filled his pipe, reached up to the rack above the mantelpiece, chose two others, filled them with tobacco and gave them to his sons. The riveted duo watched their father light a newspaper spill from the fire to ignite his pipe, drawing in, making the tobacco smolder, sending fire flakes over the bowl.

Then he lit their pipes in turn and sat back in his chair. He smoked. They smoked. The room filled with the aromatic smell of tobacco and a blue haze hung in the air. Deftly knocking his pipe on the hearth, he replaced it on the rack and retired for the night. His green-faced sons singed their fingers stubbing out theirs.

The boys tried to work out how their father knew of their tobacco experiments while carrying out their nightly boot cleaning task but Johnny was violently sick. Con gypping and holding his nose gathered rags to mop up the mess, supervised by their unsympathetic mother. Finally with the footwear polished and lined in a row, the would-be-smokers escaped. Not a word passed between father and sons but Jean saw him wink at her mother when he pulled on his boots in the morning.

Margaret gleefully asked this and that. Jean obliged with more anecdotes lulling her sister into believing there was a chance that the marriage would be accepted. However she refrained from saying there was no singing at home. The lid of the treasured piano hadn't been opened since Margaret left. Mary and their father didn't play any more.

* * * * *

Winter gave way to a gentle spring and on to summer with Edinburgh's floral parks in full bloom. Occasionally, dressed in their finest, Margaret and Ben explored the affluent streets of Morningside selecting a house for the future. It was one of their favourite games and, they daydreamed of living in one of the imposing square houses with a brass name plate on the front entrance.

Ben was becoming highly regarded in his profession, enjoying his work, continuing to read and research. Margaret was always at his elbow learning as much about medicine as her husband. It didn't cross her mind that she might have become a doctor. She had wasted the opportunity to become anything much but she had Ben. She was sorry her actions had cheated Jean and Mary of the same opportunity. Margaret didn't dwell on it. She was expecting another baby and was preoccupied with delaying telling Ben until the early months had passed.

* * * * *

A telegram arrived informing Ben that his father was very ill, requesting him to return to India without delay. He didn't hesitate, organised his work, booked a passage and left without his wife.

CHAPTER 8

Edinburgh, Newhaven and Gorebridge

Ben had been gone two months. Every day Margaret penned a few lines talking as if he were beside her, for she missed his friendship as well as their lovemaking. She posted the scribbles weekly without getting any reply. Thinking long and hard she wrote,

> *My Dearest Ben,*
>
> *I hope my letters have reached you. I cannot understand why you have not replied. I trust nothing disastrous has happened. I am miserable without you but the good news is that we are to have another child towards the end of May. Please, dearest try to get home for the birth. I am well and trying not to worry.*

The money you left is dwindling fast and will not last much longer and your banker's drafts have not arrived. I am sorry to trouble you with such mundane things when you have pressing business where you are.

I saw Doctor Sinclair from the Infirmary the other day. He was asking when you would be returning. He sends his regards. You are certain to be able to return there when this emergency is over.

My days are lonely without you so do write soon.

Your loving wife

It was imperative Margaret found a job while she could disguise her pregnancy but prospective employers were suspicious. Why would a young married, well-spoken girl be looking for work of any kind? The claim that her husband was abroad led to more questions. The truthful explanation ended any possibility of employment. Margaret became used to being almost thrown out, but that was nothing compared to the lewd suggestions. The situation was getting her down and if anything happened to this baby she didn't know what she would do. With enough money to last barely a few more weeks she was prepared to do anything, provided it was respectable.

* * * * *

High up in the accounts department of the big store Margaret's sister, Jean, surveyed the shop floor. Customers chose anything from clothes to furniture. Dockets confirming purchases whizzed beneath the ceiling in containers suspended on wire which Jean emptied. She added the totals quicker than they could be written down. Some of the young male clerks tried to confuse her by mixing up the carbon copied slips of paper, but it was good humoured and Jean entered into the spirit of it, testing them in return. It was not long before she was promoted. Her maroon rainbow-edged ledgers with precise figures in red, blue, black and green ink, double and triple entries, ruled and balanced totals were works of art. Jean tried to make Margaret a small allowance until things looked up but by the time she'd paid her train fare to the town there wasn't much left.

The accounts manager was putting the world to rights complaining that an acquaintance of his couldn't find anyone willing to manage a fish shop. It was out of the town, in a coastal village north of Edinburgh. The hours were long; the wages small but there was a flat above the shop. Jean seized this solution to her sister's problems.

* * * * *

Margaret breathed, ate and slept surrounded by the all-pervading smell of fish. She hated the towing of heavy wicker baskets and the draughty fish sheds where the fish wives gutted and cleaned the catch. She was willing to turn her hand to anything but follow the navy and white uniformed fish wives with a basket on her back to peddle the catch in Edinburgh. No one heard her grumble but they didn't hear her prayers. Her quick wit endeared her to the shop's customers who joined in the friendly banter. The takings rose and business flourished.

Margaret forwarded her address to Ben but little else. There seemed no point until he replied to the host of letters she'd already sent. The inquisitive village postmistress, skilled at wheedling out information, soon discovered that Margaret was expecting news from her husband who, she said, was in India. In next to no time the local women were waiting as impatiently as Margaret for a letter to arrive. Some couldn't have read it, but they didn't care who her so-called husband was. It was high time he wrote. If he didn't she wouldn't be short of friends.

* * * * *

Perhaps Ben was ill? God forbid that anything should happen to him. Lack of sleep and the subconscious fear that he might not return was eating away at Margaret. She touched her swollen stomach, the unborn child the sole tangible link with her husband.

Working in the fish shop grew more difficult and there were lots of good-natured jokes about how much longer she would be able to squeeze her bulk behind the counter. Margaret joined in but if she could not work she would be homeless. Jean's Sunday visits kept her sane.

They strolled, arms linked, past rows of fishing nets drying by the harbour.

Jean asked, "I wonder whether you'll have a wee girl or boy."

"Ben would like a son but I think if I could choose it would be a girl."

"I hope it's a girl with your curly hair but with my patience!"

"What cheek! I can be patient."

Jean scoffed, "Not so I'd notice."

"Well I'm trying."

"You certainly are!"

"Wait until I've had this baby. You'll not escape so easily. Anyway I've had enough of walking. It's easy for you. You've not got this weight to lug around."

"You said it," Jean joked ducking out of the way of her sister's playful swipe. Margaret wished her sister could stay forever but work called for both of them and there was always next Sunday.

* * * * *

Margaret's mother knew from experience the difficulties of this late stage of pregnancy. Her husband viewed their daughter's conduct as shameful. Marriage, anywhere but the Catholic Church, put Margaret's immortal soul in danger. He didn't know how to deal with the dictates of religion and the love of his child. His solution was to give his wife a few extra pounds 'just in case' and ask no questions.

* * * * *

Margaret displayed the best of the catch on a fishmonger's slab in the shop window. Shining silver scaled herrings, white cod, and delicious oak-brown kippers lay alongside orange-crumbed dressed fish and bright yellow smoked haddock. There were few customers at this time of the morning. Her face flushed and a clean white apron concealing her shape, Margaret sat on a stool with her back to the door sorting money in orderly piles for the busy day ahead.

"Maggie."

The women filleting the fish stopped, their quicksilver knives idle.

"Ma . . . Oh Ma, I'm so glad you've come."

"Away you go lassie! We'll mind the shop," said a gruff voiced woman, speaking for all of them.

The bare room Margaret called home was devoid of any comfort except for the clutter of well thumbed books by the bed. Jean witnessed her mother's tears. Margaret was ashamed to be the cause.

The decent woman blamed herself for not preparing her daughters for the ways of the world, but she had married young and had little experience of life outside the home. Her husband was a good man but his refusal to have anything to do with their daughter distressed and exasperated her. She used the extra money and prudent savings from the boys' wages to rent a small room above a friend's shop. Her sons attended to the rest.

Margaret gave in her notice at the fish shop and went to the little room in Gorebridge. A bed with the cover crotched by her mother, a wooden cupboard, chair, open fire, sink and a jar of delicate snowdrops picked by Jean completed the cheerfully curtained room. The boys, now men, joshed with each other, and were duly told off by their mother. The work finished they sat squashed together on the bed eating broth, pressing Margaret into refilling her bowl more than once to feed the giant child she must be having. It was like old times and the following morning Margaret would have slept on, but Jean woke her with a letter from India.

"Well Maggie . . ." Jean said troubled by her sister's obvious distress, "What does he have to say?"

Margaret dropped the letter on the bed, "He's not coming back."

"What do you mean not coming back?"

"Read for yourself . . ."

> *My Dear Margaret,*
>
> *I have received so little news of you. Your letter saying that you were contemplating leaving Edinburgh surprised me. I assumed that you had abandoned your foolish plans and returned home to your father.*
>
> *My father is no more and all duties and responsibilities pass to me. I cannot leave India. My future is here. You must remain with your parents until our child is born. I will send for you both to join me, meanwhile I have instructed the bank to pay your allowance.*

The brief business like letter with its audacious instructions riled Jean but her concern was for her sister, "What ever will you do?"

"I don't know . . . I thought this was home."

"It is. Maggie, stay with us. You've managed so far without him."

"But it wasn't meant to be forever. At least he's sent instructions to the bank so I won't be penniless and can repay mother."

"The money doesn't matter. It will break mother's heart if you leave."

But Jean sensed that Margaret had already made up her mind.

CHAPTER 9

"You're almost there hen . . . one last push." The new born cry with its rush of love put an end to Margaret's long labour. Laughing and crying she kissed the delicate face with its button nose and counted every tiny finger and toe. "Dinne worry lassie she's all there" said the midwife, putting the baby to Margaret's breast to quicken the milk.

Jean, who had been waiting on the draughty stairs with her hands clamped firmly over her ears, crept into the room. "Oh Maggie she's gorgeous . . . What a mop of hair! She needs a brush already."

"If you like you can hold her" Margaret said, wrapping a shawl tightly round her daughter.

"I don't know if I dare. Maybe I'll drop her," but their mother couldn't wait; cradling her grandchild she searched for a family resemblance.

"She's awfi like you were Jean . . . except you hardly had any hair."

"It's still baby hair. I wouldn't wish that on anybody," Jean complained taking the baby.

"For goodness sake hold the bairn without squeezing the life out of her. Steady . . . steady . . . mind the heid!"

Lapsing into the language of home Jean said timorously, "I'm trying Ma but I'm awfi feared I'll hurt her. Oh . . . she's so soft. See Maggie, little blue veins on the rim of her forehead and eyelids. Open your eyes baby so I can see their colour."

"They'll be blue, silly" Margaret said with maternal authority. "All babies have blue eyes . . . then they change. Don't they ma?" Her mother didn't know if this applied to babies with Indian fathers.

"Well I want her to have blue Riley eyes like ours!"

"Stop it you two! You're no bairns!" said their mother for once glad of their bickering. "Jean, it's no a doll you're holding. Tuck in the shawl . . . Maggie, you have to give the wee girl a name."

"Ma It doesn't matter what I choose. Ben will decide."

"Goodness knows when that will be! We must call her something!"

"Jean, you choose."

"Do you mean it?"

"Yes but don't be upset when Ben changes it."

Jean didn't think it would happen. He was gone for ever. "I'd like to call her after me, but one Jean's enough. Let's call her Jessie. We'll share the same initial."

Jessie slept throughout their deliberations. Indeed she slept on through the procession of adoring uncles and Mary, who had long since charitably forgiven past differences.

A parcel containing a pink, lacy matinee coat arrived from Nan, Margaret's eldest sister. Her husband Davey was doing well as a cabinet maker in Colchester. Their daughter Sheila was a year old. The enclosed note invited Margaret to stay. The girls would be company for each other in the coming years.

Margaret guessed from her mother's happy singing that while she rested Jessie was regularly taken to her grandfather. She had no idea that he paid the rent and all her expenses.

* * * * *

A telegram arrived from Ben. The baby was to be named Pavia. Most people complimented Margaret on the unusual choice. Jean preferred Jessie. Eventually Pavia ceased to be a novelty, acknowledged by Ben and cherished by her Scottish family.

Letters began arriving regularly from India. Margaret read out some of the everyday happenings. Jean was not impressed, calculating that her brother-in-law was deviously preparing Margaret to join him.

Pavia was quite a handful, crawling madly at nine months; making a dash for the stairs at every opportunity. "I'll be glad when she can walk." Margaret said, retrieving her daughter for the umpteenth time. Jean, who had done her share, agreed, but their mother advised that then they'd really have to be on their toes.

* * * * *

Jean spent the lunch hour combing the grand Edinburgh stores for a teddy bear. They were all the rage and outrageously expensive but the boys chipped in to buy one for Pavia's first birthday. The toddler slept with the golden bear chewing its ears, refusing to be parted from it.

* * * * *

A package arrived containing the necessary papers for Margaret's passage to India. They were to sail from Southampton in four weeks. "We're going to your daddy . . . across the sea on a big ship." She said excitedly to Pavia.

"Train . . ." Pavia said as if she was trying to correct her.

"No darling that was to Aunt Nan's but we'll go on the train to catch the ship." Margaret was having enough trouble explaining to a child. She didn't know how to broach it with her mother.

Pavia did it for her that afternoon in infant drawl. Margaret filled in the rest. The details of the proposed journey escaped Margaret's mother, who couldn't understand her daughter's faith in a man who had technically abandoned her. She hurried home to enlist her husband in putting a stop to this rash adventure.

A heartbroken Jean was sent by their father to bring Margaret and Pavia home. There was no mention of the past but a great deal of discussion surrounding the wisdom of travelling unaccompanied to a disease ridden country so far away. The consensus was that Margaret and Pavia remain in Scotland. The family would continue their support and perhaps in the future, Margaret would be able to resume studying. It was a safe sensible solution but held no appeal for Margaret. Travelling so far was exciting; yearning to be with her husband she didn't see India through their eyes.

* * * * *

Ben sent a money draft and suggestions for clothes to be bought for the voyage. The weeks flew past in a plethora of entreaties and fraught packing. Pavia, fretful and miserable, clung to her granny who travelled with them to Southampton. All too soon they were on the dockside exchanging kisses and inadequate words, "Maggie I canny bear to let you go but your duty is with your husband . . . Pavia deserves to be with her faither. You will have to make a different life but . . . Oh how I'll miss you both. I canny stop worrying . . . Write as soon as you get there to let us know you're safe. I'll pray for you . . . God only knows if I'll see you again."

Margaret looked over the side of the huge liner. Far below on the quayside carnival crowds waved; among them, her mother, a small still figure, searched the lines of passengers high above. Margaret called to her but the sound was whisked away on the wind. She moved Pavia from astride her hip holding her above the rail. Seeing her granny she almost slipped from Margaret's grasp and had to be pulled to safety.

In those seconds Margaret lost sight of her mother but the festive quay was awash with a sea of identical bobbing black hats. Then there she was, arms wide, pleading to the empty air. Margaret mouthed hopelessly, "I love you" while the gangplank rattled on board and the vessel's deep resounding horn signalled the end of any change of mind.

She hurried aft. The spectators on shore were beginning to drift homeward but the lone figure of her mother, dwarfed by cranes and pulleys, remained staring at the ever widening strip of water tearing them apart. The ship, guided by sturdy tugs, headed for the open sea.

Pavia whimpered. A fellow first class passenger suggested the nanny be sent for to take the child below, for the wind was getting up and they'd catch their death of cold.

The cabin steward was waiting but Margaret sent him away. The enormity of the decision to leave Scotland and its effect on her mother laid bare by the terrible parting, brought on a deep sense of foreboding. Lying on the bunk, resting her frozen cheek against Pavia's, mother and daughter fell asleep on tear-sodden pillows.

* * * * *

The practicalities of life on board took over. There were cocktail parties, dinners in the opulent dining room, deck quoits, bridge, and a host of entertainment. Margaret was the sole passenger in first class without a nanny or companion but she wore the appropriate evening dress, cocktail and deck outfits. Her manners were perfect, and she cultivated an air of understated wealth.

The ship passed through the Mediterranean docking at ports in countries that had once jumped out from the pages of Margaret's school books. She didn't go ashore, preferring to spend the voyage with Pavia, who, shepherded by the steward, navigated the decks like a seasoned sailor.

Egypt unfolded as they sailed through the Suez Canal and into the Red Sea. The distance and exotic landscapes steadily increased, together with the heat and the flies.

INDIA

CHAPTER 10

Bombay to Bareilly 1935

"Bombay in the morning," Margaret whispered the words over and over into her pillow. Tomorrow she would be in Ben's arms. Sleep evaded her and dawn with its promise of a new life an eternity away. Pavia was fast asleep, her peaceful breathing scarcely audible against the noise of the ship's pulsating engines taking them ever nearer the shore. The long lonely voyage and dreadful separation from her family vanished as, through the cabin porthole, Margaret watched the rosy fingers of dawn creep slowly across the sky.

Energised with anticipation she put on the green crepe dress she had worn for her wedding and, unable to find the pins for her hair, gathered it up inside a wide brimmed hat. Pavia protested sleepily but was speedily dressed and carried on deck. The ship docked majestically, eliciting a spontaneous cheer from passengers and crew.

A loud babble of voices floated up from the quayside where a multitude of people of every shade of brown from deep dull black to rich coffee cream scurried like insects far below. Red, orange, white and black turbaned heads swarmed everywhere. Enormous nets filled with a hotchpotch of cargo swung out wide of the ship to hang in mid air like drunken trapeze artists. Half naked sinewy men competed with the peak-capped pristine, white uniformed port officials whose glinting whistles marked their authority. Orders were barked, arms waved and whistles blown in an attempt to control the mass of writhing humanity.

Margaret fruitlessly searched for Ben. In Edinburgh he stood out from the crowd. Here he was indistinguishable among so many of his countrymen. Maybe he wouldn't recognise her as she was failing to recognise him? Tears pricked her hot eyes threatening to mingle with the stinging sweat, forming small beads on her forehead.

She made her way down the gangway carrying Pavia, who dislodged her mother's hat releasing a cascade of copper hair. Away from the shelter of the covered deck the unremitting sun pierced Margaret's blue eyes, blurring the buzzing scene in front of her.

On the quay, hordes of men pressed forward, hemming her in. Fingers touched her hair, rough voices called out to one another. Terrified, Margaret could go no further! Pavia began to scream! Ben was there. His servants cut a swathe through the crowd, lashing out with wooden canes, striking the bodies of the venturous.

Margaret winced to hear the dull thumps of the canes hitting their targets and the ensuing sharp cries of pain. The noise reverberated in her head. Pavia began kicking and crying louder and louder, everywhere was in motion.

An umbrella appeared from nowhere shielding them from the rising sun. A woman stepped forward and, under orders from Ben, took Pavia from Margaret. Immediately the frightened child renewed screaming, refusing to be quiet until reunited with her mother. Robbed of her charge the servant truculently trailed behind them to the waiting car while the growing rabble emitted a frightening cacophony of sound. Once inside, with Ben seated beside her, Margaret asked nervously "What are they saying?"

"Don't worry, it's nothing."

"But why are they so interested in me?"

"They are common people . . . easily influenced. We have a legend about a beautiful fairy with red golden hair who brings good fortune to everyone she has contact with. They believe in such things and think it might be you."

"But are you sure we're safe?"

Ben laughed, "They are not threatening you . . . merely calling out Charu, Charu . . . which means beautiful." Gazing into Margaret's eyes he took her small white face in his healing hands, "I give you Charuni as your Indian name. You will always be my beautiful one." With her pulse racing Margaret sank into the mahogany-coloured leather upholstery.

The chauffer drove along Bombay's sweeping marine drive. Numerous horse drawn carriages followed behind, too many for Margaret's belongings, but the endless retinue of servants took advantage of the extra space to ride in style.

The teeming city with its imposing architecture, riot of colour and contrasting squalor assaulted Margaret's eyes. Their cavalcade stopped in front of what appeared to be a gothic palace, covered with carvings of monkeys, peacocks and lions. Domes and spires sprouted from the roof and stained glass windows studded the entire building. She was amused by a plaque, which proclaimed the building to be Bombay's railway station; an imposing statue of Queen Victoria trumpeted the power of the Raj.

Immediately they stepped out from the car filthy, rag-clad beggars thrust out their open palms for money, gesturing towards their mouths. Some waved mutilated limbs; others pushed emaciated infants with huge hungry eyes in Margaret's face. She had no money or food to give so strove to keep Pavia out of their reach while Ben's servants beat off the clutching hands. Uncomfortably hot, and thirsty, with no idea where they were going, Margaret blindly followed Ben. There were so many things that she wanted to ask her husband, so much to say after all this time. His brief touch in the car was enough to reawaken her desire for him.

Coolies competed to assist the luggage-carrying servants, hindering any possibility of smooth progress. Indian travellers made way, British passengers turned their backs.

The guard paced the platform where a throbbing steam train was ready to depart. The last servant jumped on board as the guard dropped his flag and the train lurched forward. They were off.

Margaret gasped at the inside of their private carriage. It was like a doll's palace with ornate curtained windows, a brocade covered couch, easy chairs and a carved writing desk complete with pen stand. Silver filigreed glass lamps dotted small tables. Tucked away was a bedroom with a washstand and bijou bed made to scale.

Servants deftly brought trays with glasses and jugs of water. Dishes of sweet pastries, sticky white balls of syrup, fiery mixes, nuts and dark aniseeds were spooned in turn into Margaret's hand. She tried to be polite but the mixture of tastes and hot flavourings made her nauseous.

It was difficult to juggle the food, while restraining Pavia from touching everything within reach and listening to Ben's running commentary. "Our journey will take approximately three days. The servants travel separately but will attend to everything we require. The ayah is the woman who took Pavia from you at the port. She will look after our daughter, amuse her and generally perform the daily tasks required for a small child. You will not be troubled by such trifles."

Margaret reacted strongly to this suggestion, "I'm certainly not going to hand Pavia to some unknown servant to look after!"

Ben said firmly "This is the custom and so it will be. The ayah will follow your instructions. Indeed she will always be in your presence unless you choose otherwise." With that he held Pavia for the first time cooing and petting until she returned his affection with chuckles and infant caresses.

"Dada . . . Dada" Margaret repeated.

"Papa," corrected Ben.

The ayah brought a cup of warm milk and, after a little persuasion from her mother, Pavia allowed the servant to feed her.

Heavy eyed with heat, Margaret was losing the battle to stay awake and reluctantly retreated to lie on the bed. She must have slept for hours for on waking the muted lights of the sleeping quarters highlighted the sleeping figure of Ben. She opened the room's divider. On the other side Pavia was curled on a soft cot with the ayah asleep on the floor. All was well.

Peeping out through a chink in the bedroom's heavy brocade curtain Margaret's reflection bounced back at her. The train clattered noisily through a railway station lit by flaming brands attached to the sides of low buildings. On the platform groups of men huddled beside burning braziers which illuminated their faces like renaissance paintings in Edinburgh's art galleries.

Ben was different now, in control, not the spontaneous lover who threw caution to the wind. Margaret had presumed so much without asking and the journey to his home was much longer than she anticipated. She was looking forward to meeting his family and had made up her mind to like them, especially his sisters. Maybe his mother would be at the station to meet them. Margaret blinked away the tears. It didn't matter when and where the journey ended, as long as Ben was there.

She rested her head on the tepid window swaying with the movement of the carriage. Isolated from anything she had ever known, with no clue as to where she was heading, she was filled with misgivings.

* * * * *

Ben organised the servants who boiled water for drinks and washing, cooked food and kept Pavia fed and amused. The train chugged deeper into rural India passing scattered villages with houses made from mud and straw, interconnected by dirt roads. Women in brightly coloured saris, frequently with babies slung to their back, gleaned the fields, or walked balancing bundles of sticks on their head in the direction of the village. Buffaloes pulled ploughs with barefooted farmers guiding the furrows, bullock drawn carts laden with produce wound down dusty lanes.

Alarmed by the sound of banging overhead Margaret opened the carriage window and looked up. Scrawny men, surrounded by cloth bundles, were travelling on the roof. They were equally surprised to see a Memsahib boldly looking up at them. The rail route was often blocked by a cow wandering onto the track causing the engine to stop or slow to a walking pace. The men on the roof leapt off, standing in lines parallel to the track to urinate

Customs and a language with which she could make no connection bombarded Margaret. She recognised from the way the servants, porters and officials deferred to Ben that he was powerful and important whereas it was as if she was invisible.

The ayah didn't understand her. Margaret tried using signs and gestures which resulted in the servant doing as she was accustomed. Time after time, in sheer frustration Margaret sent the woman back to the servants' quarters only to recall her. Ben didn't intervene, unaware of his wife's increasing sense of uselessness and segregation.

The train arrived at a station named Bareilly at twilight. A horse-drawn carriage was waiting for them. Ben said it was a tonga. A pleasant change from the closed car but the whine of mosquitoes overloaded the oppressive air. They didn't seem to bother Ben but Margaret wearily pulled down the sleeves of her travel jaded dress in a vain attempt to fend off the multitude of voracious insects. The ayah fanned Pavia who kept attempting to climb over the side of the carriage. One advantage of the car was that you could close the windows.

The tonga driver was clean-shaven and smartly dressed in a tunic with matching trousers. He carried a light whip, drawn upright in salutation on Ben's approach. Ben clicked his fingers; two tall liveried young men, armed with long polished canes, stepped forward and bowed, "Charuni these men are your bearers. They will accompany and protect you at the cost of their lives when you go abroad."

What ever would she do with these people? All she wanted was to be alone with her husband.

Margaret's homesickness increased as they drove through the town. They passed groups of English ladies escorted by servants, presumably shopping. She nodded and smiled but they gaped rudely at her.

There was no sign of Ben's family when the tonga stopped outside a grand hotel, but the owner greeted him like a friend and supervised the off-loading of the luggage.

"I have business which will keep me in Bareilly," Ben explained sketchily, "rest and get used to my India."

Margaret hid her disappointment behind the requisite smile.

CHAPTER 11

Bareilly 1935-1936

Light forced its way through the gaps in the wooden shutters making patterns on the sleeping figure of Ben. Margaret was caught in delicious nights that sent her senses reeling, turning her world up side down. She stretched lazily listening to Bareilly waking. Dogs barked at bleating goats rousing the town; the tinkling flock led safely into the countryside by some vigilant goatherd. Then all was quiet except for the gentle mooing of meandering cows and the soft sound of air blown through velvet muzzles. The peace was broken by the rasping cough of camels loudly complaining at being harnessed to carts at the start of the working day. Pigs squealed in rage, chased from a feast of yesterday's rubbish by an unknown neighbour. Voices called, some smooth and low, others harsh and coarse until everything drowned in the ringing call of the Mullah from the lofty mosque.

* * * * *

Margaret saw little of her husband. Business took him to Aakesh, his family home, but he refused her repeated requests to accompany him. His mother and sisters were there so Margaret wasn't necessary. He needed her to remain in Bareilly to take care of him.

Take care of him! What a lame excuse! There was a surfeit of servants for everything in the hotel. Some were busy from morning to night squatting on their haunches, using short-handled brushes made from fine twigs, to sweep the floor. They were careful not to raise any more dust which, to Margaret's dismay, constantly formed a sandy layer on everything. Tongue flicking lizards roamed the hotel walls, white ants ate the doors, gigantic crimson cockroaches lurked in the kitchen.

She was wasting away, plagued by persistent diarrhea, increasingly frightened to eat the spicy food in case she hastily needed to relieve herself. Embarrassed by her predicament, and with no one to confide in, Margaret spent days in idleness, playing with Pavia, walking or reading in the hotel's private garden.

She wondered miserably what Jean was doing back home in Scotland, probably working too hard but at least she had a purpose. Margaret wrote her sister long letters but it wasn't the same as talking together. This was the longest they'd been apart. Her mother often said, "Stop blethering, Maggie" but here she was mute.

The real India bore no resemblance to the place Ben had described in the stories and legends he'd related in Scotland. He made it sound like a magical country where everyone spoke English. Margaret was shocked by the poverty littering Bombay's pavements but Ben said fatalistically, "The poor are always with us. Don't trouble yourself about it. They are untouchables. You won't come into contact with them."

It was easy for him to say but she couldn't ignore the men, women and children of all ages, wrapped in rags, eking out a dire existence when she had so much. Margaret didn't know what she would do if she had to walk past them in Bareilly.

* * * * *

A new maid was to bring morning tea. Almost shouting at Ben, Margaret exclaimed, "I don't want any more servants! I want something to do!"

He retorted, "You have something to do. You are my wife. That's what you do."

"Well it's not enough."

Ben shrugged, "Give yourself time and it will be." That was the end of any discussion.

Margaret grudgingly sipped the tea and nibbled sweet biscuits brought by the maid. *Bed tea*, aptly named, a harmless indulgence, to be enjoyed propped by an assortment of bolsters and pillows before rising. She'd written and told her mother about it.

"Memsahib, will it please you to take a bath?"

Margaret jumped. The slightly built servant was so quiet she had forgotten she was in the room, "What . . . is . . . your . . . name girl?" she asked, emphasizing every word.

The maid looked down at her feet in a gesture of respect, and replied humbly, "I am called Muni."

"Well Muni, where did you learn to speak English so well?"

"Sahib arranged it in order that I could help his British wife. It was a great honour for my family. I worked very hard at my studies, as I had been so favoured. Please God I will serve you well."

"I'm sure you will," Margaret replied amiably. The maid's decorum inhibited any demonstrative show of friendship between them.

"If you permit, Memsahib, I will prepare you for your bath."

Margaret wasn't certain what that meant but it was bound to be better than her messy attempts with bowl and bucket to keep clean.

"Please to sit?" Muni said indicating a dark wooden chair that was evidently used for this purpose. The maid massaged rose-scented oil into Margaret's hair, scalp, neck and shoulders, modestly helping her out of her night gown and into a tub of heavenly scented water. Then she withdrew leaving the memsahib soaking her cares away.

At last someone who could speak English, but it was more than that. Muni reminded Margaret of Jean. She couldn't explain it. There was an air about the maid's movements. When Muni returned Margaret readily asked questions and advice as if they had known each other for years.

Glowing from the massage and with renewed spirits, Margaret joined Ben in the breakfast room. "What kept you so long?" he said curtly.

"I didn't realise the time. Is it today we meet your mother?"

"What ever makes you think that?"

"The maid . . . I thought you had sent her to prepare me . . ."

"All the women in my family have a personal maid. It's no more than that."

"But . . ."

"Charuni, I am opening a clinic here and have attracted many sponsors. The rich will pay but the poor . . . For you I will treat them for nothing." Ben made it plain that he was pleasing her but was in no hurry to grant any request to meet his family.

She asked Muni where Ben's home was and discovered that Aakesh was in the countryside, some distance away. Surely it would be better if she stayed there. She would have his family for company. He would be able to get on with his work and it would be less expensive. Puzzled, she put it to Ben.

"My dear," he condescendingly answered, "you have joined an elite, aristocratic family of the highest caste. There are many responsibilities that go with this position. Money is not a consideration. I have been remiss in not teaching you more about your duties and conduct as my wife."

"I'm trying to learn" Margaret mumbled apologetically, but again her husband failed to detect the homesickness in her voice.

"Charuni, your work is to supervise the servants who have positions in the household according to their caste. Our caste is similar to your class system but possibly more refined. It defines ones role in society, which person you marry, where you live and the very food you eat. Here the hotel servants get on with their routine. You do not need to interfere, merely alert them to your presence. Our personal servants must follow your command."

Margaret nodded obediently but Ben's lecture wasn't over, "For instance, my dear, you must have noticed that there are servants to carry out the lowly jobs?"

Lowly jobs . . . What ever did he mean? She asked him. Ben's lip curled in disgust, "Cleaning toilets and other waste. You must have no contact with them but instruct another to check the work is done."

Who would she ask? He didn't say but continued to give reams of information, stuffing Margaret's head with noise.

"A dhobi collects the laundry and returns it ironed ready for use. Others attend to us at meal times, clearing away when we have finished. I have employed a Brahmin cook to prepare our food. We have our bearers and of course there is the ayah, our driver and a couple of general servants to run errands and such like. They will always keep a respectful distance and you must encourage this or they will become confused and take liberties."

Did this include Muni? If so where would Margaret find a friend?

Ben modulated his tone, "It is very important that you allow specific persons to handle our food and touch you and Pavia. The ayah and bearer, along with your maid and members of our family, are the only people who can touch the child. My daughter's feet must not come into contact with the earth outside the hotel and its grounds for fear of infection. Of course your maid will attend to your needs. Keep her close by you." He caressed Margaret's cheek easing the tension between them. "My dear, to me this is quite enough for you to do. Don't worry, you will get used to it in time. It is what everyone expects and works very well if you follow convention." He left abruptly without kissing her.

Before India Margaret and Pavia slept in the same room, from opening their eyes to going to sleep they were constantly together. She was the first thing Margaret saw in the morning and the last thing at night. Now Pavia's nights were spent with the ayah. This was one change Margaret quietly resented. Sometimes, when Ben was away, she smuggled her daughter into bed with her, then she didn't feel quite so lonely.

The woollen comforter given to Pavia by her Scots grandmother had long since disintegrated, replaced by a gold engraved bracelet from her father. Pavia twisted this round and round on her chubby wrist if she was tired. Today the delightful toddler was bursting with energy, jumping off her mother's knee calling, 'Jaldi jaldi,' and running off to play with the ayah.

* * * * *

Muni was Margaret's salvation, a discerning supporter, guiding her memsahib through the intricacies of the household. Mistress and maid were comfortable in each other's company and their conversations soon assumed a natural flow. Concerned that her mistress was very thin Muni ventured to ask, "Memsahib, are you well?" Margaret explained that she was continually suffering from a runny tummy. "Let me help you, memsahib, for in summers even we suffer from this. A diet with bananas and papaya fruits can help. I will also make you a special pink tea."

"Pink tea, I've never heard of such a thing."

"It is made with green tea, cardamom, cinnamon, saffron threads, almonds and honey. Sweet and soothing, it will quickly make you feel better."

An exotic cocktail made from tea. Margaret would have to write to tell her mother about it. Anxious to relieve the restricting condition Margaret suggested they go to the market to buy the ingredients.

Muni rang a small silver bell to summon a bearer. The maid spoke quickly to him and he left returning with an umbrella and a companion. Margaret had no money, but Muni told her that as the wife of such a prominent man it wasn't necessary. There was a way of doing such things.

Bareilly was an English garrison town. In the past it had been one of the sites of the Indian Mutiny and a scene of fierce sectarian fighting. At present Hindus and Muslims lived side by side and it was an important trade and travel centre. Margaret had high hopes of making friends among the British colony.

It was nine o'clock when the little party left the hotel and already growing hot when they got down from the tonga in Bareilly. The ayah carried Pavia and their fearsome bearers deterred the inquisitive as they headed towards the market.

Small wooden carts and anything with a flat surface were used to make improvised stalls. The more permanent fixtures had a straw roof and were a mass of red, orange, black, brown and brilliant yellow powder. The colourful heaps spilled over into one another merging into bright marbled streams. Muni explained these were ground spices used in cooking and took pinches of the most common ones holding them out to her mistress who cautiously sniffed them. The ground cinnamon, cardamom and coriander tickled Margaret's nose making her sneeze, sending clouds of fine powder into the air. She refused to sample any more but instead tried to repeat their Hindi names. Mistress and maid giggled like children at her tongue twisting efforts.

Muni pointed out oranges, apples and bananas. These fruits were familiar but the yellow ball-like raspberries, red tinged guavas and prickly topped pineapples were unknown to Margaret.

"Memsahib, this area of my country is famous for mangoes but they are for summers . . . never eat them, or peaches, unless at home. They cannot be safely washed here in the market. Fruit that can be peeled without washing is safe to eat outside," Muni demonstrated by peeling a banana and holding it out to Pavia who took a bite, then ate the rest. The maid peeled another, "Eat memsahib . . . it too is good for you."

"I'm not sure," Margaret said nibbling round the edge. She would have eaten more, but Muni nodded as if to say that's enough.

Two English ladies accompanied by servants sauntered ahead of them. Margaret quickened her pace treading between cloths of nuts and dried fruits covering the ground, calling urgently, "Excuse me! Excuse me!"

The women stopped. They were used to seeing the overheated face and inappropriate clothing of recent arrivals but whoever this was didn't know the form. It simply wasn't done to call out like that in public.

Margaret enquired shyly, "I wonder if you can tell me where I can find a good dressmaker. I find my clothes are most unsuitable for this heat."

The ladies, who Margaret deduced were in their late twenties, were always pleased to pass on the benefit of their knowledge. They saw it as their duty to oil the wheels of colonial tight knit society. Margaret's *faux pas* was forgiven and they strolled along dispensing advice.

It was not the done thing to go shopping with a young child in the heat of the day but of course this once wouldn't matter. Everyone could see she was new to India. They complained of the heat, that summer was the worst, the servants and the deplorable lack of standards before one of them pried "You didn't say what company your husband was in?"

"Oh he's not in the army."

"Sorry, I thought from your speech and retinue that you were the wife of a British Officer and we hadn't come across you in the military cantonment."

"You must be the new missionaries?" deduced her companion.

"Well no", Margaret replied, "My husband belongs here."

"You surely don't mean he's a native, an Indian?"

"Why yes. My husband is doctor Atrey."

The more forceful of the two women replied, "In that case we will not be expecting you to call."

Margaret's face flushed deeper. She turned from the retreating figures and returned to the hotel. In the evening she recounted the incident to Ben who assured her he would take measures to prevent it happening again.

He questioned Muni and the bearers about the insulting behaviour of the British women towards his wife. Enquiries among the garrison's servants easily identified them and their husbands' rank. The slight would not pass unpunished.

The next thing Margaret knew was that they were moving to a splendid bungalow, in landscaped grounds belonging to a wealthy relative of the Nawab. The same man had arranged the exotic train carriage to bring Margaret to Bareilly. He had been educated in England so the building reflected this. The spacious rooms were a fusion of chintz-covered couches, ornate mirrors, ivory carvings and embroidered panels and wall hangings. Margaret had admired such things when visiting the homes of wealthy students in Edinburgh but didn't expect to live amidst such treasures.

Stung into action, Ben arranged for a tutor to teach Margaret Hindi and a smattering of Urdu. It was important his wife developed the appropriate accent and mannerisms of his caste.

A quick student, Margaret welcomed the challenge, trying out her linguistic skill on Muni, mastering enough phrases to begin to instruct the other servants.

* * * * *

Satisfied with Margaret's rapid fluency in Hindi and increased confidence in managing the household Ben organized a drinks party. Invitations were hand delivered to British officers, high-ranking civil servants, their wives and prominent district society. The two officers whose wives had dared to publicly cut Margaret were not on the guest list. The army would deal with them.

Muni found an excellent dressmaker who made clothes for the wives of senior British officials. Margaret ordered a flattering eau-de-nil dress for the party. Servants decorated the garden with hanging lanterns. Informal clusters of intricate wrought iron tables were arranged on one of the lawns and a carpet of scented flower petals led from the main entrance.

The turbaned house boy announced each guest and, with gloved hands, collected their proffered cards on a silver tray. Everyone who was anyone came. Whiskey and gin flowed freely, with sherbet, soda and refreshing lime drinks for the more abstemious.

Neat understated British wives, adept at small talk clucked "My dear what a splendid evening . . ."

"Can't imagine why I've not bumped into you before . . ."

"You have a child? Sorry, I didn't think . . . Of course you have. I have two and that's quite enough in this climate . . . boarding school can't come too soon for me."

Margaret smiled graciously easing her way through the conventional chitchat of her countrywomen knowing that their true opinions would be discussed elsewhere, probably at the numerous tea parties from which, so far, she had been excluded.

Talking with the strikingly bejewelled Indian wives was more testing. Margaret overheard them talking about Aakesh, Ben's family home but the subject was dropped when she joined them. Instead Margaret was profusely congratulated on her grasp of Hindi and, charmed by her modesty and intelligence, invited to call.

Honour was satisfied. Ben had ensured that his wife had access to the most influential society in the district.

* * * * *

The low roofed clinic in Bareilly housed a pharmacy and was the only one in the area with separate facilities to treat the poor. Ben was joined by two other experienced doctors and a recently qualified junior. They trained proficient medical orderlies who were often poached by the military hospital. Every day the line of patients grew longer, sometimes stretching out into the narrow road. Margaret wanted to help but Ben forbad it. Instead she busied herself raising money at tea and garden parties to fund the enterprise.

Liberal Indian society found her amusing; donated money but avoided any references she made to Aakesh.

Margaret didn't know why but she did know that caste was supreme, providing a strict framework for social interaction.

She had learned so much since she landed in India seven months ago and grown accustomed to life with a mainly absentee husband. Indeed it was a relief to be freed from Ben's constant instruction. Although her health was much better she was still troubled by the vagaries of the climate. Materially she wanted for nothing but she had to ask. This was galling for in effect she was trapped without personal money and tolerated by British women because of her husband's powerful position.

In Britain and its territories class was extremely effective at politely marginalizing outsiders while keeping the native population in their place. Margaret wasn't certain what her place was. She often thought of her family in Scotland but this was unsettling, weakening her resolve to make the most of the life she had chosen.

* * * * *

Margaret was enjoying a rare evening with Ben, "Charuni I have built an English House for you with furniture and fittings from abroad. You will keep your own servants when we transfer there."

"Transfer . . . !" She echoed incredulously. "Where is this house?"

"Where else but in the grounds of Aakesh . . ."

Pregnant again, Margaret was terrified of giving birth without her mother's support. The summer months' soaring temperatures and dripping humidity made her irritable. Bathed in torrents of sweat, it was as much as she could do to sit still. She'd planned to have Muni with her at the birth and, if there was an emergency, the military hospital was nearby.

"I didn't need an English house to meet your mother," she said petulantly.

"Charuni, Charuni . . ." Ben said, shaking his head as if she was a child. "My mother is in charge at Aakesh. She runs it according to our tradition. I wanted you to have a separate place of your own before we reached there."

Margaret didn't understand what he meant. She didn't want to live separately from Ben's family. Divided from her own she expected to find the support and companionship she badly needed from his. "It's the baby . . ." she explained. "I've waited this long to meet your family. I'd rather wait a little longer in Bareilly until after the birth."

Unfortunately this brought another rebuke from her husband, "Are you forgetting that I am a doctor . . . as good as any with the British? I will be with you. We move in a week."

CHAPTER 12

Aakesh 1936

Cloudless blue sky and flat fertile fields stretched way into the distance on either side of the road leading out of Bareilly. Occasionally, copses of ancient oak-like trees with a few optimistic traders crouching beneath bountiful leaves drew Margaret's attention from the discomfort of the journey.

"Aakesh . . ." Ben proclaimed as they approached the drive of a magnificent stone mansion dominating the landscape, surrounded by a high wall. Carved balconies arranged in tiers ran round its upper storeys and everywhere there were trees: thick leaved banana, banyan, pomegranate, limes, lemons, oranges, apples, peaches and grove upon grove of mangoes.

He reeled off the family's assets: land as far as the eye could see from the uppermost balcony of the mansion, twenty one villages, wells, flour mills, property in Moradabad, Lucknow, Delhi and Calcutta. This extensive description of his wealth was wasted on Margaret who was searching the skyline for signs of British residents. There were labourers in the fields and the villages that housed them. This was Ghandi's India.

"The trees make me think of Edinburgh and the Botanical gardens" Margaret said, but she didn't say how she longed to be there. The nearer they got to the mansion's huge gates the more her apprehension increased.

Ben picked up on her mood, "Why so sad, my dear one? See what a rich husband you have and how much I love you. The English House is sheltered within these walls. I wanted to bring you here when it was worthy of you," but Margaret saw no shelter behind the mansion's solid walls trimmed with a tangle of spent jasmine and roses.

India bloomed endlessly, its sensuous nature unrelenting, heightening emotions. Margaret was acutely aware of her husband. She had given him everything but yet some vestige of her soul remained untouched by his influence. Would it last in Aakesh?

The car drew into a leafy courtyard where ornamental fountains played into raised pools. Almost five months into her pregnancy Margaret found it difficult to alight in a ladylike manner. She needn't have worried. There was no one to greet them.

Ben strode ahead. Margaret followed him into a long room with high windows where pankah-wallahs, seated cross-legged on the tiled floor, pulled the hanging cords of suspended fans. After the savage sun the constant breeze and thick stone room were refreshingly cool.

An imposing woman dressed in white, seated on a throne-like chair inlaid with ivory disdainfully regarded Margaret. Two graceful young women dripping with gold and jewels were seated beside her. The vulgar intrusion of noisy footsteps and a pregnant British woman in a crushed cotton dress didn't belong here. Ben bowed low and touched his mother's feet. She laid her hands on him in blessing but there were no reassuring hands when Margaret attempted to do the same.

Ben introduced his eldest sister Vartika and her husband Hiten. Margaret bent to perform the foot touching ritual but Ben forced them to bow to his wife. Maintaining an aspect of civility Vartika said maliciously in Hindi, "My brother, you treat your wife like her British Queen. Beware! Even she may yet be forced give up the claim to our India . . ."

A crying child put an end to any further remarks. The mother, scarcely more than a girl, and the ayah failed to pacify the little one. They must have crept in at the back of the room.

Margaret expected Ben to call them forward but he went to them. The tilt of his head and raised voice indicated his anger. A stifled sob and swish of kingfisher silk signalled the trio's departure. Vartika's sly smile was not lost on Margaret but it vanished with a blistering look from Ben.

His family excluded her by speaking Hindi. If they had spoken more slowly Margaret would have stood a chance of understanding and joining in the conversation. Ben had said that his sisters and brother-in-law were fluent in English, his mother less so. Margaret asked Ben for permission to summon Muni to translate, but he refused. The maid hadn't travelled in the car with them; without her Margaret was trapped with no where to hide.

"Perhaps I can help? These formal welcomes are so tedious . . . made worse in this heat. I am Suleka, the youngest sister. Do take my fan."

The straw plaited fan resembled an axe head but, when wafted, cooled her face.

"My brother has told me all about you . . ." Suleka said sympathetically. "It is his wish we become friends," but Margaret was losing faith in her husband's wishes.

Pavia, bored with being confined by the ayah, began running up and down the room. Ben caught his daughter and threw her in the air "Go to your dadi" he said, sitting the exuberant child on his mother's lap. "This is your grandmother. You must call her dadi."

Margaret tried to explain, "Dadi is papa's mother . . . Granny in Scotland is mine." Pavia's lip trembled.

Once again Suleka came to the rescue, holding a bracelet to the sunlight, dancing the green gems on the wall. Pavia reached out for it, saying please in English and Hindi, entrancing the company, especially her grandmother who remarked, "Not only is this daughter beautiful, but like her father she has great intelligence."

Margaret couldn't help thinking there was something more in the supposed compliment. That was the trouble with India, layers of meaning underneath the obvious. The trick was to feign belief then work out the significant. This didn't come naturally but she was learning.

Ben refused to be delayed any longer. He had been supervising the design and building of the English House for three years and wanted Margaret to see it before nightfall. He hurried her outside where the Bareilly bearers, servants and Muni were lined up in front of the entrance. Margaret's heartfelt "Namaste" was sincerely returned. Ben whisked her inside closing the door behind them. The scent of recent lime wash, saffron and wood added zest to his kisses.

They toured the house. A black rosewood table with twelve matching chairs took pride of place in the dining room. Margaret ran her hands across the smooth polished surface, stopping short in front of the silver candelabra ready to be lit in the evening.

"See, I have selected everything myself," Ben said parading the contents of a dresser: crockery from England, Sheffield cutlery, Edinburgh crystal, porcelain from China and damask table cloths. Chandeliers twinkled in the drawing room. Chinese silken drapes framed windows. Golden brocade high backed sofas, chairs, a chaise lounge, carved tables and lamps were arranged to their advantage. It was as if Margaret was walking through a grand furniture store. If it wasn't for the kisses she would have cried with loneliness.

The study was different. Behind the mahogany door, row after row of shelves were filled with books. Tagore nestled alongside Shakespeare, Keats, Byron and Shelly. Medical tomes nudged history and philosophy; the tooled titles of old friends inviting Margaret to linger. An oval burr walnut desk with a leather top and hive of drawers was positioned near the window. Stationary embossed with *Mrs. Margaret Atrey*, inkwells and pens were ready to be used, but a red tartan-covered book, small enough to fit in a hand, caught her attention. Ben picked it up, "Take it Charuni . . . you can read to me like you did on the night of the poetry prize."

Burns poems, a reminder of home; if Margaret knew exactly where Aakesh was perhaps she could adjust until it became home. She asked Ben if there was an Atlas or maps so she could plot how far she'd travelled. He said he would acquire some but warned "Charuni, you know exactly where you are. You are my wife; in my world." That's what she was afraid of.

Ben admitted the servants, who began lighting lamps and preparing the evening meal. Tired by the day's events Margaret retired early.

* * * * *

In the magic interlude before day-break Ben came to her. They made love as the sun broke through the night sky and birds chorused in the morning. Resting he said, "I am the happiest of men. My son will be born in this house."

Margaret laughed, "How can you be so sure we will have a boy?"

"We will. He will be brave and bold with a mind as sharp as a razor."

Their intimacy was cut short by a servant pounding on the door, "Sahib, Sahib come quickly!"

Edinburgh had taught Margaret that temporary desertion by her lover was one of the hazards of being a doctor's wife. She passed that day foraging through the library and occupying Pavia and fruitlessly hoping for a visit from Suleka. Every time the outer door opened one of the houseboys became increasing jumpy. Inherited from service with Ben's mother, his dialect was impossible and Margaret was uneasy about questioning him. She despatched Muni to find out the cause.

The maid was gone for hours and on return avoided looking at her mistress. Exasperated Margaret said "Muni, I mean to know."

"Memsahib, it is better that you do not ask and I do not tell."

"You have found out? Haven't you?"

"An ayah in the main house raised the alarm."

"And . . . ?"

"She discovered her mistress hanging by a scarf."

Margaret had a hunch that Muni was holding something back. She continued probing; dragging out that the victim was the young woman who had left the room so suddenly on their arrival. Under relentless questioning, it fell to the maid to expose the brutal truth. The young woman was Ben's Indian wife and the crying child his daughter.

The threat of all manner of curses would not alter Muni's story. On the verge of collapse, Margaret was forced to accept it.

CHAPTER 13

Muni was sent on countless errands to find Ben but the walls of silence and subterfuge in the main house were impenetrable. Sobbing uncontrollably, her thoughts racing, Margaret paced up and down . . . a child younger than Pavia.! No wonder they stayed in Bareilly. Was he sleeping with that woman while she made a fool of herself? The shame of it! If news got out into British society she'd be the joke of the garrison. Her Indian hostesses must have known. There was a slight chance they were sympathetic but even if they were they wouldn't be able to help. They too were owned by their husbands' families. Life was cheap and with no protector, friends or money she could be locked behind the mansion's gates for the rest of her life or, worse still, murdered at the whim of this powerful family. Why did Ben uproot her from Scotland, establish her in Bareilly then shift to Aakesh, where she counted for nothing?

She fell on her knees in an agony of indecision; pounding the unforgiving tiles with her forehead, peppering them with blood. Muni rocked her like a child. The maid, more than anyone, knew that one wrong move and her mistress would be swallowed up by the river of India without leaving so much as a ripple on the surface. Their lives, including that of the unborn child, depended on the memsahib.

Over the next few days, Margaret read and reread the numerous letters from her mother and Jean. Their forgiveness for the hurt she'd caused them and their words of endearment chastened her. Yet paradoxically she drew strength from them. Ben's Indian marriage was a religious union unrecognised by the British. She was his lawful wife and would fight with whatever means she could to secure the position. She owed it to those closest to her to find a way out of this mess.

* * * * *

The English House, that Ben had boasted was built with love, was based on deceit. Since the fateful morning of the attempted suicide no one had visited or enquired about Margaret and the unfortunate girl lived on. Margaret christened her 'The Impostor'. She didn't want to know the girl's real name but she couldn't hate her. Blameless adversaries, they were thrown together, pawns in the machinations of the family. Margaret refused to be marginalised, or live in some kind of *ménage à trois*.

She had to break out of this convenient prison and assert her presence in the main house.

* * * * *

"Memsahib, it is some days since you tasted food." Muni said offering a small bowel of rice. Margaret had no appetite but to please the maid she ate a little.

"Muni, today I'm going to buy saris."

"But Memsahib the heat . . ."

"I've made up my mind."

"And Pavia . . ."

"Will be left to sleep . . ."

"Memsahib the car is not available. We could go by tonga."

"Bareilly is too far away to go by tonga."

Muni laughed, "We will go to Aakesh."

Margaret said, "But we're already *there*." Muni explained that Aakesh was also the name of the nearby town with ancient buildings, a famous mosque, temples, excellent schools and colleges, a hospital, markets and a railway station that connected to Bareilly, Delhi and Lucknow.

"Memsahib, for us it is an easy walk. Daily you can see the women going to market from one of the balconies."

"Oh Muni I feel so useless . . . I thought I was miles away from anywhere."

"You are miles away from your own people but you have Pavia, and me and soon another child. We will be your people."

"You are Muni . . . you are," Margaret said gratefully.

Afternoon was for resting, especially with the late monsoon. Margaret relied on this to slip away but nothing stirred in Aakesh without her mother-in-law's knowledge. Going at this time of day would also limit the possibility of creating tittle-tattle among British women in Aakesh town. If there were any, they too would be resting in their cloistered cantonments.

Muni believed her mistress had come to her senses and, like an Indian bride, accepted the situation. She would ensure she wasn't cheated in the town's bazaars.

Margaret hung on to the side of the tonga. She must have been mad to set off. Would she ever learn to take advice and a measured view?

Ever attentive Muni said, "Memsahib I have water and fruits. Stop and eat."

The tonga driver pulled off the road. The bearer lifted out a basket from under the seat. They picnicked at the roadside in the shade of a banyan tree looking out at the baking countryside. Margaret flexed her swollen fingers and toes. "Muni, what would I do without you?"

"Rest mistress . . . Let the sun pass."

Refreshed, they travelled on to the town. Muni's chosen shopkeeper sent for a chair. Honoured by Margaret's patronage and flattered that she spoke to him in his own language, he served hot sugary tea that the maid prescribed fit to drink.

An accomplished sales magician, the shopkeeper swirled a rainbow of cotton and silk over the counter. Some fabrics were plain, woven to catch the light, others sported gold leaf patterns, paisley and intricate traditional designs. Muni was quick to point out that in summer, cotton made the best saris, with gossamer silk for more formal occasions. Winters required heavyweight silk for warmth. Margaret didn't know where to start, but the astute maid suggested she choose two or three sari lengths to take today. She also suggested that the shopkeeper bring his most exclusive goods to Aakesh. This was the way local business was conducted by wealthy families. Public buying of saris was not suitable for ladies of the Margaret's rank.

At the end of their transactions a bill was made out which Muni checked item by item, negotiating a hefty discount.

Ben arrived home unannounced the same afternoon. Margaret's absence and Muni's questioning of the servants in the main house were reported to him by his mother. The findings would be unpleasant but of no consequence. Margaret would return. Her child was here; besides where else could she go? His mother had the gate keeper beaten.

Ben sent for Pavia but his little girl was out of sorts, unwilling to sing or be amused by her father. Her dark brown eyes mirrored his but she had a knowing way of looking at him, and for a second he was shamed. He sent her away and was reading in his favourite chair when Margaret returned. He expected recriminations but none came. Curious to know where she had been, he was furious with the reply. "Shopping" he repeated, "risking our unborn child for trifles! Let me see this shopping that might have cost so much." He passed the packages to Muni who dextrously unfastened the tightly knotted string unrolling the acres of brown paper. "Saris, you bought saris?"

"Lots to wear at home . . ." Margaret gave him the bill.

The discount was good but he said she should have tried for more. Rubbing the material through his fingers, he approved of the quality. "Well done my Charuni" he said, calculating the advantages of a sari-clad British wife. "Wearing these you will attend the temple. I will instruct you in all aspects of the Hindu religion but when we call on the British you will dress according to their custom."

Did Ben think she was so easily charmed into submission? If so he was badly mistaken.

CHAPTER 14

"Memsahib" Muni said, "the cotton blouse you are wearing has been dyed green, the same colour as this sari. You can wear a different colour or shade and change the sleeve length according to your wish. Step into the petticoat and please to stand while I drape the cloth over it."

Muni picked up the end of the sari and dexterously pleated the length of fine cotton cloth around her mistress. She paid special attention to the arrangement of ties tucks and pleats that kept the material in place, without buttons or hooks.

"Are saris always the same size?" Margaret asked.

"The length is six yards. It is said the cloth was born on the loom of a fanciful weaver. He dreamt of a woman, the shimmer of her tears, the drape of her tumbling hair, and the colours of her many moods, the softness of her touch.

All these he wove together. He couldn't stop. He wove for many yards. And when he was done, the story goes he sat back and smiled and smiled."

"Just like me" Margaret said, pleased at how comfortable it felt over her changing shape. Under the maid's tuition she practised until she mastered the art of sitting, walking and carrying out tasks with aplomb.

* * * * *

The men were away from home and the women getting ready for lunch in the main house on the day Margaret made her entrance. She wore a sari that matched her blue eyes, and displayed a garnet-encrusted pin given to her by Ben. Suleka invited her to join them. The others were too stunned to object.

The meal was strictly vegetarian without onions or garlic. The strongly spiced food didn't agree with Margaret but it was a small price to pay to court her enemies. She nibbled at a selection of pakoras. "We are to have another child" she said ostensibly to Suleka, "He will be born in August."

'The Impostor' cried out in dismay. Margaret couldn't help seeing the dulled red weals gouged in her neck, partially concealed by the sari's pallu. Ben's mother dismissed the broken girl with a flick of her hand, a frightening demonstration of the woman's power and capricious nature. Turning to Margaret she addressed her for the first time in halting English, "Such information is not necessary . . . We have eyes! Your condition becomes obvious. We have need of a boy. I trust you will be strong enough to withstand these hottest months."

Vartika mocked, "You British flee to the hill stations."

"I will not be leaving," Margaret said bravely. "My husband is an excellent doctor. He will take care of me."

Vartika glowered at her, "Another delay in arranging a marriage for Suleka . . . if we can find a bridegroom . . . all because my brother married you. Ghandi is urging the British to leave India. You will not be here for ever! Maybe then we will find Suleka a husband."

Margaret wisely refused to be drawn and said reasonably, "That may well be the case. Meanwhile if my husband is not at home it will suit him if I will take lunch with you ladies and join you for the evening meal. I have asked for my household duties to be given to me as soon as possible." Wary of Ben's mother and Vartika, it was crucial Margaret sought his approval of anything involving them.

His mother craftily gave Margaret the responsibility for overseeing the cattle and the field labourers, telling her to wait until after the birth to take up such duties.

Ben refused to allow it, considering it to be menial work but to Margaret it presented a chance to break out of Aakesh. She argued persuasively, "Your mother is in good health but one day I may have to take some of the burden. What better way to learn and please her?"

Ben wasn't convinced, but said she could try it for the next month, for most of that time he would be away. He'd review it on his return.

* * * * *

Suleka was sixteen. Vartika and Hiten were fully occupied with matchmaking arrangements so she seized every opportunity to visit Margaret. She stayed for hours, playing with Pavia and listening to stories about Scotland. In return she narrated ancient Indian legends and introduced Vedic chanting. Muni joined them, chanting in a squeaky high-pitched voice, resulting in little chanting and lots of affectionate laughter.

Early one morning they journeyed in a silver decorated bullock cart to inspect the outlying farms. The animals' burnished coats and gaily-painted horns were adorned with red silken plumes and musical silver bells. The young women were seated on brightly quilted cushions and shielded from the sun by a red and gold tasselled canopy.

Suleka told Margaret that Ben had travelled to school in that very cart but as soon as he was old enough he went on horseback, riding wildly, scaring his bearers who would have been punished if any harm had come to him.

Margaret commented, "He hasn't changed."

"It is his nature," Suleka agreed, "My brother was spoiled and pampered by everyone at home. My father sent him away to school to try to correct his faults. We cried for days, especially my mother."

Margaret couldn't imagine her mother-in-law being moved to tears. Although she appeared to be old and cantankerous she was probably in her late forties. If there was any kindness in the woman Margaret hadn't seen it. Suleka was the opposite.

"You see, Charuni," she said, trying to explain her mother's behaviour, "We have land and riches but my father aimed to raise the family higher. My brother was to become a doctor and be educated in the ways of the modern world. Hiten was chosen for Vartika because he is a lawyer and would eventually administer the estates. It worked well when my father was alive but now he is no more . . . and my mother . . ." She began to cry.

"Suleka, I am so sorry" Margaret said, "I didn't know your family and culture would be as opposed to my marriage as mine was. My coming has ruined everything, including your marriage prospects."

"Charuni, I'm not bothered by any delay to my marriage. On marriage freedom goes. You know in India a woman's husband is her god. She submits to him, serves him and meets his every need. I am quite happy the day comes later." Her merry laugh returned, "Indeed, I would not mind if it never came . . . but I must take a husband to protect me in this world."

The women knew that the day would come and Suleka would have no choice but to consent. "You are brave, Charuni, you married my brother for love. I could not do such a thing."

"But I have hurt so many people."

Suleka didn't deny it. "We came to know about you through a relative who was also studying in Edinburgh. He came home having completed his degree in engineering and told my mother that my brother was involved with a fellow student."

Margaret asked candidly, "The telegram to bring Ben home . . . was your father really ill?"

"It had long been accepted that my brother would finish his education abroad. A suitable bride was chosen for him while he was very young and the necessary agreements made between the families. My father was unwell. His illness gave the excuse."

"Did he know? I mean, your father."

"He would not have associated himself with such a thing. In any event my mother was punished . . . my father had a heart attack."

Margaret's fleeting triumph turned to sorrow for her dear friend who clearly missed her father, "What possessed your brother to marry me when he had a wife already? Then to return and father a child . . ."

"Charuni, Indian men take a wife for all kinds of reasons, rarely for love. We do not know each other until after marriage and then, if we are fortunate, love grows. In his way, my brother loves you. My mother expected him to forget you when his desires were met at home . . . even after he began constructing the . . ."

"But he betrayed me!"

Margaret's raised voice drew the attention of the bearers. Muni told them it was girl's talk so they moved out of earshot.

Suleka put her hand reassuringly on her friend's, "From what you have told me I think life in my country is very different from yours. Here the men are in charge and we women are answerable to them. We have to marry to be secure. Marriages are arrangements to promote families and provide children. As you have seen, wives enter their husband's family and belong to them. It is not uncommon for a bride to be poisoned, smothered or burnt to death in a mysterious accident. You must have read in the newspaper. Brides disappear or suddenly die.

It comes to light when the girl's family asks to see her and can be many months after the wedding.

"Brides who fail to deliver suitable dowries or provide sons are at great risk; more so when they are disliked, or disapproved of. Be glad that Sati has been outlawed or we could find ourselves riding with our dead husband to be burnt alive on his funeral pyre."

"Oh Suleka, the very country goes against me!"

How could Suleka explain these things? It was as it was. "To be a woman in India is a precarious business. I ask you to take pity and be tolerant of my brother's first wife. My mother chose her. If you drive her away what will become of her and her daughter? You would be made to pay for such a thing. Your family are far away and my brother is not always at home. As long as he loves you, and is by your side, you will be protected. Let us pray you have a son . . . God willing I will always be here to help you."

Suleka's timely warning confirmed that Margaret's fear was not irrational. Ben was often at his clinic; moreover there was talk that the British had invited him to join the army. She was safe until the baby was born. But after that who knows? In the blinking of an eye her life could be snuffed out. She resolved to redouble her effort to gain visible status and recognition outside Aakesh.

CHAPTER 15

Ben's mother advised Margaret to drink slightly salted lassi, saying it was a coolant in the summer and good for the baby. Margaret was sceptical but it proved to be the case. The creamy yogurt drink was delicious and quite addictive especially when made with ripe mangoes. She sipped it in the shadow of the balcony, mulling over whether to invite the wives of British residents to tea. If Ben had been asked to join the army there ought to be some positive response.

A cloud of dust rose up from the road caused by a troop of mounted soldiers escorting a car. The outriders wheeled into the drive in perfect formation. Margaret recognised the vehicle as belonging to the Collector, the British official charged with managing land and district taxes for the government. She went to meet him in the receiving room of the main house where she found him respectfully talking to Ben's mother, who presented Margaret.

"Mrs Atrey, do forgive my unannounced arrival but I was in the area and took the opportunity to call in person. My wife would have asked you to tea but she is frightfully busy these days and unfortunately I've been in Delhi."

"Then perhaps you would take tea with me?" Margaret said cordially. "It will allow me to show you the English House. My husband built it for me and is very proud of it."

"I'm afraid it will have to be some other time," he replied bowing to Ben's mother. Margaret was sorry she hadn't changed into English clothes but he sat while servants brought water and snacks. A fellow Scot, they spoke of Edinburgh and their home country.

"Mrs Atrey, you realise that your husband is greatly respected and an accomplished doctor."

"Naturally we are delighted," Margaret replied diplomatically.

Somewhat caught out the Collector admitted, "I don't know if this has ever happened before . . . I'm not certain how it will work out in practice." Clearing his throat he added, "You should be able to attend social functions but I'm not certain of the protocol. I have asked my wife to check out the situation. Women are so much better at these things than men."

Margaret managed to keep a pleasant expression. The Collector had a duty towards her but the rest of the women in Ben's aristocratic family didn't move in British circles.

The short visit officially recognised her status, however it also infuriated her. She was being politely warned to stay away from the social scene until 'her situation' was cleared. She would wait and see what happened. At the moment no one would respond to an invitation to tea at Aakesh.

* * * * *

Each morning at sunrise Margaret offered water to the gods and performed Puja in the family shrine. Suleka took her to the local temple which was a racket of tambourines, drums and cymbals. The burning incense and rhythmic chanting of the priests brought the same peace Margaret had experienced at Mass. She prayed for safekeeping and the birth of a son. Outwardly a devout Hindu, she exchanged Catholicism for earthly survival and, to atone for her sins, fearlessly distributed food and alms to the dozens of beggars crowding the temple precinct. A memsahib performing rites and prayers in a Hindu temple was unheard of, attracting pilgrims who donated gifts and money.

The tardy monsoon took its toll. Leaves drooped limply from the trees. The very air scorched the ground locking Margaret indoors. Temple servants enquired daily after her health at the main house, much to the annoyance of its occupants.

A purple blackened sky heralded the breaking of the weather. The deluge veiled the landscape. Margaret and Pavia danced on the balcony lifting their faces up to catch rain. Muni scuttled indoors to sort out woollen shawls for the changing season. In the merriment Ben arrived soaking wet, calling for a bath.

* * * * *

Margaret changed seats. Perspiration drenched her. Muni fanned, pankah-wallahs fanned, water was brought, lassi was brought but, bigger with this pregnancy, sitting, standing, and lying, day or night there was no rest for Margaret.

Ben diagnosed that the baby was in a good position, with the head engaged. He said, "Charuni you are so huge there's no room for me," and took to sleeping in his own apartments.

This made her feel like an enormous elephant and permanently crotchety. "I know your first wife and child live in the main house and you have a duty to them . . ." Ben made as if he was going to say something but changed his mind. Goading him to answer she said, "I ask you not to take your pleasure there and that they do not come into my presence."

"Charuni, a man cannot always control where he takes his pleasure! I have not availed myself of her since you arrived in India. Be satisfied to be my true love."

She wanted to believe him but it would always be like this, the uncertainty, unless of course she gave birth to a son.

The next day was brightened by the arrival of a letter from her mother. Margaret read some of it aloud to Suleka:

"We have such a lovely scene, the view from the kitchenette window across the fields. I never tire of looking out at odd moments. It is always changing, sometimes horses and sheep and today some beautiful cows. They are kept so nice and clean.

I enjoy feasting my eye on two or three shades of green and gold, the corn and the grass, the cottage in the distance but I am quite satisfied watching the onions, potatoes and lettuce all coming up so nicely and in good order. You know what your father is for order. Well you can picture what the garden looks like.

I can't think of any more now but I would love to see your bananas and peaches growing."

"Your mother sounds quite poetic, I wish one day to meet her, but Scotland is so very far away."

Margaret replied wistfully, "It is."

* * * * *

The traditional protection for the mother and unborn child held sway over modern foreign ideas. Ben's mother arranged for a special birth chamber to be set up without windows. Margaret would be confined indoors to prevent evil spirits harming her or the unborn child. She agreed to the latter but being incarcerated in the main house was more terrifying than defying Ben's mother. She persuaded Ben that a room with a small window at the back of their quiet house would make the birth easier. Medically he couldn't see it made any difference but agreed. Luckily the bed was placed in an auspicious position so it didn't have to be moved.

Just as she'd resigned herself to being pregnant forever Margaret's waters broke and the baby was born easily. The first cry sent Ben crashing into the midwife and Muni. "Sahib, this is not for you," the maid said quickly gathering up the contaminated bed linen.

Ben saw only Margaret, propped up on pillows looking down at her naked newborn baby. Lovingly pushing back her sweat entangled hair he revealed his wife's radiant face. Triumphantly, she said, "You have a son."

Ecstatic, Ben held the baby for a few minutes before the midwife and Muni chased him away. This was women's work.

The midwife cleared the room, destroying the polluted birth bedding and clothes. Muni tenderly oiled and massaged mother and son with turmeric, outlining the baby's eyes with kohl to ward off evil. Margaret would have to be purified before any of them returned to the household.

The whirring of the crickets and harsh call of night birds were eclipsed by the bangs and squeals of fireworks lighting up the sky for miles around. Ben was announcing the birth of his son. Margaret drifted into sleep accompanied by the sounds of celebrations.

* * * * *

Careless of custom when it suited him, Ben showed Pavia her brother and agreed to call the baby Saurabh:

a poetic name meaning fragrance. Margaret hoped he wouldn't change it for something more forceful when the euphoria died down. His mother finally intervened barring him from the room. Nothing must imperil the rituals for the welfare of her grandson. Margaret didn't mind. She was safe.

CHAPTER 16

1936-1939

The parched earth was renewed on the back of the monsoon and by October milder weather returned cosseting mother and son. The Scots winter following Pavia's birth had been bleak, with the windows curtained in ice, but Margaret would have traded all the luxury in the world to be with her mother and Jean.

Suleka visited, bringing Pavia. They came in the morning and again in the evening around six o'clock. Baby Saurabh fascinated his big sister. She gently played with his fingers and toes planting sloppy kisses over his squirming face. He kicked out his little bowed legs in protest. One day he peed up into the air spraying the bed. Pavia leapt around shrieking gleefully asking him to do it again, making the grown ups laugh. The company of Suleka and the joy Margaret found with the children alleviated the months without Ben.

* * * * *

On a warm evening towards the end of February, drowning in the scent of flowers, Muni massaged Margaret with seductive oils and, piling up her mistresses hair, threaded the trailing plait with jasmine. Ben was coming home. Tonight they would make love for the first time since Saurabh's birth.

Ben entered the apartment pausing by the open window. Margaret breathed in his presence. He looked at her in the same way as he had done in the days of spontaneous abandon when they worshipped each other to distraction.

She remained still, her eyes cast down, subjugating herself to him. His magnetism drew her, compelling a response. She slowly lifted her gaze from his feet to his head. Her pulse quickened. He took her hand and led her towards the bed. She moistened her lips and kissed him, pressing her body against his as he taught her in the early days of their love making. Pleasure showed in his eyes and she felt his excitement through her silken sari. She was in control, deliberately tantalising him, letting the unwinding silk expose her white skin.

Ben pulled the pins from Margaret's hair. It fell on to her bare shoulders. She was on fire . . .

Afterwards, they slept, her hand resting on the spent damp body of a fulfilled lover.

They got up late to the sound of their son's hungry cries, throwing the orderly house into chaos. No amount of cooing and rocking by the ayah would satisfy him. Ben withdrew to his own apartments. Margaret's breasts were already leaking milk when the rooting baby fastened on her nipple.

"It is good to see the Sahib at home," Muni said tactfully, picking up last night's abandoned sari and uncovering a heart-shaped box hidden by the scattered bedclothes. Margaret opened it. A cornflower sapphire ring lay on a bed of white satin.

"You've found it!" Ben said joining her from his dressing room. "I meant to give it to you last night but somehow didn't find the time." He slipped the ring on her finger. "Not even this can do justice to your eyes. It is your birthstone. See the open setting . . . the stone must touch your skin. Wear it always."

The scintillating jewel dwarfed Margaret's hand. "This is too precious for every day. What if I lost or damaged it?"

"Do not spoil my gift with your sensible ways. Enjoy it. Don't keep it in the box to be stolen. I leave today for Delhi. My Charuni, I don't know when we will spend another night together."

* * * * *

At ten months old Saurabh was walking, investigating everything. His legs couldn't go very fast so he dropped to the floor and crawled away to hide. His ayah retrieved him but the word 'No' in any language didn't affect his behaviour. His birth appeared to achieve a mellowing of relationships. Sometimes Margaret caught a glimpse of 'The Impostor'; recently a twinge of pity softened her harsh attitude but not enough to acknowledge the woman or her child. Life rolled along aided by Ben's letters directing Margaret's work and leisure.

* * * * *

The Collector called to let Margaret know that Gandhi was preaching Satyagraha through out Northern India: peaceful protest based on love and self sacrifice. It couldn't last. The elected assembly granted by the British was, in his opinion, a sop to appease the masses. A minority would have the right to vote and the official saw no end to the rising demand for Independence.

Margaret liked to be kept abreast of events from a British perspective. She needed to think ahead and if ever there was an emergency she was confident the Collector would let her know. She couldn't rely on the family. Vartika had taken to ignoring her.

In the English House the supervision of ayahs, bearers, general household servants and the children left Margaret very little time to herself. Since Saurabh's birth she had remained in Aakesh and needed a legitimate excuse to make contact beyond its walls. There was nothing to preclude the resumption of her duties, including the inspection of the fields. She had a notion to do it on horseback and wrote to Ben to ask his permission.

* * * * *

Margaret had almost forgotten about riding when Hiten, her brother-in-law, curtly informed her that suitable horses had been bought, a groom engaged, lessons arranged and Suleka and Pavia included.

"Horses are so big and sweaty," Suleka said. "Charuni, I can't think you want to do this. What happens if we fall off?"

"We will go very slowly. The groom will hold the horse's head. The bearers will be with us."

"I cannot sit astride a horse!"

"We can have special saddles so we sit in a ladylike way or we can wear shalwar kameeze. The loose top and trousers is perfectly suitable."

"No I cannot do this. Muni will learn."

"Memsahib . . . I too am not wanting it."

"I'm sure you'll enjoy it"

"No!" said Suleka firmly.

"Mem . . . saaaab . . . please . . . not me."

"What a pair of spoilsports. You don't know what you're missing" Margaret said, trying to win them over. It didn't work. She wouldn't make Muni try. That left Pavia, who loved the white pony chosen for its gentle temperament.

Over the months mother and daughter became proficient horsewomen. Pavia rode daily in the grounds, with a groom by the horse's head holding a long rein. Margaret regularly trekked through their estate outside the mansion, riding a game chestnut mare, accompanied by a groom and bearer. It was a startling sight in a mainly Muslim area but her modest dress and intuitive sense of justice led to harmony among the common people. The land and cattle prospered. Ben's mother shrewdly allowed her to get on without interference.

* * * * *

Ben wrote from Delhi saying he expected any nationalistic trouble to be restricted to the cities. However the Hindu Congress party under Nehru had won eight out of the eleven provinces, leaving Muslims clamouring for a separate state. Spasmodic violence broke out in Bareilly, a historical remnant of Islamic rule. Ben proposed Hiten arm the bearers as a precaution. Margaret was convinced it was hooligans using the civil unrest to legitimise their criminal activities. She sympathised with both communities, but Hiten restricted her rides, and armed bearers accompanied her.

* * * * *

Two year old Saurabh followed Pavia everywhere. Margaret had to reprimand her daughter for playing too near the deep well in the courtyard. A stern 'talking to' often worked but Saurabh had to be physically carried off the well's wall. Margaret almost smacked him. She had a violent headache. The pain was so severe it made her short tempered and dealing with a naughty child impossible. Alternately feverish or shaking with cold, she went to bed.

The fever raged through the night. In the delirium Margaret was by the sea at Queensferry with the salty waves lapping around her feet. She cried out for her mother, snatching the empty air. At other times she fought, fending away Muni and Suleka who slept on charpoys beside the bed. The devoted women washed their friend's burning body, and administered quinine according to Ben's urgent telegram.

* * * * *

The malaria fever broke leaving Margaret emaciated but she refused food believing it was poisoned. Suleka sweet-talked her by sampling each dish. Muni wrapped morsels in chapattis or spoon-fed her mistress. Their loving patience saw off the fallacy but Suleka didn't deny the possibility.

New mosquito nets were fitted above the beds and Margaret requested the return of the children from the main house. Days passed. Weak and fretful she was unable to extricate them. Suleka said that she would ensure their return but there was no hurry until Charuni was well.

* * * * *

Ben wrote ordering the construction of a badminton court to be used as part of Margaret's convalescence. Suleka encouraged the playing of the game in the cool morning, leaving her friend to rest in the afternoon. Muni was designated the role of umpire although she had no idea of the rules and awarded points to which ever player dropped the shuttlecock. Margaret became frustrated by Suleka's genteel approach to the game, "Suleka, that's not the idea . . . you're supposed to try to win"

"But Charuni, you are so weak. I don't want to tire you."

"I'm getting stronger!" Margaret replied slamming a point past her uncompetitive opponent.

Suleka yelled, winning her serve, "Okay! You've got yourself a match."

Their noisy games could be heard throughout both houses. Pavia pestered her dadi to watch. Ben's mother was unimpressed by the useless exercise but asked that Pavia be given a racquet to join in. The adult sized racquet was too big for her small hands but until a child sized one could be bought she used two hands to practice. It was the beginning of Pavia's return to the English House, first for refreshments and then to stay. A few days later, to Margaret's intense relief, Suleka brought Saurabh and his ayah.

* * * * *

An outbreak of diphtheria was wreaking havoc through the villages claiming the lives of more than twenty children. Most of the British children were away in school and those that were left were taken to the hill stations. On one of his regular visits the Collector advised Margaret to do the same. She asked Ben's mother for permission, expecting it to be refused.

"Charuni, I can't accompany you . . . and Suleka is needed for on-going wedding arrangements but *you must go* for the children's health. Hiten will arrange for you to stay in Nainital. You will be safe among your own people there. Take Muni, ayahs, bearers, servants and anything else you need from here."

CHAPTER 17

Spring in Nainital 1939

Seven mountainous snow-capped peaks ringed the breathtaking valley of Nainital. Hillsides were splashed with the sumptuous lodges of Maharajas against a backdrop of green trees and bright blue sky. Little wonder the British flocked there from the northern plains in summer.

The thrill of English voices, bungalows with sweeping drives, manicured lawns, carelessly abandoned croquet mallets and tennis courts. All manner of British outdoor bits and pieces littered the gardens, including an assortment of formidable looking bicycles. Travelling in a tailored woollen coat and dress, Margaret blended easily into the colonial scene. Hiten had rented Barum Cottage, a delightful wooden bungalow situated off the main Mall road. There was plenty of room to house the servants and bearers. Within hours it seemed as if they had been there forever.

Nainital increased Margaret's nostalgia but the children were in robust health, their cheeks reddened by mountain sunshine. She began formal lessons with five years old Pavia, based on a school morning, and the incubation period for diphtheria passed. Afternoons were for recreation. A trim pony and cart were hired for outings. They made a splendid party: Muni, ayah, Margaret and the children, accompanied by bearers, rugs, umbrellas, wicker baskets crammed with delicious food, and all the paraphernalia necessary for jaunts, picnics and boat rides on Nainital's azure lake. It made up for missing Suleka's wedding. Margaret knew Suleka would understand and it was probably better for everyone that she didn't attend.

Margaret's Indian surname was a target for talk in local circles. Consequently she received no invitations to call and issued none. It made her angry. The effect stranded her on an island of servants, children and domesticity. On the plus side she bought riding boots, jodhpurs and jackets for herself and Pavia.

Margaret had hoped Nainital might be more enlightened. To amuse herself she hired a horse and as soon as it was light rode stealthily into the feathery white mist hanging low in the valley. Diamonds of soft damp dew clung to her flowing hair and sparkled in the horse's mane. Mountains, trees, land, blurred in cloud revealing little of what lay beyond the path she'd chosen.

All at once the sun was up. She was in the middle of a kaleidoscope of anemones, geraniums, candulas, aconites, primulas, orchids, colour on colour, too many and varied to name. The horse cut through the fragrant spectacle sending an extravaganza of nectar-seeking butterflies pirouetting skywards. The faint dark line marking her passage was closed over, erased by bounteous grass.

She rode on serenely thinking of nothing, enjoying the solitude. A group of noisy riders gingerly negotiating the nearby slopes shattered the moment. No doubt they were the latest British soldiers seen swaggering in the town. Whistling and calling they attempted to catch her up. She was put out by their raucous behaviour but amused by their attempt at riding. Clasping reins and digging their heels into the horses' flanks, they were sweating as heavily as their mounts.

She condescended to wait, chatting amiably while the men tried to control the frisky horses. Once more on level ground, with the calming influence of Margaret's horse setting a steady pace, the soldiers regained their confidence. Some took the opportunity to flirt with this mesmerizing woman who had appeared from nowhere.

Quickly bored with their banter and the slow pace of the ride Margaret cantered away. Her companions' horses dashed heedlessly after her. Their riders gamely hung on, fighting to remain in the saddle. Margaret glanced back at the ensuing chaos, so far no one had fallen off, but any posturing would be painful for the next few days.

* * * * *

She received a letter from the magistrate. A landowner claimed to have witnessed the horse chase across his lands.

He accused Margaret of reckless riding and cantering her horse on the Mall Road, which was against the local byelaws. She hadn't considered the ownership of the land but did the man think she was a fool? One was lucky to ride at all through the main road's hectic traffic! The 25 rupee fine was extortion! She wouldn't be riding again. Pregnancy had put a stop to that. She avoided payment by returning to Aakesh.

CHAPTER 18

Aakesh 1939

Ben was waiting in the courtyard. He looked washed out as if a painter had begun to rework a canvas. The image was there but the colour gone. He pinched Saurabh's cheeks. Pavia pushed her brother away to get a share of her father's affection and began to tell him of their holiday. Ben put his hands on his daughter's shoulders quietening her, "My darling child. I thought you'd never return."

"It was just the sickness" Pavia said, "but papa, Where's dadi?"

Yes, Margaret thought, where was their grandmother? She must have missed the children. They certainly missed her.

"Mama please can we go to find dadi and Aunt Vartika and . . ."

"Shh Pavia . . . everyone will be here. They must be busy." Margaret sent the ayah to find them but Ben called the servant back. Pavia took her sulks to Muni. Margaret grumbled "Don't think you can return and take over the children."

"They're mine. I will do with them what ever I choose." The flash of anger was gone. "Let us go in," he said unhappily. "The servants can amuse the child. Usually there was no shortage of servants to play with Pavia but today no one came forward. Muni and the ayah took the children.

Ben led the way to the study where he slumped into his chair. "My Indian wife and daughter are dead . . . lost in the diphtheria outbreak. By the time word reached me it was too late. They will no longer trouble you," but Margaret saw they troubled him.

She had wanted nothing more than to get rid of 'The Impostor' and her child, but not like this. Death was too cruel. She was glad there was no grave. Maybe they would meet in another life?

Ben came to Margaret's bed and while she comforted him he discovered there was to be another child, to be born in the autumn. It was a sad beginning.

* * * * *

Hiten gave Ben a malicious letter from the landowner in Nainital, intimating that Margaret's flirting and irresponsible actions had come to the attention of the magistrate. Ben read the impudent letter and half-heartedly reproached her "Charuni, you must take better care of yourself. You are not Indian and so at present your constitution is more delicate."

"I am as strong as an ox. Look how I recover from bouts of malaria."

Hiten warned, "The stiff fine imposed by the magistrate will not be forgotten. I suggest it is paid."

"I've no intention of paying it."

"Vidyaaranya, tell her . . . think of the family name."

"I'm adding a new member to the family name," Margaret said sarcastically. "Let's think about that. I might not return to Nainital."

* * * * *

The 'Impostor's' death bought some stability but it was no guarantee of Ben's long term fidelity. After the taste of freedom in Nainital the rigid culture of Aakesh began to grind Margaret down. Under these black clouds she went into labour earlier than expected. Muni was with her but as the hours passed the maid became increasingly worried. The midwife could do nothing. Margaret screamed out in agony. Ben intervened sending his near hysterical mother away; keeping Muni and the midwife to assist him. The baby was in a breech position; too late to turn, delivered wrapped in his mother's pain. There was no cry.

Ben worked speedily, clearing mucus from the infant's mouth, expertly rubbing the blue floppy body until with a series of splutters, the baby drew breath. Ben's cheeks were wet with emotion, "A son! . . . Charuni, we have a son."

Margaret experienced none of the euphoria that accompanied the births of the older children. Torn, hovering between life and death she didn't expect the baby to survive. Some twisted logic accepting it as fitting punishment for her treatment of Ben's dead wife and child.

Once more there were fireworks but Ben stayed at home ministering to his wife and son, checking their heartbeat and respiration. On the following dismal day the baby was placed with its ayah, but immediately he was out of sight Margaret sent Muni to bring him back, refusing a wet nurse. The sickly baby lived, forcing his depressed mother to love him.

Ben's face grew soft when he held his son. He named him Rajeev. Pavia and Saurabh were far too boisterous to stay quiet for long so their visits were curtailed. Margaret rested.

Paternal custom was again derailed by Ben who supervised the care of his son. It seemed to Margaret that he wanted to spend every second with them. He read poetry to her. His deep melodic voice made the verse come alive. Sometimes they read the *Gita* together, discussing its teachings. She learned lines off by heart to please him. They shared ideas, laughed together at the amusing antics of their older children and prayed for an improvement in the health of their youngest. Margaret was as happy as when they first met in Edinburgh, long before any physical intimacy took place. There was the uniting of minds.

* * * * *

Margaret didn't question Ben's lengthy stay at home and was taken aback when he said, "I was invited to join the British Army before war broke out in Europe. It was an honour and it would have been discourteous to refuse."

"Why didn't you tell me?"

"It was for me to decide. You are used to my being away and I thought it would advance the family."

"I still haven't met the Collectors wife! You're good enough to die for my country but not good enough to take your wife to the mess."

"You have been here long enough to know how these things work. The war in Europe is not going well. Ghandi is opposed to Indian involvement but Jinnah's Muslim League is inclined to support it. The British will not talk of independence until the war is over and Jinnah hopes this will gain him influence. If Indian troops are required there is a possibility I will leave with them."

"Leave India! But you can't . . ."

"My Charuni, you know I must. You are British and an officer's wife. Hiten will protect you and God willing all will be well and things will go on as before. Let us see. It may be that Suleka will move here for a few months. You must miss my sister since her marriage."

Of course she did but that wasn't the problem. Ben's family would believe she had something to do with his decision to join the army. His mother and Vartika must hate her. Hiten in charge meant impending loneliness; for how long? Margaret couldn't ask Ben to shirk his duty. In the world of men and politics he was true and noble. She admired him for that.

The final command to rejoin his regiment came, as she knew it must. Over the last weeks they had said their sorrowful goodbyes in private. The staff car was waiting. Ben kissed the children, saluted his mother and assembled family. The driver slammed the door shut sending a cold shiver down Margaret's spine. Nothing would ever be the same.

CHAPTER 19

1940

Hiten went through Margaret's accounts in detail, cynically intruding into every aspect of her life. She acrimoniously answered his queries and he paid the creditors. He was an excellent administrator. Electricity was to be installed throughout both houses, and they were to have a wireless and telephone. However with Ben abroad he was able to exert a frightening level of control.

Letters made Margaret's day. Ben's, from North Africa, overflowed with affection and enquiries concerning the children and of course his usual guidance. She learned from Scotland that Jean and their brother-in-law Willie were in the Royal Air Force. Willie hoped to become a pilot. Margaret's mother didn't like him being so high above the land, writing that he'd have done better keeping his feet on the ground and joining the army like Nan's husband. The unpretentious letters worrying about Margaret's health, grumbling about the weather, the war and the shortage of things in the shops bridged the ocean.

Jean wrote enclosing some photographs. In one she was wearing the latest bobbed hair-cut and a short coat with a fur collar. Another showed her perched on a high hedge beaming, put there by some fun-loving young pilots out on a spree. She looked terrific, not at all like the sister Margaret knew. Jean described dances, trips to the mess and a free and easy attitude between men and women, unwittingly reinforcing the difference between their cultures.

Thinking of Jean brought on a wave of homesickness Margaret hadn't experienced in a long time. Uncertainty was everywhere and it was difficult to keep track of the people she loved. She made offerings to the gods for their safety, throwing in a sprinkling of 'Hail Marys' to cover all the angles, trying hard not to think further than the present.

* * * * *

Margaret couldn't believe Ben's latest letter. Surely he wasn't expecting her to leave the children so she could work as a volunteer with the British. It was bad enough their being without a father but to be without both parents? Well the idea was ridiculous. However he meant it and had written to his mother and Hiten.

Already Pavia and Saurabh led their bearers a dance, leaping over the well, hiding in the stables, or sneaking out of the main gate. They were unaware that once outside the protective walls of Aakesh they risked being kidnapped for ransom or prostitution. Ben's mother ordered the harassed servants to be beaten on more than one occasion for the children's naughtiness. Margaret was appalled to see them strutting round the main house, haughtily demanding the servants attend to their whims. Thankfully Rajeev was different, gentle and quiet, but he picked up all manner of coughs and colds. He was happy to be nursed by his dadi, making no attempt to crawl after his impish older brother and sister.

Margaret asked Ben's mother to be firmer and punish Saurabh and Pavia, not the servants. This brought a tirade from the devoted dadi. Saurabh was her eldest grandson. One day he would be lord of the estates. Superiority and authority was his. He would exert it where he chose.

Margaret remonstrated with her but she commented witheringly, "You have no knowledge of these things. Why should you? It is not your birthright. Because of this you will always be an unsuitable wife. My son required an Indian wife . . . The girl I had chosen, such an obedient girl, trained from birth to obey her husband . . . but she is no more . . . And you? You want to know too much . . . never content with what you find. Rather than continually meddling you will be better served with your own people. Be satisfied that my grandchildren love you but they will never be Britishers!"

How could she say such wicked things after all these years? Was nothing to be forgotten or forgiven?

Ben's instructions to help with the war effort ran contrary to Margaret's desire to remain with the children.

She increasingly feared for her safety. If the family wanted rid of her, it was working. She applied to work as volunteer at the Garrison in Bareilly.

That done the priority was to make provision for Muni's future. There was no way Margaret could make the maid independent so she sought a marriage with a valued and respectable servant in the home of Ben's aunt, who was extending her household. The aunt was delighted to acquire such a talented maid. Hiten would be most unwise to disregard the arrangement.

Margaret was giving away a friend, the woman who had saved her life and if called on would sacrifice her own. Muni begged to be allowed to remain but Margaret denied the tearful pleas, "Don't hate me Muni. I can't take you with me and I can't leave you at Aakesh unprotected."

In the privacy of the English House mistress and maid embraced each other as equals. Their awful parting was dry eyed. "Memsahib, think of me with love as I shall surely think of you" Muni said, burning the words in their hearts.

Worse was to follow. The garrison Commander at Bareilly telephoned thanking Margaret for the offer of help but he had plenty of volunteers. However there was an urgent need at Nainital. He had taken the liberty of contacting her brother-in-law who could see no problem in sending on the necessary credentials. Captain Atrey would approve of such a prestigious posting. The Commander looked forward to renewing his acquaintance when he returned from overseas. A car and trusted Sepoy were to be sent on Sunday to take Margaret to the train.

So soon . . . she considered feigning a malaria attack, God knows she'd had plenty but it would only delay the inevitable; to renege would shame Ben and give Hiten more ammunition against her. She would have to cope with the separation. Nothing she thought of made it any easier. Unable to make the weeping children understand why she was going without them, Margaret fought back the tears and caught the night train to Nainital.

CHAPTER 20

Nainital 1940-43

Returning to Barum Cottage was a mistake. Margaret rattled round it miserably. Last time she was here Pavia and Saurabh had chased down the wooden corridors, racing in and out of the rooms, filling the bungalow with noisy play. She hadn't the heart to stay and supervise the unpacking. The capable bearer would do it properly whether she was there or not.

She rode aimlessly down to Lake Naini and sat idly in the saddle while her horse drank the clear water. The rippling reflection merged with the towering hills and traffic on the main road. Nothing was clear. Muni had recounted the gruesome legend of the Lake's peculiar colour and how Sati, the wife of God Shiva, destroyed herself by fire because of a slight against him by her father. Shiva flew over the lake carrying the burnt body to its final resting place on mount Kailash. However the corpse shifted in his arms and the goddess's eyes fell into the water colouring it a mythical blue-green.

Margaret hadn't thought of it before but maybe Ben's mother considered her to be a slight on the family. Love and barbaric cruelty were strange companions woven through India like endless unfinished threads. If Muni were here they'd laugh away such melancholic dark thoughts.

Deep in thought Margaret left the serene lakeside and turned onto the busy main road. A policeman grabbed the horse's bridle. "How dare you put a hand on my horse without permission?" Margaret challenged, wheeling the animal's head, pulling the bridle from his grasp.

"Memsahib . . . you are causing confusion on the crowded road . . . not looking where you are going!"

Margaret's blood was up. She glowered down at the man who was rapidly losing authority while his voice rose higher with every word, "Memsahib, please to give me your name?"

"My name . . . ? My name is Atrey. My husband is Captain Atrey, an officer in the British Army, at present serving overseas."

The man shrivelled in front of her but a gathering of spectators hemmed in both horse and rider. The high-spirited animal chomped on the bit. Margaret drew upright in the saddle, tightening the reins. Flecks of foam gathered at the corners of the horse's mouth. Brandishing her whip threateningly she pushed through the gawping mass. In a fit of pique Margaret returned the mare to its owner and stormed into Barum cottage banging the doors behind her. She was to report for duty for the first time that afternoon and the morning had done nothing to calm her nerves.

The single storied Military Hospital was surrounded by lawns. Every blade of grass stood to attention. At strategic points, carved flowerbeds were placed like buttons on a dress uniform. Nothing was left to nature. Margaret approached the dazzling white reception area where a khaki dressed, clean-shaven young man shuffled papers behind a desk. A fan whirred above his head rustling the pages. He was in no hurry to acknowledge the woman waiting impatiently.

"Mrs Margaret Atrey," Margaret said, "reporting for work as a volunteer auxiliary nurse."

"Well I don't know where we'll put you!"

"Young man, I am the wife of a distinguished Indian officer. How dare you assume that I will be quartered at your discretion? I have my own bungalow off the Mall road."

A junior officer came into the lobby. The clerk's manner immediately became deferential, "Sir, I was explaining to Mrs Atrey that I did not know where she would be quartered, her being married to an Indian."

"I'm sure Private Jackson meant no offence. I believe the Colonel would like to meet you," he said politely steering Margaret into an elegant furnished room. The Commanding Officer rose to greet her.

"Mrs Atrey, I am delighted to meet you," he said, shaking her hand. "My name is Colonel Charles Thorpe. I had the good fortune to meet your husband in Egypt.

What a lucky coincidence you've been posted here. Won't you join me for tea? I'll introduce you to matron later."

Tea was served on the veranda. Colonel Thorpe chatted easily. He'd met Ben in Cairo, "Your husband is a first class surgeon, saved the lives of countless of my chaps." Then he added tactlessly, "Forgive me but you're not what I expected."

Margaret raised her eyebrows, "Well Colonel, what did you expect?"

"I'm very sorry, that was damned impertinent of me."

"I'm sure you meant no harm. I have become used to the reaction my marriage evokes."

"Your husband is a very fortunate man. Please accept my apology for being so crass." Discomforted by his earlier remark Colonel Thorpe tried to make amends, "Look, I expect to be posted out shortly. I don't like to see a British woman alone in these troubled times. My wife is here. I'm sure she will do whatever she can to help you." The Colonel's manner convinced Margaret that he meant what he said. She wasn't sure his how his wife would feel about it.

Matron was formidable. She was also brisk, proficient, and highly professional. The hospital ran like clockwork. Margaret was to be working almost exclusively alongside a group of Anglo-Indian volunteers.

* * * * *

The patients suffered from malaria, typhoid, and a multitude of fevers, ulcers, wounds and broken limbs that festered in the heat. The men were an easy-going bunch but on recovery returned to the merciless jungles. Some had been hospitalized two or three times, wise-cracking that they were on holiday.

The death of a soldier, and the realisation that his parents would receive the news at the same time as the cheerful letter she had written for him made Margaret feel particularly low. She was grateful to be asked to go roller skating by some of the nurses. Her usefulness on the wards and obvious education led to an increasing number of invitations to join them. Their jolly company helped to fill the lonely hours without the children.

The Flatt, on the Northern side of Lake Naini, was a popular place for recreation with a thriving market and famous boat house as well as the roller skating rink. Margaret laced up the skates and timorously stepped out, held up by her colleagues. Eventually she wobbled after them jerking her arms mechanically or whirling them madly, trying to emulate their fluid movements. She was beginning to make progress when her legs were knocked from behind and she landed on the rink with a painful thump.

A dark haired man gallantly helped her up. She took a steady look at him. Beneath his tan, lines of fatigue creased the skin at the corners of his brown eyes. Margaret intended to tick him off but he got in first, "That's what you get for messing about with soldiers on horse back."

"Excuse me! I've got better things to do with my time!"

"My heart is broken! I can see you've forgotten me."

"Forgotten you?" Margaret searched her memory without any luck.

"The last time I was in Nainital you almost unseated me . . . riding off with hardly a backward glance."

"Gosh was that you? It was yonks ago! I bet you were sore for days."

"More like weeks!"

"Well if it's any consolation I was reported and fined."

"Serves you right . . . I'm not sure I should introduce myself to a law breaker. By the way I'm Tommy."

"A likely story . . . Every man in the British army is called Tommy."

He laughed, "It's true! I'm with the Bush Warfare School."

She quipped, "I've heard you have to be slightly mad to be with them. Well Tommy I'm Margaret . . . Margaret Atrey" she said, as the other girls skated towards them. She introduced him.

He said "I'm hoping if I teach your friend to skate, she'll teach me to ride"

They told him she was pretty hopeless. Some of them had to go on duty so they couldn't wait. He wanted to start immediately. Margaret agreed so they left them to it.

"I hope you know what you're taking on" she said.

"That's the fun. I don't."

After an hour spent teaching her with nothing to show for it except bumps and bruises Tommy said, "Look, we don't seem to be having much luck with the roller-skating. Why don't we give it a rest and go to the mess? "

"That's a bit rich. You're just ashamed to be seen with such useless skater in front of your friends."

"Not so. You're the best looking nurse on the rink. It's a pity you can't stay on your feet long enough to prove it."

She drank gin fizz for the first time. Tommy was entranced and told her he'd never met a girl like her but Margaret didn't feel like a girl. There were days when she felt a thousand years old. Tommy made her keep their pact and she arranged to go riding with him the next day.

* * * * *

They rode out as often as they could. Tommy had been in India almost as long as Margaret. He had arrived via Gibraltar with the Kings Own Yorkshire Light Infantry in 1936, and within months was attached to the Burmese militia. In and out of Burma, he'd been recruited by the Bush Warfare School. Since then he'd spent most of his time in the jungle. He'd left a fiancée behind in England. She'd married his best friend. Away from home for five years, he didn't blame her.

"That's war for you" Margaret said, telling him how she missed Ben and the children.

She was in a quandary. Surely there could be nothing wrong in enjoying Tommy's friendship? Then why did she have scruples when he asked her to spend a whole day with him?

They set off by car to explore lofty Naina Peak, climbing the first quarter of a mile on foot through the shade of tall trees, the heavy green canopy lit by the plumage of gaudy birds. Putting on warm jackets they ventured higher into more rugged mountainous terrain. The high altitude made the going tough and Margaret rested on a pile of boulders looking down the mountainside where the land basked in the warmth of the afternoon. Tommy climbed higher calling her to follow him. She scrambled up to see the awesome Himalayas ranged along the horizon, their snow capped peaks tinged pink by the rays of the sun.

"Margaret I'm leaving tomorrow. I want you to know you've got me through a difficult patch in my life . . ." The air between them was electric. "I can't go without telling you. I love you. I didn't mean to. It started out as a bit of a lark to get my own back . . . If you weren't married . . ." He pulled her closer, kissing her.

"Tommy don't . . ." she said breaking away, but the enjoyment of the lingering kiss pricked her conscience. If things were different, well who knows? Always happy in his company she instinctively trusted him. His posting was a blessing, removing temptation, but the brightness in her life was going with him.

She couldn't let him walk away and agreed he could contact her through the army, making it plain they could only be friends. They shook hands at the door of Barum Cottage. Margaret was ashamed to admit she wanted more.

CHAPTER 21

A fleeting return to Aakesh

Margaret thought the infrequency of Ben's letters was caused by the war but the tone had changed. Surely he couldn't have found out about Tommy? It was a friendship but the kiss . . . Ben couldn't possibly know its effect.

Cut off from the children, Margaret wrote regularly to Suleka and Ben's mother asking for news of them. She also sent advice for the care of the animals, work in the fields and maintenance of the English House. Suleka replied briefly saying that the children were in good health and getting on with their studies at home.

A letter from Ben asking Margaret to sort out the children's formal education quelled any worries. She was to search out prestigious schools for Pavia and Saurabh. High ranking British and Indians frequenting Nainital were rich enough to pay and the schools reflected this. Why hadn't she thought of it before? She'd bring the three children here! She was baffled by Ben's other suggestion, that she qualify as a nurse once the older children were settled in school.

It couldn't have been more opportune. Margaret was due some leave and had a trunk ready packed with presents, sweets for the children, and a warm winter coat for her mother-in-law, tea for Suleka and token gifts for everyone else. She threw in a copy of bank transactions at the last minute for Hiten's scrutiny.

* * * * *

Pavia and Saurabh competed to be near their mother, pushing each other out of the way until she made them stop. Little Rajeev appeared slightly confused. Poor thing, Margaret wasn't certain he knew who she was. She bowed to pay respect to Ben's mother who neatly side-stepped on the pretext of talking to a servant. The attendant was shocked by the rebuff. The Memsahib's kindness and generosity were well known. He valued his position so his face portrayed nothing. Neither did Margaret's.

Hiten, bolstered by his mother-in-law's actions, accused Margaret of discrepancies in the accounts. There had been another letter from the magistrate! He could find no record of the fine being paid. Was it because she intended to continue ruining the family name? He'd written to Ben.

"You have no right!"

"I have every right. Vidyaaranya, or as *you* call him Ben, has given me power of attorney. After all I am a lawyer. Long before you arrived I was running the family finances."

"Still you should have written to me, not my husband."

"Write to you! May the Gods forbid that I am answerable to you! There are many changes in the arrangements for the estates. The common people attending the animals remain. The servants in this main house obey our respected mother's instructions."

"And in the English House?"

"Dismissed . . ." He said cynically, "All is agreed. We need to use money wisely if the children are to be educated."

Margaret was livid. On the surface it seemed a reasonable proposition but what if this boldness meant Hiten knew of some weakening in Ben's affection? It was too awful to contemplate.

Rajeev edged his older brother out of the way, snuggling close sing-songing "Mama, mama . . ." Margaret took him by the hand and, leaving the meal uneaten, with her older children following, withdrew to the English House.

The red and black tiled entrance was dull and neglected. Cobwebs crisscrossed the corners of the rooms. Dried curled leaves carpeted the floor, blown in where a shutter hung open. Rajeev watched Pavia and Saurabh kick their way through the piles of leaves filling the air with dust.

Margaret went through the rooms. Drawers were half opened, their contents rifled through. There didn't appear to be anything missing. This wasn't the work of djinns or the petty theft of disgruntled servants. It was much more menacing than that. Thank goodness Muni was out of this. The English House was being left to decay and in this climate would quickly become uninhabitable.

Saurabh checked under his bed. His boxes of toy soldiers were where he'd left them. He was quickly engrossed in lining them up to fight.

Pavia's room was also undisturbed. She blew the dust off the book cover of the *Naughtiest Girl*, sent by her Aunt Jean, and settled down with it like a forgotten friend.

Later, with the children sleeping beside her in the marital bed, Margaret tried to put her emotions to one side. One night in Aakesh was enough. She couldn't stay. There was no hint in Ben's letters of what awaited her. Did he know, or was this the way he intended her to find out? Either way Hiten's control was established with or without Ben's consent. Powdered glass in her food could be his next move.

Rajeev's curls and Pavia's long hair were entwined on the pillow, one black the other brown. Saurabh sprawled across the bed. Independent and proud even in sleep; so like his father.

And Tommy, where did he fit in? The children would always be first and what ever the state of her marriage she must keep them close while their father was out of the country. Schooling provided the perfect excuse. Hiten couldn't object to that. She'd show him Ben's letter, say they had places, drop a few names and tell him her leave expired at midnight. She fell to sleep making lists of things to take to Nainital in the morning.

CHAPTER 22

Nainital

A suitable elitist school was no problem but Barum cottage proved too small to house an extra child, servants and provide adequate space for study. Margaret found the ideal bungalow in its own ground on a hillside overlooking the town. On such a peaceful morning it was difficult to believe the disruption facing India. Margaret opened the *Times*. Gandhi was grabbing the headlines again. He had been arrested with other national leaders the day after Congress passed the 'Quit India' resolution and, since then, held in Aga Khan Palace Jail. The article went on to say that he was fasting in protest at the British occupation. Didn't he know there was a war on? Indian troops were dying in defence of the very country he was trying to break away from. Margaret shook the paper and turned the page, searching for news of the North African campaign.

Ben's dutiful letters were short and business like. It was hurtful but she was confident they would work things out when he returned to India. He mentioned Tobruk, El Alamein and fighting Italians. He'd been decorated but didn't say what for. She'd have liked to have had more details to tell the children. She was always talking to them about their father, preparing them for his return. Margaret prayed he was safe but after such a long separation Ben was no longer the focus of everyday life.

Events closer to home were more worrying. The Japanese had swept through Asia taking Singapore, forcing the British to withdraw from Burma. The entire East was imperilled. In the tranquil garden, with the children in school and Rajeev playing, war seemed so far away. Tommy was in the thick of it. She wouldn't know if he lived or died but couldn't forget him.

She casually opened a hand-delivered letter brought by the houseboy. It contained a summons to attend the Magistrates court. A British woman enrolling children in a prestigious school was a regular occurrence but a British woman alone, with an Indian husband, was bound to arouse interest. Someone had capitalized on it.

British men who took Indian mistresses were viewed as rather risqué but it was socially acceptable, provided they were discrete. Legitimate marriage was rare and so far Margaret hadn't come across another British woman married to an Indian. The injustice and hypocrisy in both societies always made her angry. She took up her pen and wrote to the District Commissioner.

Dear Sir,

I request your just intervention in a decree issued against me some years ago. My husband, Captain Atrey, is on active service in the Middle East and has been away from India for a number of years without leave. At his request I have been working as a volunteer helping to nurse the British troops recuperating here, travelling between Nainital and Aakesh the family home. At present my children accompany me and are in school.

I am being harassed for the non-payment of a fine of 25 rupees in connection with an allegation that some years ago, I cantered on a horse down Mall Road breaking a byelaw. I considered the fine to be excessive and intended to write to you at that time. However I had to return urgently to the plains and the incident slipped my mind. I recently returned to put my children into school and resume my work as a volunteer nurse.

The complainant, a Mr Mehte, has exaggerated an incident when, as a novice rider, I returned by horseback to Barum Cottage, which, as no doubt you are aware, is situated on Mall road. Taking into consideration the number of people who do go very recklessly on horseback, I consider it most unfair that I have been picked out from the crowd. I wish you to take account of my husband's services and those of myself in the W.V.S and accept my apology.

*I thank you for what I am sure will be
your worthy consideration of my position with
regards to this unfortunate incident.*

*Yours faithfully
Margaret Atrey*

She sealed the envelope with a flourish. India had taught Margaret many things including how to effectively slice through bureaucracy and deal with paper tigers.

The letter wasn't a lie, more a convenient distortion of the facts and gave her something to do. She was bored with her own company, besides which she felt useless lazing around with so many injured men flooding the military hospital. Ben's plan that she should train as a nurse held some appeal. The only drawback was leaving Rajeev with his ayah for long periods, but at least they would be together. She resumed voluntary work to see how things went.

* * * * *

The ayah was doing a splendid job but Pavia and Saurabh were rebelling against the restrictions of school. Margaret was requested to meet the Mother Superior on more than one occasion to discuss their behaviour. This made no impression on the arrogant children who claimed, in their defence, that the other pupils taunted them. Saurabh said fiercely, "They say we are British. We're not. We're Indian."

"And they won't do what we tell them so Saurabh beats them up."

Margaret tried to explain that, unlike Aakesh, at school the pupils were equal. This reasoning was nonsense to Saurabh and Pavia.

Reverend Mother's patience was sorely tried but the children's charm saved them. She had a soft spot for Saurabh with his exceptional intellect and appealing smile. What would become of him and his sister if the Japanese invaded India or the British left? Their mother would be in a perilous position. The Irish nun was impressed by the charity of this woman who found good in people, irrespective of their race or religious belief. The children attended mass as if they were good Catholics. It was possible their souls would be saved, but their mother lacked contrition and without it she was damned.

The nun tried to dissuade Margaret from seeing troops unaccompanied while undertaking welfare work. She cautioned that this might put temptation in the way of young men who had been away from home for so long. Margaret scoffed at the possibility. She was simply doing her duty.

The soldiers nicknamed Margaret 'Scottie' and were grateful for the unstinting work she did in supporting them. Some men had left for India missing the birth of their youngest child. One asked what she missed about Scotland, "Not the children" she said, "mine are with me but lots of things, the smell of the sea carried on the cold wind, the soft rain of spring and the stinging whipped rain of winter. Most of all I miss the sound of my mother's voice and the touch of her hand on my forehead." Married or single, child-free or parent, the general assent of the men drew them together.

* * * * *

A soldier wounded in Burma arrived on the ward. Margaret asked if he'd come across a Sergeant Waters. "Have I? . . . I almost stood on him lying in the undergrowth. He gave me a poke in the ribs with his rifle. Pardon me nurse but I nearly shot my lot. Then I made out the whites of his eyes and stupid grin. Poor sods, they've got their work cut out. I don't think they'll all come back, but I hope he bloody does. I've got to get my own back on that bugger!"

Margaret's worries were insignificant compared to the increased suffering she witnessed daily. Off duty she dropped in at the mess. It was good to have some light-hearted contact with adults. A group of squaddies loitering outside made lewd comments, offering 'to see she was alright', nudging and winking at each other. Their leering made her blush so they did it all the more. They'd be posted out pretty soon so it wasn't worth making a fuss, but she stopped going.

The majority of her spare time was spent amusing Rajeev and helping Pavia and Saurabh with their homework. The lively twosome easily achieved academically and fellow pupils were attracted to their company. Although popular in school, the children were rarely asked to the homes of their classmates. Margaret issued lots of invitations to tea but few were taken up.

She hoped Ben would return from Egypt before she put Saurabh's name down for Sherwood, a boarding school with a lengthy waiting list. He would need to use his influence to get his son in. Pavia would change school first but not as a boarder. She was Margaret's rock, an extension of herself, the much-cuddled Edinburgh bear propped up on the pillow, a reminder of Scottish love. Three year old Rajeev continued to contract every childhood ailment and was often curled up in some corner of the bungalow with his head in a picture book. It was difficult to separate the children but schooling was too important to let sentiment rule.

Once the children were in bed Margaret faced another night alone. She was having problems getting to sleep and after the servants retired relaxed with a late night tot of whiskey. It would never do to let them see her sipping the golden liquid.

She was roused from a deep sleep by a noise but the bungalow was quiet except for the creaking and settling noises made by the building as night passed and the temperature changed. Drowsy from the whiskey, she heard a man persistently repeating her name. Something must have happened to Ben! Where was the night door servant? She'd forgotten he'd been unwell and been sent to the servants' quarter. She unlocked the door.

A man burst in, dragging her into the hallway forcing her against the wall. Margaret tried to scream but the hand violently slapped across her mouth choked the cry. Blood trickled down her throat. Sour breath filled her nostrils.

He panted in her face, "You've not had an English man, just a bloody Indian . . . Well what's he got we haven't? I'll make you shout. You'll be begging for more.

One at a time, or all at once " He fumbled with his trouser buttons. The hand viciously keeping her quiet hampered the unfastening.

Paralysed with fear she realised he was not alone. A second assailant fell to his knees, tearing at her nightgown. She was no match for his strength.

A third man moved out of the darkness into the lamp lit hallway. Oh God! They're soldiers! How many more? Margaret's eyes beseeched him for help.

"I'm off," he said, "I was looking for a bit of comfort. I don't want any part of this."

His so-called friends swore at him and forced Margaret onto the floor. She implored God to keep her conscious.

Out of the darkness, screaming like a banshee, Saurabh launched himself at the soldiers. They kicked him to one side but the noise woke the servants, who gave chase. Once inside the barracks it was impossible for them to follow and identify the drunken louts. There was nothing to be done until daylight. The house was locked and a door servant posted.

Margaret shook from head to foot. It wouldn't matter that she fought the fiends who abused her. She would be portrayed as having enticed them. There were plenty of witnesses to testify seeing her drinking unaccompanied in the mess. British soldiers would not be blamed for offences against such a woman, especially one married to an Indian. No one must ever know, especially Ben. There would be no mercy shown for allowing such a thing to take place.

She staunched the blood pouring from Saurabh's nose and washed his cut hands. Six years old, fearless in defence of his mother, he began to cry. She calmed him, made him warm milk and put him in her bed.

The rancid smell of the men made Margaret vomit. In the bathroom buckets of water were lined up ready to be heated for morning baths. Tearing off the remains of her nightdress she poured them over her head, cleansing herself, ferociously scrubbing her body, purifying and absolving it from the men's vile touch. Climbing into bed she spent the endless night next to the innocent warmth of her son.

At daybreak the servants opened the house. She went out onto the veranda. The birds sang and the world went on as before, but she was silently screaming.

The postman brought a letter. On seeing the Memsahib's bruised and swollen face he enquired if everything was all right. Margaret said it was nothing: a tumble from a horse. Within the hour the gossip would circulate Nainital. She gambled that sober, the assailants would be grateful not to be reported, and leave her alone.

She turned her attention to the post, recognising with dismay Hiten's precise handwriting on the envelope. Enclosed was a letter from her father:

> My Dear Maggie,
>
> I am sorry to tell you that by the time you receive this letter we will have buried your beloved mother. She died suddenly, in her bed, from a thickening of the heart. God keep you safe. I remember you in my prayers.

The light was going out on Margaret's world.

CHAPTER 23

Margaret vainly attempted to claw back some semblance of normality, for the sake of the children. Notes were despatched. One to the hospital claiming that a fall from a horse meant she would be absent from duty for a few days, and another to the children's school saying they had a minor stomach upset. She silenced the servants by threatening that the Sahib would blame them if, on his return, he found they had failed to protect his family. Naturally Saurabh told his big sister but Margaret made them swear to keep the secret so 'the bad men' would not return.

Then she set about ensuring they enjoyed a fun filled holiday, recounting stories of brave knights fighting dragons and rescuing damsels in distress. "Just like Saurabh" Pavia said, then put her finger over her lips. "Yes my darling just like Saurabh." Margaret replied, imitating the child and covering her lips.

The bearer made wooden swords and the children acted out imaginary scenarios, stabbing bushes, servants and each other with great gusto. Rajeev clapped and cheered. Saurabh was their champion. Pavia gave him a scarf, which he fastened to his sword, flourishing it triumphantly, galloping round the garden on a pretend steed. Most of the daring boy's cuts and bruises were concealed by his clothes. Those visible by the end of the week looked as if they were the result of adventurous play.

Margaret scarcely ate, compulsively scrubbing her defiled body and weeping in the bathroom. The day the children returned to school she escaped into the bedroom. For years she'd expected to die, killed by the climate, childbirth or Hiten's ambition, but God had spared her, taking her virtuous mother. What right had she to live on?

She took the scissors from the workbasket and slid the razor-like blades across her white wrists, drawing blood . . . Once more deeper. Rajeev's crying infiltrated the curtain of despair. She hesitated . . . turned the scissors . . . mercilessly hacking her hair. It rained down on and on until the weapon clattered to the floor.

Margaret must have slept for she was woken by a man's voice rising above the children's chatter. Manically brushing at the hairs stuck to her face she was unaware that Pavia and Saurabh were in the room. They were swiftly removed by their bearer.

A maid entered. Margaret said distractedly, "Muni . . . Is that you? Muni . . ." but the nameless maid continued to sweep, gathering the golden crop and throwing it on the fire where it hissed and was gone.

A sliver of lamplight crept under the door. Margaret overheard Pavia trying to explain to Rajeev that mama was ill and sleeping but he kept asking, "Where is she? Where is she? I want to see mama *now . . .*"

"She's in the bedroom,"

"Mama, mama" Rajeev wailed, rattling the door, "Let me in."

Margaret opened the door. Rajeev flung himself at her, banging his head. She kissed it better while he patted the shorn tufts of her hair.

Pavia searched for a hair brush but Saurabh stared sullenly at his mother, "Mama you don't look like you. You are an English Memsahib."

Margaret gasped at his perception. It was true. It was time to put aside the saris.

* * * * *

Training to qualify and juggling the children was demanding, but it left no time to brood. Margaret successfully passed the first batch of exams. The consequence would almost certainly be a posting to Kohat on India's North West Frontier, hundreds of miles away. What on earth was she to do with the children? The history of the area was steeped in bloody rebellion. Fierce tribal resistance and inhospitable mountainous terrain had repelled invaders over centuries. The straggling border touched China, Jammu and Kashmir in the north and Afghanistan in the west. It was a world of lawlessness and intrigue. The British maintained a strong presence overseeing movement through the Khyber Pass, the legendary gateway to South Asia. Sick at heart, it was futile of Margaret to think of taking the children there.

Coincidentally a friend of Ben's family, a hydro electrical engineer on business in Nainital looked her up; from him she learned that Ben's mother was unwell. Margaret wrote to Hiten:

> *Whose treatment is she under? If she likes, you can send her up here and I'll have her treated in the military hospital. You will need to send warm bedding with her and she must travel in warm clothes as winter is setting in. I hope to have news that Doctor Sahib will be home very soon.*

The letter elicited no reply. Margaret arranged with the school for Pavia and Saurabh to become temporary boarders as soon as her posting was confirmed. Their howls of protest could be heard throughout Nainital.

* * * * *

Weeks passed with nothing sorted for Rajeev. Margaret was contemplating keeping the bungalow, hiring an English tutor and leaving her son there with his ayah. It wasn't ideal but it was preferable to sending him to Aakesh to stay with his ailing dadi.

* * * * *

Snowflakes fell like shining stars onto the shaggy pines and leafless silver oaks. Christmas came and went. Huge log fires burned day and night turning the bungalow into a haven of cuddles, hot drinks, thawing fingers and toes from building snowmen, sledging and sliding. Margaret continued riding into the white wilderness with Pavia and Saurabh but the worsening weather often prevented it.

The New Year brought more snow. She put off making a decision about Rajeev. She had written to Hiten to tell him of the Commissioner's decision to quash the fine. The reply was from Ben saying in future all bills would be paid direct. Her husband asked why she needed more money from the account. Was it to finance more amusement in his absence? Even Hiten couldn't have got this news to him so quickly. She read on. He'd been to the Punjab, Lucknow and Aakesh! He must have been in India at least a month!

Was she some kind of toy to be picked up on a whim, always answerable to someone? If this was love it was the wrong kind. Tommy too could have easily taken advantage of her. She wouldn't have resisted and where would that have left her?

Rajeev sheltered in the porch, waiting for a cuddle before his mother left for the hospital. The little man didn't like her returning to work in the afternoon. Margaret ruffled his curly hair. "Be back to tuck you up" she said, stepping out into a gale-force wind.

A car slithered up the tree-lined drive, ran off the road and became wedged in a bank of snow. The driver got out and walked round the vehicle throwing his hands in the air. The passenger harangued him through the window. A man got out. The deep snow rooted Margaret's boots in the ground. Her heart stopped. Ben! Flecks of sparkling snow landed on his army greatcoat. Grey hairs streaked his black hair, a dark sculpture in this fairy tale landscape.

He immediately took control, "I have arranged with the hospital for you to have a short leave. Shall we go?" He headed towards the bungalow. Rajeev's screams brought the servants wading through the drifts. Not knowing who he was, a hullabaloo of fists followed. Margaret yelled "It's, your Sahib, my husband!"

Ben knocked a poor man down and drew back his arm to hit him again. Margaret dragged at his coat sleeve to stop him. "You should be grateful that the servants are so vigilant in their protection."

"The devil that lets you down will pay for it!" Ben said cuffing the nearest, then, stamping the snow from his boots, he installed himself as master of the house.

The ayah pushed Rajeev forward but the boy wouldn't pay homage to his father, refusing to touch his feet. Ben asked, "Do you know who I am?"

The sometimes timorous boy shook his head. Ben lifted him up. Rajeev studied the face so close to his. "Papa . . . ?"

"Yes . . . Papa . . . Go play while I speak to your mama."

"Go play!" Margaret said, her hands on Rajeev's shoulders, "Is this all you have to say to your son!"

"I have pressing business with you that does not concern the child." The ayah led Rajeev away.

Margaret marched over to the desk and angrily pulled a sheaf of papers from the drawer. Brandishing them at her husband she shouted, "Is this it! Aakesh . . . anything and anybody before your wife and children! You want the recent accounts? Here they are! The originals are lodged at the bank. I send Hiten copies."

She lifted her head defiantly, "I have done all you asked. The children are in school. I have tried to keep in touch with your family but they have stolen our English House so I have no home at Aakesh. What more do you want from me?"

An assertive English woman was not the reception Ben expected. "My Charuni I intend to spend a few days with you and the children before returning to Aakesh and then to the Punjab to rejoin my Unit."

She asked hesitantly "Did you ever think of me or has time and distance erased me from your heart?" There were to be no answers. Always his way . . .

"Where is my eldest son?"

"The children are in school!"

"Well take them out of school!"

"But they'll be back at tea time and the car is stuck."

"You have horses?"

"Well yes . . ."

"We'll ride there."

They rode morosely to the school. An unspoken truce was established in Reverend mother's study. The nun discussed Saurabh's potential. Oxford, Cambridge or Edinburgh was well within his grasp. Pavia's too if Colonel Atrey chose to take the unusual step of educating his daughter overseas. Ben made polite noises.

A glib tongue held no sway with Reverend Mother but she was not totally immune to persuasion. The children were granted a holiday to celebrate their father's safe return.

Ben swung Pavia onto the horse with her mother. Saurabh would have none of it. A miniature version of his father, he was the man around here. A block was brought so he could mount unaided. Ben swung up behind him and took the reins with Saurabh holding onto the horse's mane. He rode far too fast for Margaret to keep up, endangering himself and his son on the slippery road. They were laughing by the fireside when she reached the bungalow.

"Papa, why didn't you wait for us?" Pavia said.

"Men don't wait for girls . . . do they papa?"

"Of course they do," Margaret said. "Saurabh, you must always wait and look after your sister". She knew his father wouldn't wait for anything or anyone. *Why* had he really come to Nainital?

They didn't talk except to the children. Ben gave them liberty to do as they pleased; flying paper aeroplanes at the ayah and generally causing a nuisance. By bed-time even Rajeev had stopped looking at his mother for approval.

Ben asked Pavia if she liked school. She replied with a torrent of fictitious stories illustrating how much she loathed it.

"How would you like to go back to Aakesh?"

"Really, papa?" she said, her eyes widening.

Saurabh chimed in, "What about me?"

"And you of course, old chap."

The boy dashed enthusiastically through the bungalow, gathering his favourite things. Margaret was perplexed. According to Reverend mother they were enjoying school. It was unthinkable they should abandon their studies on an impulse. Saurabh would be ruined if his grandmother encouraged his wayward nature. Margaret tried to discuss it but Ben's mind was made up. They would be tutored at home. He further justified his position by reminding her that she would be in Kohat for most of the year.

That night Margaret spread an embroidered cover on the bed and, using her intimate knowledge of Ben's body, oiled and massaged him. This cheap tactic wasn't love making but she had to try to change his mind. Saurabh must go to boarding school.

Ben confessed, "I was not prepared for this. Three years apart is a long time for any marriage. People change. I came to ask you for a separation."

"I have done nothing to cause you to put me to one side." She pleaded, "Once more must I lie alone?" He spent the remainder of the night in another bedroom. Margaret had her answer.

The instant Rajeev realised his mother wasn't going with them to Aakesh he began to cry. Pavia and Saurabh asked their father to let them stay. Boarding school wasn't so bad and they could be with their mother in the holidays, lots of their English school friends did that. But their intractable father spirited them away before their tears had time to dry.

A shoe lying here: woollen hats and scarves tossed to one side: books, pages open by the side of beds: crumpled cushions where the children sprawled reading gave the illusion they were outside playing. Pavia's bear missing from the pillow told a different story. Margaret didn't even have that for consolation.

Ben's promotion and return from overseas would have made it possible to delay her posting. What was so urgent that it couldn't wait while they sorted things out between them? In the haste to get away he had left his light travel bag, empty except for a crumpled letter. Margaret read,

> *My Dearest, Atrey,*
>
> *You will now be at home with your wife. Do not forget me and the nights we have spent together under Egypt's stars. I had never known what it was to fall in love. I thought it could never happen to me. I was too wrapped up in my work to become involved with such foolishness but these last two years with you have been worth everything. When will you send for me? Will I have to wait for this wretched war to end? Be kind to your wife when you tell her.*

It was signed Olivia, the address a military hospital in Egypt. Improbably it was from a woman who sounded so like herself. Tearing it to shreds Margaret watched them curl to ash on the fire's dying embers.

CHAPTER 24

Delhi February 1943

Margaret was posted to Delhi. Maybe Ben had fixed it so she could visit the children. Road and rail links were good. There was a train to Aakesh and she could take a tonga to the house, a journey under ninety miles instead of the hundreds she would have to travel if she'd been sent to Kohat.

Letters were getting through to her, forwarded from Nainital. In his, Margaret's father admitted to being lonely since his wife's death. She sympathised but the ache inside her was made worse by the living. She didn't ill wish Ben but prayed for some kind of severance from him. Margaret couldn't expect her father to understand, or Nan and Mary. Her sisters were happily married and praying to be with their husbands who were away at the war, while she was seeking a solution to her own marriage. Ironically, she might see their husbands before they did. Her father had mentioned that they were on their way out East, and had promised to look her up, if they got the chance.

Margaret knew Nan's husband Davey but Mary had been too young for courtship when Margaret sailed for India. It would be great if they could get together, then she'd get the real low-down on what was happening in Scotland. Writing letters passed the time and she was disappointed if a day passed without receiving one, but today's was most surprising:

> *Dear Nurse Atrey,*
>
> *Sergeant Waters gave me a note to give to you if I reached Nainital. I'm sorry but it was months ago and the hospital there said you'd been posted out. They wouldn't give me your address but offered to send a letter on, so I hope this reaches you.*
>
> *Sorry for the delay,*
> *Sandy Green*

The enclosed grubby envelope contained an equally grubby scrap of paper:

> *Dear Margaret,*
>
> *Excuse this pencilled note. I know you are married and can only ever be a friend to me but I will never forget you as I think you are the most*

*generous woman I have ever met. I would give
anything to meet you again.*

*I can't tell you much about what I've been
doing, except to say that I have seen things
I never thought men could do to others. The
memories of riding out with you and our time
together by the lake kept me going.*

*Don't worry if you can't write back. I'll
understand. Meanwhile God Bless You,*

*Your loving friend,
Tommy*

Thank goodness for Tommy's straightforward approach
to life. There was no address to reply to so she wrote care
of The Bush Warfare School, enclosing the Delhi hospital
address.

The discovery of Ben's affair with Olivia and his
barbaric removal of the children had crushed her. Scot
and Indian, Hindu and Catholic, Margaret had striven to
yoke the opposing cultures but lately she despised the
grovelling and pretence. Tommy didn't deserve to be
caught up in this but she didn't want to give him up. Maybe
she was no better than Ben? She hadn't had an affair but
Tommy's kiss had warned her of the risk she was taking. It
was silly, for they hardly knew each other and might not
meet again. However, while she remained married there
was a slight chance she might rescue the children. Yet, she
felt unfaithful to Tommy in trying to save her marriage.

A change of location to the busy city hospital was
welcome. Margaret didn't know how long she would

stay but the central quarters were perfect for shopping. However, she was feeling unwell and couldn't make the most of it. She spent her time off duty resting. No doubt it was nothing and would pass. A letter from Ben led her to believe there was a possibility of retrieving something from their relationship. She replied at once.

Lady Irwin Hospital
New Delhi

My Dearest Ben,

Thank you so much for your letter and the note and drawing from Pavia. I am so glad you are OK. I was worried at not hearing from you for some time.

Well your letter was short but full of news. I am puzzled when you write that you are alone with the children. No my dear, Suleka gave me no news of you. I don't know why I feel so jealous but I can't bear to think of you with anyone else. Later I'll be with you. Please excuse this outburst. I thought I was getting hard natured but I believe you will always be able to break me.

My dear, my final exams will be on the 15th of this month. I hope I am all right until then, but these haemorrhages are taking a lot out of me and now my temperature stays up all day. I think its just weakness because I can't eat much food without being sick. Of course, now you are back in India, I eat neither meat nor eggs, and as this is the main food available here, I often go dinnerless. I don't know. I simply can't look at the meat. It reminds me of the many operated bodies I see in the ward.

My dear, I sent my father's air graph just because I thought you'd like to read it. I don't know why he mentioned that my nursing would be useful to me when I returned home.

Tell me the truth, are you anxious for me to go and leave this land? These miserable days without the children make me realise how near to heaven I was with them. The beauty of the life I led has only struck me now. Up till then I saw only the hardships. Oh Ben you will never realise the torture in my heart! So much so that I feel life so hard that death is very welcome. No, it is not the work I have to do. It is very interesting and I like it. If only the circumstances had been different and I was with our children. Day and night I am haunted. I just want to die unwept because I have lost those who would have cried for me and respected my name in death. You could change it all.

My thoughts are for our children and your happiness and contentment that is the prayer of my heart.

Love to you and the children
Charuni

* * * * *

Ben telephoned. He was coming to Delhi and bringing Pavia. Margaret wasn't going to waste a second in wondering why. She went shopping, flitting from stall to stall in the market buying ribbons and pretty slides for her daughter's hair, gaudy glass bracelets, embroidered handkerchiefs, books and aquamarine patterned cloth to make Pavia a dress. They could go to the tailors together. Ben would book them into a hotel. She'd pack a bag . . . be ready to go with them. They could talk, sort out the differences. And most important, she would be with Pavia.

What should she wear to meet them . . . something to make an impact? Margaret held dress after dress in front of the mirror before choosing a white blouse with Swiss embroidery on the collar to team with a grey suit. She always felt attractive in that. She took leave, pushing any doubts aside.

Winter was fading fast but some days were cool with occasional rain. The hospital gardeners, warm shawls draped round their bony shoulders, were hard at work sweeping debris from lawns and weeding flowerbeds. Margaret's visitors were due at her quarters by eight o'clock. She set a small table so they could breakfast together but it was after nine and the tea had grown cold in the pot.

Ben left Pavia in the car with a woman who he claimed to be a governess. Margaret waved to her daughter from the veranda, but Pavia was out of the car, her plait coming loose as she raced across the grass. Margaret would re-plait it tonight and tomorrow and . . . Pavia sobbed,

"Please mama, please come home." Come home! If only it were possible. "Mama, don't you love us?"

The barb struck home, "Of course I love you . . . I always will . . . But there's a war on . . ." Margaret tried to explain . . . soldiers needed caring for . . . she wouldn't be allowed to leave . . .

"We'll come to you!"

Margaret pushed back the strands of hair hanging down her daughter's tear-stained face. "You can't stay here my darling. But we'll be together soon." She pulled Pavia close, kissing the top of her head. Ben must see what this separation was doing. How could he be so hard? Punish her, but not the children. She'd give up everything and go to Aakesh, if he'd let her.

Ben said that it was time to go.

Pavia obediently took her mother's hand. Margaret let it go to pick up the bag. The child skipped on unaware of the drama unfolding between her parents.

"Leave it." Ben growled but Margaret picked it up. "I *said* leave it."

"I won't leave it. I can do without the clothes but the children's presents . . ."

"The children don't need your presents."

"Don't be ridiculous. I chose them especially . . ."

"You're not coming. My mother is ill. Treatment is expensive . . . I need to secure the property. The family have arranged for me to marry a well-educated high caste lady, a teacher and owner of a private school. She brings a substantial dowry. You must grant me a divorce."

Instinctively Margaret made a dash for the open door. Ben barred the way. She beat him with her fists but he caught her hands contemptuously pushing them away. She dashed after him calling out as if he were a thief, "Give me back my children . . . There will be no divorce!"

Powerless to prevent the car from driving away she was hounded indoors by diving malevolent crows disturbed by the commotion. Why hadn't she seen through him? Hadn't she learned anything?

Haemorrhaging, she stumbled into the bathroom cursing God and her husband. Someone was coming . . . running down the corridor . . .

CHAPTER 25

Before she let the servant in Margaret had checked that the miscarriage was complete, and mopped the bathroom with white towels. The deep red blood wouldn't rinse out. The servant said she was sorry. Margaret wasn't sorry. She was worn-out and relieved, relieved another child hadn't been born amid scandal and disgrace. She bribed the servant to dispose of the towels in the hospital waste and not to report it.

Why hadn't she recognized she was pregnant? It could only be Ben's child, the result of the last attempt to save her marriage. The bungled rape was too long ago to be the cause. Either way the evidence was gone, flushed down the drain before too many questions were asked. The miscarriage had been merciful. She'd bleed for a couple of weeks, like a heavy period. That's how she'd think of it.

* * * * *

Ben's intention to sue for divorce had largely died down when Mary's husband Willie contacted Margaret. However there was speculation, always speculation, so she arranged to meet him at India Gate. The prominent sandstone and granite war memorial commemorated the lives of 90,000 soldiers in the British Indian army, who lost their lives fighting in World War 1. The landmark, in New Delhi, was easily found.

Jean had written describing Willie as being well over six feet tall, saying that Mary was lucky to have such a dashing husband. Margaret stationed herself by the side of the wide tree-lined road leading to the Viceroy's Lodge on Rasina Hill. Willie was sure to see her there. She waved down a Rickshaw carrying a likely looking candidate, "Willie?" she queried.

The airman grinned and shook his head, "Wish I was." The hunt for Willie turned into a hilarious game with rickshaws slowing and airmen shouting "Have you found Willie?"

She was feeling rather silly when the genuine Willie strolled towards her, smiling broadly, "You must be Maggie?" he said, giving her a bear hug. "I hope you are. If not it's been nice meeting you."

Jean was right. In uniform, his pilot's cap perched jauntily on his blonde hair, Willie was quite the man about town. "As you're not beating me off, I need to tell you that the hug is from everyone back home. I've to write and let them know you are okay as soon as we meet up."

Margaret decided to forgo showing him the sights, steering their steps away from the busy road and onto the green lawns of the fountain-parks bordering India Gate. She wanted to know what was happening in Scotland but Willie got in first telling her of the birth of his son who was to be called John, after Margaret's brother. Willie hadn't seen the baby. The disappointment was in his eyes. Mary was sending a photograph. He asked if Margaret minded her father marrying again.

"Father hasn't told me. No one has," she said, hurt and angry that his recent letters hadn't so much as hinted at the prospect.

"Look Maggie, I'm certain he will in his next letter."

"Yes, when it's too late for me to say anything."

"Apparently it took everyone by surprise. You knew he was working in London?"

"Yes . . ."

"Well that's where he met his wife."

"He soon forgot my mother."

"Now Maggie, you wouldn't want to spoil his happiness. It's been pretty bad at home. Your father was lonely. These days who knows what tomorrow will bring?"

Willie described the changes in the country since the outbreak of war: women driving ambulances; working on the land and in factories, replacing men everywhere except down the mines. He told her about air raids, the blackout, and shortage of everyday items. Describing a friend's wedding he said the bride's dress was made of parachute silk but the cake was an elaborate cardboard model covering cheap Madeira. Eggs, flour and dried fruit were rationed.

"Do you know Maggie, I've eaten heaps of fresh fruit since I arrived. My favourite's papaya . . . makes my mouth water . . ."

"Papaya's mine too . . . though I'm dying for strawberries from my father's garden. As a British Officer you'll want for nothing."

"And a good job too! A country boy made good, that's me! What about you? Is your husband still overseas?"

"Actually he's in the Punjab."

"Good, then I'll get to meet him."

"Meanwhile, to Delhi's sights" Margaret said, quickly hailing a rickshaw.

Willie admired the classical bungalows, shady trees and wide airy roads of Lutyens New Delhi but the labyrinth of the Old City, filled with ghostly history, intrigued him. Over the next few days they explored the sandstone citadel of the Red Fort and the ancient towering Qutab Minar where monkeys roamed in place of Sultan's armies.

"Just stand looking interested" Margaret said, lining up her box camera. "I expect you to be able to name the places we've been to before I send the photos to Mary."

"Don't do that! I'm supposed to be having a miserable time."

Margaret pulled his leg, "You boys in blue have no idea what that is."

* * * * *

Willie's last evening was to be spent in Chandni Chowk, once the grandest market in India with a canal running through the middle of the main street, as part of the city's water supply. At night the moon and stars shone on the surface. Chaos, and cripples wailing 'baksheesh' had long ago usurped this oasis. Willie reached in his pocket but Margaret warned him to leave the money where it was. A few annas meant the difference between life and death. They'd be mobbed in the resulting scramble. Fierce looks and no money sent the menacing beggars skulking into the shadows.

Confused looking cows wandered freely, dogs slunk by. Animals and humans poured onto streets that spawned an excess of filth and abject poverty. Willie filled his upturned hat with ripe guavas but spent so long holding his nose because of the open sewers that he threw the fruit away. He'd had enough of 'Old Delhi'. The Mullah called the faithful to prayer. Willie hailed a rickshaw to the Officers Club.

* * * * *

The Club, blessed with deferential servants and refined voices, contrasted sharply with the babble of the streets. Willie mopped his brow, "I shouldn't want to get lost in that place. You might not get out alive!"

Margaret grinned. Sitting here under the fan with a gin fizz had a lot going for it.

"The past is gone, Maggie. You can't get it back. None of us know the future. If I did, I don't think I'd get in another aeroplane. Live for today, that's my motto, tomorrow may never come."

He tried to offer advice but for Margaret today and tomorrow involved her children. She was stuck in limbo.

* * * * *

"I was thinking . . . Maggie, what will you do when I leave tomorrow?"

"Have a rest from all this jaunting and drinking," she flippantly replied.

"Have you thought of going home . . . to Scotland?"

"A lot lately . . . It's the children . . . I'd not get them out of the country. Also I've no money, except what I earn."

"The scoundrel! Doesn't he maintain you?"

"Don't be too hard on him. Ben wanted to send me home to my father but how could I go? He offered me an allowance but I came with nothing and I want nothing from him, except to see my children."

It was after one in the morning when Willie gave Margaret a brotherly kiss outside the nurses' quarters and told her to "Keep smiling."

She thought how Mary and the children must miss him. For years she had missed Ben in the same way, but not any more. Margaret sighed, resigning herself to the present, and turned in for the night.

The following morning she was ordered to report to matron, immediately! The dustless office smelt of efficiency and military polish. Margaret stood to attention in front of a peppered haired authoritarian woman. "Nurse Atrey, it has come to my attention that you have been entertaining a man at your quarters. You of all people should have had enough of men to last a lifetime!"

Matron's colonial world thrived on malicious tea party chitchat. Always in the wrong, Margaret didn't care any more. Let them think what they liked. They would anyway. However she wasn't going to jeopardize Willie's reputation, or risk his being carpeted to satisfy some petty scandalmonger. She began politely, "Ma'am, don't some people know there's a war on?"

"Nurse Atrey, may I remind you where you are? I want an explanation, not your observations!"

Margaret answered heatedly, "That man is my brother-in-law! He's been bombing Europe while some people with cushy numbers pushing pens in Delhi have nothing better to do than pull him down. He won't be here again. He's off to bomb the Japanese!" She turned on her heels and left.

The notice of her posting came the following day. Matron announced that in order to allow Nurse Atrey the luxury of a clear conscience, and an opportunity to play a greater part in the war effort, she was sending her to Manipur. There, she would be too busy to entertain anyone, including her brother-in-law.

CHAPTER 26

Nainital April 1943

At the British withdrawal from Burma courageous men and women working in mission hospitals fled in front of the merciless enemy. Ill-prepared for flight, they journeyed through treacherous jungle, climbing mountains and crossing rivers. Many travelled for as long as twenty-nine days to the Indian state of Manipur, where they had arrived sick and exhausted. Those who were well enough immediately offered their services to the medical staff. They were snapped up, for there was a dire shortage of nurses to look after the influx of civilian and military casualties across Manipur. Tents were converted overnight into primitive hospital wards. The torrential rainy season turned the tented clearings into quagmires. Transport in any form was bogged down by the treacle-like mud.

This was where matron proposed to send Margaret. The arduous conditions and close proximity of Manipur to Burma and the Japanese didn't frighten Margaret. Her fear arose from Pavia's unhappy face as the car drove away in Delhi and the boys, her lovely boys. Saurabh's bright eyes, Rajeev's lisping stories. When would she see them again?

* * * * *

By some administrative fluke Margaret was posted to Nainital and quartered near the hospital. Aakesh, a hundred miles away was within reach! There could be no justification for Ben refusing access to their children. Margaret crawled out of the perpetual abyss that dogged her and wrote to Suleka,

> *My Dear Friend,*
>
> *It is so long since I heard from you. I have the good fortune to be posted here. Please intercede with your brother on mine and the children's behalf. I miss them dearly. If I could spend a few days with them either here or at Aakesh I will be forever indebted to you.*
>
> *Nainital is safe even though news of the Japanese is alarming.*
>
> *Your affectionate sister,*
> *Charuni*

Suleka, who was staying at Aakesh because of her mother's worsening health, wrote saying her own daughter was enjoying the company of the children, especially Rajeev, who was patience itself. Margaret didn't want her son to grow up so quickly! There was no coded invitation to meet the children. On the contrary Suleka said,

> . . . the atmosphere in the house is most uncomfortable. I do not think that things go well for my dear brother and his new wife. She is not happy here and certainly not compliant. I fear my mother and Vartika misjudged the whole sorry business. It appears that urged on by Hiten an advertisement was placed requesting a wife for a widowed army officer with three children. My mother and Vartika then sifted through the candidates. You will not be surprised to learn that many families wanted to introduce their daughter. It would be very advantageous to have the family name with all its connections. Sandyia was chosen. She came to Delhi the last time you saw Pavia. The marriage went ahead without any problems but it is clear that it will never work. My brother is away from home with the army. He was last in the Punjab but I have no news since.
>
> I miss your company and you will always be my sister. I will always do the best for the children. They are much loved here and used to you being away. I do not think that they realise what has happened. Let us hope they never will.

Margaret needed no reminder of the agony of the last meeting with Pavia. Greed for money, land and power would surely be the undoing of Hiten and Vartika. For years they had continuously dripped their poisonous slander, exaggerating and manipulating whatever they could to defame her; pandering to Ben's weakness, flattering and encouraging him to indulge himself. His agreement to their duplicitous plan, entrapping a woman into a bogus religious marriage, disgusted her. Margaret had mistaken Ben for a man of substance but his selfishness and infidelity destroyed those who truly loved him. She prayed that one day she would be avenged. Meanwhile it was safer to stay away.

* * * * *

Countless new faces blurred into those of Willie and Tommy. Margaret searched the lists of the wounded. The faith and energy of youth chipped away with every dying patient. In the day Margaret's devotion to her patients was paramount but the nights off the ward were for oblivion. Locked inside herself she drank alone in the deserted mess, anaesthetising all feeling, getting through another day without her loved ones.

She arrived on night duty to a packed ward and another poor soul, legs covered in ulcers, shivering with fever under the mosquito net. She shone the night lamp towards his bed. It couldn't be . . . "Tommy?"

"You're all I want to see," he said closing his fevered eyes.

Tommy was too ill to care when the American cargo plane had picked him up from Yunnan. The months spent undercover supporting the guerrilla activities of the Nationalist, Chinese army of Chiang Kai-Shek were gruelling. He'd seen and done terrible things. The rescue plane landed at some American base. He didn't know where but he could smell India as soon as they opened the hold.

Somewhere along the way his old instructor, Mike Calvert, contacted him. Promoted to the rank of Brigadier with the Chindits, he was rooting for Tommy to join him. There was a vital job to be done and Tommy's guerrilla experience with the Chinese equipped him to do it.

* * * * *

Tommy recovered slowly, walking Margaret to the hospital when she was on duty, waiting to collect her when the shift was over. He slept while she was at work. She slept hardly at all. Liberated from guilt, she expected no commitment from him other than friendship. She had grown up under Ben's influence, a drug she couldn't get out of her system, but the addiction was over. Tied to him by their children she pondered what she would do if he asked her to return. Fate had brought Tommy back into her life. He was everything honourable, but was that enough?

In the dense jungle, Tommy had seen planes swoop low, skim the tree tops, and climb high into the open sky. He fancied trying to join the dare-devil crew that flew in them. He played for time to make a decision. In any case he wanted to settle his future with Margaret; so far he'd skirted round it. He approached her cautiously, "When my girlfriend married that was it. I wasn't looking for anyone. Don't get me wrong . . . there've been plenty of women . . ."

"I don't need to know that!" Margaret said wondering where this was leading.

"What I mean to say is . . . I don't expect you to forget Ben . . . We've nothing to apologise for . . . our lives hold good memories as well as bad. I've rented a place for a few days and I want to spend them with you."

* * * * *

The bungalow was orchestrated to provide a service much in demand. It came with a manservant who lit the oil lamps and made curry and rice before leaving. Being together in the evening without work or company was a novelty. Margaret sipped her drink. Tommy downed his, "Do you want to use the bathroom first?

"Yes please," she said, undressing privately. She so wanted it to be perfect for Tommy but the map of silver stretch marks on her abdomen would forever be evidence of motherhood and past love. She covered them with the bed sheet. Tommy moved it aside exposing her body in the mellow light "Don't be sad, Margaret. I want you as you are. We don't need to pretend."

They talked and caressed and when the moment came he made love to her, not with the selfish haste of a young man, but with experience that came from having lived life to the full. She responded with the generosity and wonder of a woman discovering the complexity of mature love.

On their last day Tommy gave her a battered parcel held together with fraying string and sealing wax, "I got this on my last mission."

Margaret reverently peeled away layers of blood and mud-spattered paper. A creamy yellow silk kimono spilled out, eclipsing the sunlight streaming through the shutters. She slipped her arms through the wide sleeves.

"Dreaming of you wearing this kept me alive" Tommy said, tracing the embroidered flowers down Margaret's back, sighing into her hair, "Marry me." She pulled away. He said earnestly, "Don't be afraid. I want to spend the rest of my life making you happy."

"But . . ."

"Hear me out. When this war is over I'll stay in India. Together we can fight for your children."

CHAPTER 27

Delhi April to November 1943

No sooner had the temperate spring weather brought flowers back to Nainital than Tommy disappeared and Margaret was sent to Delhi. After the happiness of being with him the loneliness intensified. Did fate control their destiny? Margaret didn't know but the antidote to this misery lay in trying to take some control. She began divorce proceedings and wrote a desperate letter to Suleka,

> My Dearest Sister in Law,
>
> Do not think the worst of me. I am put to one side. Ben has made a new life. I must make a home in India and fight for my rightful contact with Pavia and the boys.

Please encourage them to write to me. I do not know if they have received the many letters I have sent them. Surely Ben has not prevented them from replying. I beg you to forward an address for me to write direct to Pavia. My nursing was to be a temporary thing to help with the war effort. Now it seems to be all I have.

Tell my children about me. Don't let them forget me for I love them with all my heart and would agree to anything to have them by my side. I have sent some more small gifts for you and your children for I don't believe I will ever see them.

Suleka replied,

My Dear Charuni,

We must keep writing for we are all in God's hands. The children miss you especially Rajeev but he is such a gentle child, and, as you know, his health is not good. He still catches many coughs and colds. My mother, who continues in poor health, keeps him by her and he is greatly attached to her.

Rajeev attached to Ben's mother! It was too much! Margaret wrote furiously forbidding him to be left with her. The smiling children beamed up from the photographs on the writing table. These reminders of happier times were more valuable than the jewels or gold in the safe at Aakesh. Rajeev must have been around two when his photo was taken. He'd soon be four. It saddened her to think he saw more of his dadi and aunts than either of his parents. Ben did his duty in providing for the children's safety and education but his mother showed them love. Margaret screwed up the letter. She'd investigate opportunities to stay on in India after the war, separately from Ben and his family. She didn't believe in waiting for an all controlling God who played games with people's lives.

* * * * *

August in Delhi was stifling, necessitating a change of perspiration-soaked uniform at least twice a day. The proximity of the scorching city to Aakesh was the only reason Margaret didn't ask for a transfer.

The high ceilings and humming fans of Lady Irwin Hospital provided some relief but today Margaret's off duty coincided with the height of the afternoon. The rickshaw bumped along in the roasting sun. Shopping to buy cotton to send to Suleka for more summer outfits for the girls was idiotic, but it shouldn't take long.

The last time she was in Chandni Chowk was with Willie. In the early days of the war she'd tried to persuade Jean to request a posting to India and was disappointed when she refused. Margaret missed her sister but was glad Jean hadn't seen the complete mess she'd made of everything.

Now Jean would be safer in Europe. Although war was dragging on, Africa had been freed, and in Italy, Mussolini had been arrested. The allies would win there in the end. India and the East remained in grave peril.

Margaret got down from the rickshaw and walked past sprightly horses negotiating the maze of constricted alleys. In more open spaces, ruminating cows leisurely strolled along as if they owned the place, occasionally stopping to steal from the brimming vegetable stalls. Flea-ravaged pye-dogs became the prey of filthy stone-throwing children.

A tight circle of men sat cross-legged, playing cards under rickety awnings only to be scattered in all directions by a band of mangy grey donkeys marauding towards them.

Flaming stalls of gladioli lit dark shaded corners but everywhere droned with flies. The gluttonous insects massed on animal dung dropped in untidy heaps on the road, or swarmed over human excrement behind the piles of stinking rubbish picked over by the unfortunate.

Margaret moved through the market with the confidence and authority of an English Memsahib. Her grasp of the languages was sufficiently fluent to understand the hubbub of conversation between stallholders and the crowds of men gathering by the chai stall drinking sweet tea. These days they could be plotting trouble.

She was always appalled by the vast numbers of beggars attracted to Delhi from the countryside, dreaming of making their fortune. Every nook and cranny was home to pathetic shelters. Women struggled to find privacy to give birth. If it lived, the newborn infant was swaddled in a bundle tied on its mother's back and they rejoined the rest of her rag-tag brood breaking stones for the road.

Human catastrophe failed to suppress the vivacity that infused the city. Any life was preferable to none. Margaret had railed against the poverty when she first arrived but, like most people, was too submerged in her own problems to alleviate it. Gradually it passed by largely unnoticed.

She drank the last dregs from the water bottle. There wasn't enough to quench her thirst. The forbidden ice cream cart was too tempting. She rolled each creamy mouthful round her palate, savouring the cold treat. Milky trickles ran down the back of her hand. Margaret licked the sticky streams, not wasting a drop. It was irresponsible but the ice cream was worth it.

By the end of the day she was thirsty and lethargic and drinking copious amounts of water. Diarrhoea and a fiery fever confined Margaret to her quarters. The onset of a red speckled rash spreading over her chest denoted that she had most probably contracted typhoid from the ice cream. She had nursed too many patients with the disease to question the symptoms.

Ben was granted emergency leave. Delirious or semi-conscious, Margaret was unaware he was there. He returned to Aakesh where he prepared the children for the death of their mother.

* * * * *

In October, Margaret was wheeled into the hospital grounds, her arms needle-scarred from the drips that had kept her alive. The monsoon had come and gone leaving the lawns freshly green. The gardeners would begin preparing the borders for winter and the subsequent spring flowering of cannas, roses and giant chrysanthemums.

Margaret was inundated with visitors and good wishes but it was as if Ben and the children didn't exist. Paradoxically, without her, their caste offered Pavia, Rajeev and Saurabh the highest social standing. They were assured a secure future with their Indian family to love and protect them. She believed that race and class prejudice were endemic in the British. Would the children thank her if she cheated them of their heritage by exposing them to that? But how would they know the depth of her love if they couldn't be together? The conundrum had no easy solution but she had to get well to find one.

* * * * *

Margaret had been on light duties at the hospital, but was sufficiently recovered to be posted out to Kohat where she should have gone a year ago. So much had happened since then. She felt like a different person. She wrote to the children and to Tommy. Post came from Scotland but none from those who mattered most.

CHAPTER 28

Kohat 1943/45

Margaret wrapped the shawl tighter, trapping in the heat of her winter clothes. The jeep rattled through Peshawar's bazaars where spiced meat roasting on spits and warmed ripe fruits wetted her appetite. Groups of tall, fiercely independent, green-eyed Pathans, bristling with guns and ammunition, haughtily jostled shoulder to shoulder with lesser tribesmen in the maze of alleys. Out of town the road became a series of hairpin bends, in places falling away into bitter cold rocky rivers. The piercing winds sweeping down from the mountainous border of Afghanistan heralded Margaret's arrival at Kohat.

It was a friendly garrison fortified by a contingent of British and Indian troops who had served together in North Africa. Some probably knew Ben. Margaret didn't enquire but was impressed by the increase in the number of Indian pilots skilfully manoeuvring planes on the primitive airstrip. They took off with an ear splitting noise, shuddering and juddering into the sky.

* * * * *

Suleka wrote constantly trying to persuade Margaret to put off the divorce but Margaret refused to be swayed. She wanted to marry Tommy but more than that she wanted to be done with Ben. It would be hurtful and unwise to tell Suleka how much she despised him. A worrying break in correspondence was accounted for by a telephone message. Margaret replied at once,

Kohat

> *Dearest Suleka,*
> *Thanks for your very kind phone call and the wonderful news of the birth. I was sorry I wasn't here to take your call. I'm frightfully busy and telephoning is often rushed so I thought I'd write. I hope you are recovered and enjoying baby Chimini. Even though she is only a few months old I feel certain she will enjoy the company of all the children. Mother must be feeling much better with you at home. It was good of your husband's family to allow it.*
> *Try to get a carpenter to fix up some of those wooden toys. There is a delay in my pay but as soon as I receive it I will send money down*

for my children's expenses. It is so very cold here that I had to spend money on extra clothes. The cost of the cloth is exorbitant!

I am on night duty and do not get a chance to go up to the city. As soon as I can I will send you another parcel of wool.

Now be careful all of you. Love to the children.

Yours affectionately
Charuni

* * * * *

Margaret had been worried that she might be sent to Europe, alternating how she would tell the children with the fact that there might not be an opportunity to say goodbye. In saner moments she realised this was extremely unlikely for the Japanese were in a pole position to strike India. She asked her commanding officer to try to find out where Tommy was. He said that the British attitude was she was not a relative, and there was a war on, so it was unlikely that he would find out anything. The fighting and possibility of invasion was heating up, a rationale for his absence.

She strove harder to become indispensable, working more unsociable hours than anyone else. In between she packed a trunk to send to Suleka. There were soft hanks of purple, blue and pink wool to make cardigans for the girls, mouth warming cinnamon, nuts, dried fruits, almond-nougat with cherries, and delicious sweets for the boys. In addition she put in bolts of fine grey and brown woven cloth and embroidered shawls, bought from Jammu salesmen in Peshawar's bazaar. Suleka could please herself what she did with the material.

Pavia was nine, Saurabh seven and Rajeev four. She'd missed their birthdays. Their father had got what he wanted and was in no hurry to involve expensive lawyers. Margaret decided to temporarily leave things as they were in exchange for trying to get his agreement for a Christmas visit to the children.

Suleka telephoned. Margaret was thrilled, "I've embroidered names on the children's Christmas stockings . . . It took an age. I'm glad you chose short names for your girls. We can hang the stockings on the bed head like we used to . . ."

"Charuni . . ." How ever it was said Suleka knew the effect would be disastrous, "You're not invited."

"Who says so?"

"My brother . . . He tore up your letter."

"I'll telephone."

"I'm not supposed to tell you . . ."

"Don't cry Suleka . . . it's not your fault . . ."

"Friends .?" she asked, her voice quavering.

"For ever . . ."

Margaret put down the phone. She didn't feel the hot red wax blistering her hand when she sealed the string on the parcel.

In church on Christmas Eve, surrounded by colleagues carolling their hearts out, she visualised Pavia and Saurabh caught up in the excitement of bedtime; sweetly singing *Away in the Manger*. They might be too old for Father

Christmas but would play along for Rajeev. A chilling thought struck Margaret: without her there would be no need to celebrate Christmas at Aakesh.

* * * * *

Winter had penetrated Margaret's bones, increasing her dark mood. In nearby Kashmir the melting snows changed the peaceful rivers to torrents sending them tumbling down to the thirsty plains, making the passes relatively snow free. She joined some nurses on an expedition to see the renowned pink blossom of the almond trees.

April was a delightful month for an adventure. The merry band missed some of the first flush of blossom but the air was filled with the fragrance of a million spring flowers blooming on trees, shrubs and creepers. The nurses made their way to the ancient city of Srinagar where they hired a luxurious wooden houseboat moored on the river Jhelum. They followed its course through the heart of the city, past willow-shaded channels, canals and under curvaceous low bridges. Deep green rice fields, water lilies, lotus and intricate Mughal gardens littered the riverbanks. Lines of doongas, the floating homes of the river people, swayed in unison. Women, seated at the prow, pounded grain and called to one another across the tranquil water.

The crew of the houseboat tied up at regular intervals and Margaret and her friends explored the labyrinth lanes of rich red brick and carved wooden houses that stretched into the town.

There was a constant flow of activity between the water and the land. Homes, schools, shops and mosques jostled for position along the crowded banks. Endless roof gardens and orchards tumbled down towards the river; lattice carved windows of buildings added a touch of timelessness.

In the evenings the boatmen lit small bukharis. The smoke from these wood-burning stoves perfumed the air like incense. Servants brought bowls of rose scented water for hand washing, cinnamon tea and delicately spiced food; apricot stuffed lamb, fish in coconut, saffron rice, breads and fruits, relics of their Persian ancestry, washed down with sherbet.

The party relaxed on luxurious carpets or reclined on cushioned couches. The moon on the water and the reflection of the light from hundreds of lanterns, suspended from innumerable shadowy boats, shut out unhappiness.

* * * * *

Kashmir with its glimpse of paradise had been a haven of healing from which to draw the strength Margaret would need. Her father wrote with bad news: Nan's husband Davey was dead, killed by a sniper in Burma while serving with Wingate's Chindits. The remote jungle and nature of the mission meant his body lay where it fell. Nan was left with five young children. The last, like so many others, would not know her father. Willie was right, only this moment is certain.

The Japanese, building up their reserves to attack India, had cut the road link between Imphal and Kohima. Residents caught in the fighting were either killed or interned. Planes flew day and night supplying and evacuating troops or bombing the enemy. Willie was up there, and although Margaret didn't want another dead brother-in-law at least she knew where he was.

She'd wheedled out of headquarters that Mike Calvert, and his group of Special Forces were with the Chindits. Tommy must be with them. These men were engaged in hand to hand combat with the enemy, suffering terrible casualties. Horrific stories of soldiers captured by the Japanese were well known. Those who escaped were often mentally and physically scarred beyond healing.

Men living on the edge of death seldom made commitments, but Tommy had given his word and Margaret trusted him to keep it. She shut her ears to the rumble of aircraft and the possibility that he was dead. Somehow he'd find her, even in Kohat.

May brought a letter from Suleka,

> *My Dearest Charuni,*
>
> *Your replacement, Sandyia, has returned to her brother and is running their school. She has taken Pavia with her. Don't be upset my dear friend but my brother has another son. If he wants to see him he will have to go there. Saurabh and Rajeev remain here . . .*
>
> *I remain your sister. No one will ever take your place in my affection.*

Sandyia hadn't settled for rural life with its lack of intellectual company, sick mother-in-law and persistent interference from Vartika and Hiten. Why hadn't Margaret done the same, taken the children, taken control, forced Ben into fighting for them?

A son posed a threat but Hiten would protect Saurabh and Rajeev's interests, so tightly bound up with his own. Pavia gone with Sandyia was a death blow.

What to do? What to do? If Margaret had someone to help . . . but she didn't even know where Sandyia lived. She sent letter after letter to Ben beseeching him to return their daughter.

* * * * *

Depression is a poor companion. Afraid to be alone in this melancholy state Margaret took refuge in the mess where the wireless underpinned conversation. A huge cheer roared throughout the room bursting out into the night. Hundreds of voices began singing, shouting, whistling sending the noise echoing through the mountains. Berets and caps were thrown in the air. Men swung each other round, slapping backs, pumping hands and kissing every woman in sight. Giddy from dancing she asked her partner what was happening.

"What's happening . . . ? We've landed in Normandy! The Jerries are on the run. The whole bloody world has landed on the beaches, Yanks, Canadians, the whole caboodle."

Drinks were poured, toasts were drunk and Vera Lynn transmitted at full volume. Margaret was nearly late on duty.

The disinfected wards with dimmed night-lights were at odds with the festivities. A soldier groaned. The surgical pain from his amputated leg and the unusual racket outside had got the better of him. "Nurse . . . What's going on?"

Margaret told him. The ward erupted into a symphony of waving limbs, towels, pillows, bedclothes, toothbrushes and anything to hand. One by one critically ill men asked, "Does this mean we can go home?"

"Soon," she reassured them, but where would she go when it was over?

CHAPTER 29

June and July passed with more allied victories in Europe. Margaret was half listening to Victor Sylvester's big band concert in the mess when the popular wireless programme was interrupted by an announcement, "Yesterday our brave boys were honoured by Field Marshall Montgomery in a Normandy quarry . . ." Boos and cat calls drowned the rest.

"Get him off. We want news of the Japs! There's a war on here you know!"

"My brother's over there . . ."

"Somebody shut him up!"

The volume was turned up until it crackled. In standard BBC English a list of decorated men was read out, " . . . Fifth Parachute Brigade, Airborne Signals Section, Corporal Thomas Waters . . ."

Margaret said, "Corporal Thomas Waters . . . Did he say *Corporal Thomas Waters?"*

"Got the Military Medal . . ."

"He's my fiancé! But he's a sergeant? "

"He's a hero!"

The mess toasted Tommy and his comrades until the rafters rang with his name.

Secrecy was paramount throughout Tommy's missions in The East but to be transferred to Europe . . . perhaps when they last met he had an inkling of what lay ahead? Margaret wished she'd asked him more, but he wouldn't have told her. He might be half way across the world but he was alive; being together was just a matter of time.

* * * * *

She dreamt of making their home in India. It would have to be a city, probably Delhi. They'd have a summer home in Nainital; she'd put the children in school. They'd ride through the hills . . . honeymoon in Kashmir . . . the war couldn't last much longer.

France

My Darling Girl,

It's been pretty hectic here one way and another and impossible to write. Unfortunately the action isn't over. I am still on active service and expect to be on the move any day.

I hope you and the children are well and that you think of me often. I know it's selfish but wait for me. Nothing's changed. I meant every word I said when we last met,

Well sweetheart I promise I'll get back to you but it looks as if we'll have to wait for the end of this bash. Try to get a letter to me if you can. I had to drop rank but I'm due for promotion. I might make it to Officer and give you the life you deserve.

Your sweetheart,
Tommy

Didn't Tommy realise she loved him for the man he was? Rank had nothing to do with it, but she wondered why he'd had to drop rank for such a dangerous mission. The protocol used by the army to determine these things was beyond her.

* * * * *

Moving easily across cultures Margaret built a reputation as a translator. A new post was created combining nursing with assisting Indian staff taking over British roles. Margaret enjoyed the work immensely, visiting outlying districts where she made contact with civil administrators. She was getting a feel for the politics of Independence. The best openings were going to be in Delhi or Calcutta. She intended to secure a posting, or civilian job, in one city or the other. She surmised Tommy was involved in what the papers described as 'Mopping up Operations,' in Europe.

She continued to write loving letters to the children without expecting a reply. Suleka wrote, although the intervals between letters were getting longer.

My Dear Charuni

Pavia and Saurabh are with their father at Dehra Dun for a holiday. Ben is in charge of the health of many Japanese prisoners of war who are interred there. However I am expecting them back at Aakesh any day. The children have been very mischievous. They climbed to the top of a hill and could see the Japanese in the camp far below. Then they crept nearer and the prisoners saw them. Immediately the men started to encourage them to come nearer. Pavia and Saurabh were fascinated and amused themselves by hiding behind trees and rocks, then bobbing out and waving. In this way they were almost at the perimeter fence when an Indian soldier spotted them and quickly marched them away.

Of course they were unaware of the great danger they had placed themselves in. Ben was very angry and is organizing sepoys to bring them here. He will miss them. Rajeev continues to remain at home. Saurabh will be sent away to school and Pavia will return to Sandyia for her studies.

Your affectionate sister,
Suleka

It was distressing to know that Pavia was with Sandyia almost permanently but this would change when Tommy returned and Margaret gained custody of the children. Fortunately the new job was so hectic it occupied her full attention. A spell on night duty would be a break from translating. A letter came with an English stamp but, not recognising the handwriting, she stuffed it in her pocket to read in a quiet moment.

The patients settled down to sleep without incident. Every bed was full and most of the men were on the road to recovery. Devoid of their daytime personality, the slumbering men became uncanny shapes under military blankets like exhibits in a museum. She spread out the letter under the dim desk lamp.

Denaby

Dear Margaret,

My son Thomas Waters has asked me to write to you on his behalf. He has been very badly injured during a training exercise. An Officer pulled the pin of a live hand grenade. As it landed Tommy threw a waste paper basket over it and was caught in the blast.

Tommy told me you planned to marry and his army duties prevented it from going ahead. You promised to wait for him and he believes you will have kept your word. He wants me to tell you he releases you from your promise. You see he will not be much good now.

He thanks you for waiting this long and hopes life will work out better for you in the future.

Yours sincerely,
Albert Thomas Waters

The careful handwriting ran with her tears. It was some moments before she realised the doctor was there. He coughed self-consciously. She blew her nose and showed him the letter. "Poor chap, what rotten luck." The stock response but then added genuinely, "Is there anything I can do?"

"It hasn't really sunk in. I need time to think . . . get it in perspective or what ever one does when faced with this."

"Be sure to let me know if I can help." he said, continuing on his round unaccompanied. The night dragged on. Margaret's patients became Tommy, so far away, being cared for by anonymous nurses.

At the end of the shift she escaped to her quarters. Fixed a stiff whiskey, downed it in one, and then topped up the glass. She couldn't remember the exact moment she fell in love with Tommy. It evolved alongside their friendship and he had so many friends. Burmese, Indian and Ghurkha soldiers would do anything for him. He valued them as much as their British counterparts.

Faces of men tragically burnt and disfigured flashed before her; countless hands held through nightmarish pain. Tommy with his zest for life . . . the injustice replayed . . . perhaps she was a jinx? She flung the half empty glass across the room smashing it against the wall. Splinters flew everywhere. A wet stain baptised the white distemper.

The letter gave no details of Tommy's injuries or the hospital name but if he told his father what to put in the letter, there was hope. She wrote,

Kohat

My Dearest Tommy,

I seem to be shuttling backwards and forwards always searching for you. When I started to read the letter from your father I was afraid you were dead. We have both been through too much to let an accident get in the way.

My love, fight. Use your great courage. We can't be robbed of our chance of happiness. I love you and will wait forever. No one can take your place. We are meant to be together and until that day comes you are seldom out of my thoughts and prayers.

Your own,
Margaret

She addressed the letter to Tommy's father entrusting him to deliver it.

CHAPTER 30

Snow returned to the nearby mountains. Sepoys cleared paths around the hospital. Margaret followed their trail. At Nainital Pavia and Saurabh had competed to be the first to stamp their footprints on virgin snow. There'd be no snow at Aakesh to remind them. She was glad, for it hurt to remember. She walked on, running recent events through her mind. Going slowly with the divorce to win Ben over had been a mistake, confirmed by Suleka's telephone call a week ago. She said that the family knew Margaret was having an affair with a Britisher. She made it sound shocking. Margaret put the phone down.

An unsigned note had arrived yesterday. It wasn't dated and was post marked Lucknow.

> *Charuni,*
>
> *I tried to persuade you to drop the divorce and now it is too late. The children are dead to you. Be on your guard. There are those who would end your life for what you have done. My brother has filed for a divorce citing your adultery.*

It could have only come from Suleka. Ben's behaviour and adultery were forgotten by his family. Surely the courts would decide otherwise? She thought of Ghandi and how last February the whole of India had been brought to a standstill by the death of his wife, Kasturba. She died in prison in his arms. They'd been married for sixty years. He had spun the yarn for the shroud that wrapped her body. She had been a loyal Indian wife, accepting her husband's trespasses. Margaret couldn't accept or forgive Ben's indiscretions so apart from Tommy, who would grieve for her? As far as the children were concerned she might as well be dead.

Ideas and politics drew Margaret like a magnet and India was aflame with both. The gatherings of the impoverished illiterate infiltrated by opportunists were a volatile mix. Leaders, on all sides, were incapable of agreeing how an independent country would be governed. Ghandi continued to favour a united India and Jinnah a separatist Muslim state. There were rumblings of bloody sectarian violence. India was a burden the British intended to relinquish; unwise political action was inevitable.

Against this background what hope was there of a quick judicial hearing? Ben knew she hadn't the influence or money to fund a protracted legal wrangle. Let him do his worst. Margaret had a sinking feeling all was lost.

While she was out the servant had taken a telephone call from Colonel Thorpe Sahib. Margaret was to go to his office as soon as she came in.

The Colonel was with his wife, "Nurse Atrey . . . whiskey?" She declined. "Please sit down . . . As you know we are both dreadfully sorry to hear the news concerning your fiancé. I have been in touch with Delhi to try to ascertain more up to date information, without any luck."

"I'm grateful he's alive."

"Understood, but what do you want to do about it?"

"I don't know what you mean. What can I do?"

"Have you considered going home to Scotland?"

"My dear," the Colonel's wife said, handing Margaret a handkerchief, "I don't have to tell you that your fiancé will require a great deal of nursing care. We would like to help."

"My wife is right. Nurse Atrey, I have something to put to you. She is due to return to England with our children. Her original travelling companion is unavailable. You could take her place."

"Do take it, Margaret. You don't mind me calling you that? I'm Marjorie. My husband has told me lots about you since he first met you in Nainital. I'm certain we will get on . . . you could shortly be with your fiancé . . . be the prop necessary for him to recover."

"I appreciate your offer, but I need time to make arrangements. I have my own children to consider."

"I don't mean to be unkind but from what I hear," the Colonel said, "I think it most unlikely you will have any authority over your children's future. I'm sure I don't have to tell you, you certainly won't get them out of India."

"I planned to stay."

"I think you would find it impossible to manage without a husband when we pull out. And we will . . ."

His wife interrupted, "Darling we can't advise Margaret. The war will end and India will become independent. The signs are everywhere."

"The problem is I need an answer immediately to get the paper work completed."

The inertia of fear, the rationalisation of the separation and the conflict of love across continents became too much. Margaret was weary, so very, very weary.

* * * * *

Six o'clock on a glorious February Bombay morning in 1945. The powerful male monkey strolled languorously on top of the wall surrounding the hotel garden, pausing where blousy red roses bobbed in the balmy air. Head lifted towards the sun the animal sniffed, turned and fixed Margaret with its amber eyes then wickedly decapitated the nearest bloom. It munched slowly, occasionally opening its mouth to reveal splinters of bloodied petals trapped between jagged teeth.

Woodpeckers balancing on telephone wires, silhouetted against the morning light, had seen it all before but the washer-woman birds called alarmingly.

A servant threw sticks and the monkey was off, leaping lithely to join its harem in the jackfruit tree.

Morning dragged towards lunchtime. Margaret ate a small piece of bread and butter. She couldn't eat anything else. At half past three the car arrived to take her to the port.

Troop ships rode the swell in Bombay Harbour. They'd been loading all day. The pre-war glamour days of travel were substituted for stripped down vessels carrying military personnel, equipment and essential supplies.

Colonel Thorpe was there with his wife and children. He ordered Margaret's luggage to be put with theirs and saw it efficiently stowed on board.

Later she stood with his wife on deck while the Colonel's sons waved to him on shore. The eldest boy was eleven, slightly older than Pavia. He'd be in England for his twelfth birthday. Where would Pavia be? Who would be with her? Would the children be together?

The Colonel would follow his wife. Theirs would be a temporary separation. Margaret didn't know if she could endure the finality of hers. The children would never understand the price she was paying to set them free to flourish in their independent country.

Oh Ben, what have we done? Margaret's heart was breaking, her mind in torment, for she hated and loved him. She leant on the passenger rail. There was no one to wave to or to follow her. The convoy, escorted by destroyers and minesweepers made for sea. India slipped into the sunset.

THE RETURN

CHAPTER 31

Scotland 1945

The convoy avoided the risky Suez Canal, sailing round the tip of Africa. The anguish at leaving India blotted out the six weeks Margaret spent at sea. The Colonel's wife became an empathetic companion, fleeting friends for the journey. They parted in the murky dawn of Southampton, each knowing they wouldn't meet again.

The London train was packed with jolly servicemen and women, trading cigarettes and good natured banter. Margaret found a seat next to the window. In civilian clothes and having no experience of war time Britain to engage in small talk, she spent the journey looking out of the window at the colourless countryside.

The approach to London was shocking. The bombed houses; the fronts peeled back exposing blackened wall papered rooms. The intrusion of privacy in the debris of what had been once homes. Where had the people gone? Margaret had seen newsreels in India of the London Blitz and the evacuation of children but the films failed to portray the personal impact and scale of the damage. Parts of the capital were reduced to grotesque cartoons of burnt and semi-collapsed buildings, a testament to the Luftwaffe and the price of war. Yet the city was busy with purposeful people . . . Londoners getting on with the business of living . . . war hadn't destroyed that. It was silly but she wanted to cheer for the stubborn ordinary people, who held out under so much pressure.

Could *she* hold out? Hold out until she saw Tommy . . . And then . . .

* * * * *

Margaret's father was waiting at Waverly station, the brim of his flat tweed cap wedged down against Edinburgh's perpetual wind. Choking back tears, she dropped the small portmanteau she was carrying on the platform and ran towards him.

"Maggie . . . my Maggie . . ." he said, squeezing the breath out of her. Sheltered in his tobacco-scented gabardine she felt like a child rescued from drowning. He wiped her eyes, dabbed his own.

"Is this it?" he said, retrieving the case. Margaret said she'd heaps of stuff that would be delivered later.

"Then it's hame hen . . ."

"Home father . . ."

"Frances is waiting."

Yes, Frances, his new wife, who had tagged on a paragraph to the more recent letters Margaret, had received from her father. She'd hardly bothered to read or allude to it in her replies.

* * * * *

Frances opened the door. "Welcome Maggie, I'll show you to your room, I hope you like it. We've had it re-done for you."

Re-done . . . like the rest of the house . . . The only reminder of the past was the ticking wall clock. Margaret resented the replacement of the scuffed furniture and the floral bedroom wallpaper. The room had been her brothers', filled with their grubby clothes, pillow fights and emerging masculinity. The essence of her childhood had gone. What was she doing here?

She noticed a letter, post marked Denaby, on the dressing table. The writing wasn't Tommy's but it must be news of him. She ripped open the envelope.

Denaby

> *My Dearest Margaret,*
> *My father is writing to ask if I can come to Scotland to meet you. I want you to see me as I am before making any final decisions . . .*

There was a tap at the door. Frances asked, "Is everything alright Maggie? Only the meal is ready. Your father chose it. He has counted the days from the moment he knew you were coming."

"I was just about to come down," Margaret replied tersely through the closed door. She wanted to talk to her father but didn't want to explain anything to Frances. The woman's English accent and groomed appearance were the antithesis of Margaret's mother. It wasn't what she expected and she felt hurt without knowing why.

Her father was already seated at the table. He patted the chair nearest to him and Margaret sat down.

"Your father says this is your favourite" Frances said, smiling at her as she brought the barley broth to the table.

Margaret thought she'd got over her mother's death but coming here brought it back. None of this was Frances fault. Margaret knew she was trying to make her feel at home. It couldn't be easy being married to a strongly principled man, who thrived on control. Margaret recalled that her father had mentioned Frances had no children, and being so far from her London friends, would have no one to turn to. She wasn't prepared to take on that responsibility.

"I hope yon letter is good news Maggie," said her father. "Is it from Tommy?"

"It's more of a note," Margaret replied flatly, "His father wrote it."

"Does he say how Tommy is?" Frances asked.

"No, just that he wants to come." Margaret read out the note. "You see I don't know the extent of Tommy's injuries."

"Well then Maggie," her father said, obviously excluding his wife, "we'll take a look at him. You can send a telegram the morn, inviting him to stay when we take a wee walk to Nan's."

* * * * *

The telegram was sent before they set out on the country road to Nan's. They passed Grant's farm. The solidly built farmhouse, gnarled apple trees and smell of fresh manure remained the same. Margaret and Jean had been sent there to collect milk. In those days the bulky Friesian cows were hand-milked by Alec, the farmer's son who teased the sisters by squirting the animal's teats in their direction. Margaret's father said Alec had been killed at Dunkirk. His younger brother had taken over the running of the farm and was going to install milking machines. "Things change, Maggie . . . There was a letter from your husband saying you might be coming hame."

Margaret said she didn't know where to begin. "Dinne begin anywhere," her father said evenly.

"Well he's got his wish," she said sarcastically.

"Now Maggie . . . he wrote after your boys were born and when he left for Egypt. The last letter came out of the blue. I didna ken what to make of it. Mary had word from Willie. You were safe and I had to be content with that."

It was easier to talk as they walked and Margaret told her father that the divorce was progressing. She was attending mass and seeking an annulment. He was satisfied with the answers regarding the welfare of his grandchildren and kept his opinions on Margaret's proposed marriage to himself. Before they reached Nan's house at Gowkshill everything was said. He would leave it to Margaret to tell her sisters and brothers whatever she chose. As far as he was concerned the chapter was closed.

Nan's two youngest boys, their faces pressed against the window, were looking out for them. They tumbled through the door to chatter with their grandpa but stood tongue-tied in front of Margaret. Nan with her youngest daughter in tow embraced her sister. An older boy and girl stood in the doorway. "Goodness me . . . Sheila? The last time I saw you, you were just a toddler" Margaret said, kissing her niece. "And you must be young Davey" she laughed, as he dived out of the way.

Nan had been in service and the house was scrubbed bone clean with roller blinds at the windows, pretty curtains, lacy head rests and a gleaming soot-defying grate. The children were taken off for a walk by their grandpa.

"Well Maggie" Nan said, when they were out of earshot "you're hame . . . left your man and found another."

Margaret was staggered by the bitter tone, "No, Ben left me . . . I tried to make it work but . . ." Nan shrugged her shoulders. "Don't let's fight, Nan. I can't bear the memories and seeing your children reminds me . . ."

"Maggie, dinne mind me. I canny hold ma tongue . . . I keep hoping it'll be Davey off the bus . . . coming up the path . . . swinging the boys roond . . ." Nan silently cried into her apron.

She gave Margaret the standard letter from the war office that bleakly informed her of Davey's death. "I dinne think I'll ever rest knowing he's lying somewhere in the jungle" Nan said, taking the letter back and carefully folding it along the original worn crease marks. "I keep thinking it might be a mistake." She looked at Margaret, "It isn't. Is it Maggie?"

The sisters commiserated with each other, not daring to show weakness in public in case it betrayed the dead, or upset those closest to them.

They talked of other things. Jean was in Germany doing something with accounts. Margaret learned that her sister had planned to become engaged to a pilot but he was shot down. Nan hadn't met him. She didn't think there would be anyone else. "Why didn't she tell me?" Margaret asked, "You don't suppose she's still angry about Ben."

"What put that into your heid?"

"I don't know . . ."

"Tommy's the one we should be speaking about."

"I came home to nurse him but I don't know if he needs it or what kind of life we'll have."

"He's alive . . ."

"But . . ." Margaret said truthfully, "I don't know if I'm up to it."

"Well there's only one way to find out. Go to England or let him come here. "

"He wants to come. I've sent a telegram but staying with Frances . . . She's very kind but it's not the same. "

"Bide wi me . . . your man too. Faither will be relieved. Things aren't going well there."

* * * * *

Margaret moved to Nan's, sharing the girls' bedroom. Five children made a great deal of noise, filling the house, leaving no space for solitary misery. And Tommy was coming.

* * * * *

The train came and went and there was no sign of Tommy. Margaret trawled the station looking for him. The next train from Doncaster wasn't due until late in the evening. The station held too many memories of the past for Margaret to wait alone, so she caught the bus to Gowkshill. The aisle and luggage space were crammed with kit bags and haversacks. A sailor on leave gave Margaret his seat, saying that he was used to swaying on the ship so this was "a piece of cake."

The conductor made a great show of punching tickets, jostling his way up the bus, stopping to talk to people he knew, or to adjust the wooden clipboard holding an array of multi-coloured tickets.

A passenger at the front of the bus stood up, uncertain whether he'd caught the right one. Margaret recognised the voice. It was Tommy! He'd lost an eye! Burns and blast marks gouged his face! He began to shake! Dumbstruck, she elbowed her way down the aisle.

Tommy nervously gave her a crooked smile. Margaret flung her arms round him. Caught off balance they toppled onto his vacant seat to thunderous whistles and cheers.

The bus drew up opposite Nan's. Her father was leaning on the gate. Tommy pulled himself as upright as he could and limped across the road. "Now son, looks like you've seen a bit of action," Margaret's father said, taking Tommy's small suitcase. "A wee dram will put you right."

Tommy laughed, "I'm . . . a . . . b . . . beer man myself."

"We'll soon change that!" the older man said giving Tommy a brotherly pat on the back.

Nan had made soup. Tommy ate slowly, wiping his mouth with a handkerchief to catch the dribbles. He had problems coordinating the spoon and holding a cup of tea. The children were reprimanded for staring but Tommy said it was natural and he didn't mind. Margaret minded. She wanted to protect him and make him well again.

That night Tommy lay rigid in bed with his head turned away, "You see . . . w . . . what . . . you're letting yourself in for . . ."

Margaret ran her fingers over the raw puckered scars. He turned to speak but she put her finger over his lips. "You once told me you loved me as I was. That's how I love you. We'll get through this together." She kissed him again and again while he stammered out the brutal details of the accident, indebted to the surgeons for installing the metal plate in his head keeping him alive.

They didn't make love but Margaret tenderly nursed him, pulling the blinds and curtains shut to keep out the light, holding him while the spasms of pain subsided.

* * * * *

"I . . . don't . . . w . . . wwant . . . your pity . . ." Tommy stammered one day, as she tiptoed round the bedroom. Margaret hoped that the increasing clarity of his angry exchanges indicated progress but he followed her like a confused child, uncertain of today and unable to deal with tomorrow.

Nan said it was nice to have a man in the house. It gave her plenty to do. She made Tommy laugh but he couldn't do with sitting around. "I can't . . . sstay fffor . . . ever Margaret. I've got to get a job." Margaret entreated him to wait for although his speech was improving, the sudden fits of shaking made him virtually unemployable. She couldn't disillusion him. Consequently nothing was decided about their future and Tommy returned to Yorkshire for more treatment and to search for work.

CHAPTER 32

Scotland to Yorkshire 1945-1955

Nan had squirreled away the bounty of luxuries brought from India: tea, nuts, dried fruits, sweets, cloth and table linen. Sometimes she made a cake using the dried fruit but eked out the treats to make them last longer. Margaret remembered the monkeys eating their fill, plucking the fruit straight from the trees at Aakesh. Everything was dull by comparison, except the pain of separation, which was as sharp as it had ever been.

Margaret heard from Tommy. She had given up so much to be with him, but he'd had no luck in finding a job and was living with his father and stepmother in Denaby. He had written a disjointed letter but sending the address of a hospital at Mexborough, a short distance away. If Margaret could get a post there accommodation would be provided. It was a splendid idea. They could meet without the pressure of sharing someone else's home and the lack of money.

Throughout her stay at Nan's, Margaret ached to hear the voices of her own children. She consoled herself that they were better off in the luxury provided by their father, than being homeless with her.

* * * * *

> *My Dearest Tommy*
>
> *I have wonderful news. I have a nursing post at Mexborough Montague Hospital. I didn't tell you I was applying in case I didn't get it and you were disappointed. I am to have some sort of training. Of course I will have to live in as Nursing rules are still strict, but it won't be forever. I will travel straight there, settle in and if it's alright with your father, I can visit you.*
>
> *Even better I start in two weeks. It won't be long my darling. We will make a life together so keep your chin up.*

Nan and her father understood. Margaret would miss them.

* * * * *

A square woman approximately five feet tall, dressed in an ill-fitting navy blue suit and black peaked hat, marshalled the small railway station. At Margaret's request

The Letter

for a porter to unload the luggage from the guard's van the woman threw her head back and burst out laughing, "You're looking at everybody love, station master, porter, and taxi service. Nelly's the name," she said wading in to help the guard throw Margaret's endless bags from the train.

A wicker basket spilled, scattering nuts. "Looks like you've come to stop," Nelly wheezed, shovelling up the nuts with workman like hands. Margaret began to help. "Eeh lass, leave it to me . . . them fancy clothes weren't meant for jobs like this. It's not for ladies. I'll 'ave it done in a tick."

Wiping her brow on the back of a straining sleeve, Nelly produced a handcart from behind a shed, loaded it with the rest of the luggage and asked Margaret where she was going.

"A place called Mexborough."

"Last train that stops at Mexborough's gone."

"Yes, I know but I thought I'd get this far and take a cab."

"There's no cab 'ere love."

"Well can I get to Barnburgh Street in Denaby . . . Do you know it?"

"Know it? It's where I live. Hang on a minute. You're the woman that Tommy Waters met out in India? Going to work at Montague?"

Margaret was glad she'd worn gloves or this knowing woman might have noticed the faded mark of Ben's wedding ring on her finger.

After briskly rubbing her hands together the indomitable Stationmaster grabbed the handles of the cart. "Right, there's no train for a bit. Them that wants me'll have to wait" she said, setting off to walk at a cracking pace. Margaret teetered behind in high-heeled shoes, taking care to avoid the numerous stagnant puddles and potholes barring the way.

The station lay in a dip opposite the colliery. A black-watered canal navigated by coal-laden barges ran parallel to the rough road. The surrounding landscape blighted by monstrous slag heaps smoking like menacing volcanoes.

Nelly took a rest, "Look back way we've come and there's Castle." Margaret followed Nelly's outstretched arm and in the distance, shielded by trees, were the remains of a ruined stone edifice high on a hill. "That's Conisbrough, but you're alreet, we're not going among them hoity toities. Can't stand'em miself" Nelly said, striding sturdily out in the opposite direction.

Margaret was disappointed. Conisbrough looked likely to be a pleasant place, whereas rough smudged-black men with bright eyes outlined in coal dust peopled their treeless route.

"Now then love them's only pitmen" Nelly reassured. "Day shift's finished. That there's tobacco juice they're spitting. Gob it out wit' dust to clear lungs . . ."

In Bombay Margaret had mistaken the red betel juice splashes on walls and floor of the railway station for blood but there was no mistaking the thick tar-like substance ejected by the coughing miners. It made her want to vomit.

On one side of this walk through hell, row upon row of sooty brick terraced houses stretched back into the distance. On the other side identical dwellings were squashed together against the railway track, bordered by the dismal canal. A run of solid bay-windowed double-fronted shops proudly displayed their owners' name above the door. Dark grey smoke spewed in unison from countless chimneystacks. In the distance the enormous winding wheel of a second colliery was silhouetted against the mean skyline.

Thin, grimy children, playing on the mucky roadside, disappeared inside warren-like houses, reappearing with a gaggle of the inhabitants.

Nelly stopped and hammered on a door. "Anybody at home?" She hammered louder. "This must be only house in Denaby with everybody in it."

Margaret smiled grimly as the door was opened by a dapper man, with a silver pocket watch hanging from his waistcoat.

"Come in. Come in. Tha must be Margaret. I'm Albert, Tommy's dad. Make thisen at 'ome. Mother, brew a pot of tea. Poor lass'll be gasping."

Margaret wiped her feet on the clipped rag doormat. The delicate shoes and nylon stockings were ruined. What a fright she'd look when she arrived at the hospital.

A woman, her face reddened from cooking on the fire, shook Margaret's hand, "I'm Shirley, Tommy's stepmother. I'm very pleased to meet you."

Albert pulled out a wooden chair from under the kitchen table, "Sit thi sen darn. Tha shud 'ave let us know. Well you're 'ere now safe and sound. "

"I didn't mean to put you out" Margaret said, "I thought the train went to Mexborough."

Shirley cleared the remains of a meal from the table. "Tommy's father's been on the day shift but I'll soon have you a bite to eat." She produced a lace tray cloth and set a place with a china cup and saucer, plate and silver butter knife.

Albert sliced chunks of bread to toast on the fiery coals of the black lead range. A kettle steamed incessantly. The hot toast was lavishly buttered and set before Margaret. Someone would have to go without for this hospitality.

"This was my mother's tea set," Shirley explained. "Only the best is good enough for Tommy's future wife. He'll be back soon. He's gone for a walk."

Gone for a walk, Margaret thought. Who'd go for a walk in this awful place?

Shirley told her that they were lucky to have Tommy. "He's an accident waiting to happen. We didn't think he'd recover from T.B. let alone join the army . . . Hasn't he told you? He had a T. B. spine as a boy. The hospital put him in a plaster cast. Albert concocted a flat cart for him to lie on. Alice, that's Tommy's eldest sister, pushed him round on it. Florrie, she's the youngest, was in a sanatorium for months. At least he was at home."

"I married a grand lass," Albert said. "She took on children. as her own; travelled every week t' hospital at Ilkley t' see Florrie."

"Enough of that, Dad . . ." Shirley said pleased to have the attention turned on Tommy who came in through the back door

"Where's tha bin lad? We've got a visitor."

"I can see" Tommy said. He leant awkwardly on the mantelpiece aware of his rough hob-nailed boots and shoddy clothes. He put his hands in his trouser pockets. Took them out, did it again but Margaret saw his despondency at not finding work and the scars standing out like ridges on his gaunt face.

She explained about the train, skirting round his discomfort. It struck Margaret that when you returned to your parents' home you became a child again. She was the same in Scotland, but this wasn't what she'd travelled half way round the world for. She had to get away.

"Tommy, I'm expected at the hospital and it's getting late."

Albert put on his trilby hat and coat saying, "I'm off t' see Father O'Keefe. Stay 'ere lad. Keep Margaret company."

Margaret looked at him blankly. She was having trouble understanding what he said. She was fine with Shirley, who had hardly any accent, certainly not a Yorkshire one. It was Tommy's turn to explain, "The priest's got a car. My dad's gone to sort it." And, with his whippet-like father gone, he quickly, kissed her.

"I thought you'd never get round to doing that," Shirley said. "You know Margaret, Denaby wasn't what I was used to. It's been hard but I mustn't grumble." She said she'd had a daughter before she married Tommy's father. Albert was good to both of them, and she was happy. Things had a habit of working out.

Margaret instantly liked and admired Tommy's stepmother. Such open honesty. Secrets didn't belong here but how much had Tommy told her? Margaret didn't want things to work out if it meant living like this. She had tried to fit in to Ben's family and it hadn't worked. She didn't know if she could do it again but Tommy was so pleased to see her, standing taller, his face relaxed. What ever would she do? She smiled at him and said, "Tommy, the basket of nuts and dates by the door is for Shirley."

"Margaret, you shouldn't have . . ." Shirley said. "It's years since I saw nuts. We used to have them at my parents' house at Christmas, and dates. I don't think Florrie's children have ever tasted them."

Shirley carried some of the gifts into the tiny kitchen, giving Margaret and Tommy a few moments alone. He hadn't deceived her about his family. They hadn't talked much about their parents. It hadn't been important. Denaby and Gorebridge were immaterial. India was to be their home. She put her arms round him to reassure them both.

Albert returned with the priest who kept the car engine running, while Margaret said goodbye. She was greatly tempted to ask him to take her to Doncaster Station and catch the next train back to Scotland.

CHAPTER 33

The pits resembled battlefields, equally capable of mangling a man's body and mind. Margaret worried what became of patients discharged from hospital but she soon discovered the unspoken loyalty that bound the mining community together. Neighbours rallied round. Meals were cooked; children looked after, washing shared out and what ever else was needed to 'tide the family over'.

People took to knocking on Albert's door with various ailments or to ask for advice when the nurse came. "Tha might as well move in . . . Turn kitchen in t' surgery . . ." He complained but Margaret knew he liked the attention. His son had a feather in his cap having a fiancée who was a nurse.

Living in at the hospital enabled Margaret to save. The Post Office savings book was in her name. She suggested to Tommy it was changed, to include him.

"It's your money, Margaret. I can't take a penny."

"It's for us, for our home. I want to be with you more than I want money."

"I've no right."

"We have the right to be together. What's mine is yours and if anything happened to me . . . ?"

"That's not going to happen."

"I know but the divorce isn't through and well . . . you see what I mean."

He shook his head.

"Then do it for me."

They went together to change the account. Tommy's shaky signature bound them together but it increased his determination to find work. His sister Alice lived outside Manchester. Her husband was overseas and she had three children to support. Tommy decided to stay with her. Albert, Shirley and Margaret were against it.

* * * * *

Tommy hadn't been at Manchester three weeks before a letter came from Alice.

> *Manchester*

> *Dear Margaret,*
> *I am writing to ask you to send Tommy's bank book. He has found a job but will not get paid for another week and I have the children to support.*

> *Alice*

What kind of work had Tommy found? Was he well? The letter only mentioned the bank book. He'd probably had one when he was in the army but Margaret hadn't seen it. This was theirs, for their future, a statement that she'd given up hope of returning to India. She'd take it to Manchester.

* * * * *

Margaret waited patiently. Alice registered her disapproval by banging pans, chopping vegetables and over-polishing the kitchen range. Talk was impossible. Alice grudgingly offered to stretch the meal to one more but there was no invitation to stay the night.

The heavy iron sneck was lifted several times before Tommy opened the back door. He didn't notice Margaret. Ashen faced, more dead than alive he stripped off his shirt to wash in the kitchen sink. Margaret counted every rib in his drastically underweight frame. Towelling himself dry he brightened at the sight of her. "Alice got me a job, working in the mill."

"I can see that." Margaret said trying to control her anger.

"It's easy. When the cloth comes off the machines all I have to do is wrap it round me. If I stick at it I'll earn good money."

Tommy was a human bobbin! Margaret rounded savagely on Alice, "Are you blind? Can't you see what it's doing to him?"

Alice fought back, "You come here thinking you know it all! Well you can tell my brother what to do but you're not telling *me*."

Tommy tried to calm things down, "I owe money."

Margaret looked at Alice in disgust, "So it was really you who wanted the bank book?"

"I can't expect my sister to keep me for nothing," Tommy said, looking from one to the other.

Margaret threw the bank book at Alice, "Take your blood money!"

Alice ground it into the kitchen floor. Tommy shouted above the din, "Margaret it was my idea."

"Pack your bags and return to Yorkshire with me tonight or there'll be no wedding!"

Tommy hadn't the strength to argue. He slept for most of the journey back to Yorkshire. Margaret realised the foolishness of losing her temper. Tommy couldn't know what the bank book meant. She had humiliated him and alienated Alice. What if he'd chosen to stay in Manchester?

Tommy found another job in the local glass-making works. The high temperature and his stubborn attempts to do the same work as the other men made him ill. He missed shifts and was sacked. He tried to work in a small engineering factory making irons and kettles but the constant hammering of the steel press drove him mad and he had to give it up.

Margaret hated to see him dead beat with trying. She attributed her late period to overtiredness. A rest and change of scene would put things right.

CHAPTER 34

A break in Scotland

Scotland provided a ready escape. Tommy didn't question Margaret's decision to go there and was excited at the prospect of a holiday. Frances had left Margaret's father and returned to London. He was with Nan. His collection of clocks, at various stages of repair maddeningly ticked and chimed the hours away. Nan was looking forward to Margaret and Tommy's visit, especially as the clocks would be stopped. Their father said that Tommy coudna do with the noise.

Margaret tossed and turned in bed at Nan's. After her behaviour in Manchester she hadn't the heart to reject Tommy's lovemaking. He was so vulnerable. He might think she didn't want him. But Tommy was clumsy and she would have to deal with the consequences. How could they cope with a child?

She understood why women procured abortions. A foolish lonely war time fling, a careless slip and another mouth to feed, so much to lose for a moment's pleasure. At the Montague she'd nursed the results of women interfered with by so called, 'mothers helpers'. Often the result was abortion but damaged wombs, childlessness and death through septicaemia were equally common. Everyone knew but nothing was said. This way fewer people were hurt.

Margaret wasn't certain when her baby was due. Late August or September seemed the most probable. Saurabh's birthday was in August so she plumped for September. Birthdays and Christmas were the worst of times. She would have this child, not as a substitute for those she'd lost, or because of her belief in the sanctity of life, but because Tommy deserved hope.

Nan queried, "Maggie, are you sure you're alright?"

"Yes . . ."

"Well you dinne look it,"

"Well I'm fine."

Nan was rarely put off. "Maggie is there something you should be telling Tommy?"

It was as if a dam broke inside, "I'm pregnant Nan. I'll have to give up my job, and then we can't afford to live. How will we manage? Oh Nan I shouldn't put you, of all people through this."

"Life has to go on. Tommy's a good man but it'll no be easy."

"He'll insist we go back to Denaby and I don't think I can take it."

"You've got to tell him Maggie . . . whatever he does."

"Let's get Christmas over. It's such an unlucky time for us."

"Oh Maggie make the most of what you've got. The divorce's through. Away and get a special licence."

"Father wouldn't stand for it."

"Maggie, faither's changed. Leave him to me."

A joyous Tommy married Margaret in Edinburgh on an arctic Tuesday in January. Cards and telegrams from friends and family wished them well.

CHAPTER 35

Return to Denaby

Tuberculosis was in the fabric of Denaby. It must have been dormant in Shirley for years. She put the increased shortness of breath and weight loss down to a heavy cold but the persistent cough and bloody sputum worried Albert. He sent for Doctor McArthur who confirmed the disease. It was too advanced to send Shirley to a sanatorium. The doctor prescribed keeping her at home, supervised by Margaret. Tommy's youngest sister, Florrie, took over while Margaret finished working her notice at the hospital.

Margaret had already organised the conversion of one of the two bedrooms into a 'sickroom'. Florrie diligently washed Shirley's eating utensils, bedding, towels and night clothes separately from those of the rest of the household. After that the general treatment for the illness was light and air.

Light and air in Denaby! The 'sick room,' with the window opened wide let in the coal dust, blown in on the slightest breeze, making Shirley's cough worse. Albert closed the window. The room became hot. Shirley couldn't breathe. The sliding of the sash, open or shut, marked the hours.

The final stage of the illness came more quickly than anticipated. Shirley's daughter arrived from Birmingham, Alice arrived from Manchester. Tommy and Dad joined the women devotedly nursing Shirley as she had done for so many. She didn't need to be told she was dying. Mercifully by then she mainly slept.

Tommy and his sisters were resting in the kitchen while Margaret made Shirley comfortable. Albert was shovelling coal into a bucket in the yard. Margaret could hear him through the open window. A waft of scented sweet violet blew in. Margaret closed the window. She had last smelled the perfume in India on the day she received word of her mother's death. She called for Albert, waking Shirley who lucidly asked her to look after him and Tommy, and be a friend to his sisters. Shirley died before Albert and the others reached the top of the stairs.

The death dispelled any animosity between Alice and Margaret. The funeral was dignified and sorrowful but Albert, declared, "I'll not walk behind one more coffin from this 'ouse."

* * * * *

Albert took a house on Cliff View. It was further from the main road than Barnburgh Street with a high hard-red brick wall enclosing the back yard, and an outside lavatory that flushed. The street ran out of steam in a patch of open ground surrounded by a few scrubby trees called 'The Rec.' Colliery Officials' houses with neat gardens were close by. A path led to the allotments where miners indulged their passion for fresh air, growing vegetables and gaudy chrysanthemums in orderly rows; a glimmer of beauty in a cheerless scene.

Margaret wasn't the kind of wife Albert wanted for Tommy, and Cliff View was the last place she expected to be, but it was done. The first Saturday night she spent there Margaret couldn't sleep. In the morning she decided to go to mass. Tommy accompanied her as far as the local Catholic Church.

The spiritual comfort from the mass made Margaret more secure. She couldn't go to Communion. Divorced people weren't allowed to receive the Sacrament but anyone could go to mass. She'd been angry with her father for suggesting she get an annulment of her marriage to Ben. Maybe it wasn't such a bad idea?

Tommy had said he'd have breakfast waiting. The inviting smell of frying bacon greeted Margaret's return. "Don't ask where that's come from" Albert said, as Tommy put a plate of bacon and eggs on the table.

"What about you and Tommy?"

"We've 'ad ours" Albert said, running the polishing brush over his going-out black shoes.

She didn't need to be asked twice and didn't notice Tommy go upstairs.

Albert loitered by the back door. He tossed his watch into his waistcoat pocket. "What kept yer?" He said to Tommy, who had changed from his work a day clothes to wearing a sports jacket and flannels.

"We're going out Margaret, me and mi dad."

"Come on lad. Let's be 'aving yer," Albert chivvied. "Margaret, vegetables ont draining board, spuds int sink . . . meat's ont side," and they were off.

Margaret finished her breakfast. An hour passed with no sign of Tommy or his father. Where had they gone? She examined the pile of vegetables. Soft green and yellow striped caterpillars crawled out from the dark green cabbage leaves. Margaret flicked them into the stone sink, swished them down the plughole and rinsed the leaves.

Short of something to do she scrubbed the dirty potatoes and carrots with a small bristle brush lying on the wooden draining board; cut away the carrot tops, trimmed outgrowing lumps from the potatoes, chopping them into regular shapes to fit the saucepans. The onions made her eyes water. The raw meat turned her stomach. Disgusted, she gave up.

Father and son returned full of cheer and Miners Welfare beer, took off their ties and meticulously hung up their jackets. Albert began sharpening the carving knife before he realised there was nothing to carve. No Yorkshire puddings and no Sunday dinner! It was too much even for Tommy. Margaret shouted above their loud complaints, "I can't cook!"

"Can't cook?" Albert said incredulously. "Tha's 'aving me on . . ." Margaret shook her head, "By gum lass ther's nowt to it."

"But I've never needed to."

"Well tha needs to nar!"

Albert cooked the dinner teaching Margaret the essentials: the right kind of fire, glowing hot, not smoky, the timing of the vegetables and the meat done to a turn. His Yorkshire puddings rose to the top of the oven, firm on the outside, soft and creamy inside; soaked in thick meaty gravy.

Margaret copied the men, mopping the plate clean with a slice of bread. "Tha'll be alreet next Sunday," Albert said going to bed for his traditional Sunday afternoon sleep.

* * * * *

Doctor McArthur examined Margaret, peered over his half moon spectacles and said, "Well lassie?"

"It's not my first pregnancy."

"I can tell that."

Margaret briefly outlined the circumstances. The doctor thought he'd seen everything in his years in Denaby but the last thing he expected was to be treating the former wife of a fellow doctor, married to a labourer. He asked how she was coping and Margaret answered that she was finding it tough.

"No one here, apart from Tommy and Albert, knows I have children. If anything goes wrong with the birth will you send me to the Western Hospital in Balby, not The Montague?"

"Do you think Tommy's bothered what people think?"

"No but I do. I've got to start again. That's difficult enough. I don't know if I could do it if my past came out." The doctor raised his eyebrows. "I love my Indian children, doctor. I had no choice but to leave them."

Margaret hadn't known what his response would be but the doctor arranged for her to be admitted to Western Hospital for the birth.

Florrie offered to help when Margaret's time came but Albert said if Doctor Mac wanted Margaret to go into hospital it was for a good reason. He guessed why she'd chosen The Western. It was rarely used by Denaby people. Florrie could call in and look after Tommy and him instead.

* * * * *

The baby was born jaundiced and a month premature. Tommy's daughter, something for him to live for, he'd get a job. Make her proud of him. The nurses joked they'd throw him out if he asked to go down to the nursery again.

Margaret was glad to be in the clean orderly ward away from Tommy's exuberant delight. There were feeding times and sleeping times and few occasions to cuddle new babies, routine was far more important. Mothers were made to rest on their beds and gather strength for returning home. Denaby wasn't home, more like a stage on which Margaret played various roles. She was convincing but each time she picked up Tommy's daughter she felt like a traitor. She chose not to breast feed and when it came to choosing a name there was only one on her lips . . . Pavia.

Tommy named the baby Elizabeth, after the king's daughter.

CHAPTER 36

The unpredictable tremors in Tommy's limbs increased. Outbursts of rage and blinding pains in his head drove him into the sanctuary of the bedroom where he screamed and shouted like a man possessed, until it passed. Then he'd lie like a lost soul with his broken head in Margaret's lap. She often fell asleep wondering what was going through his mind, but he couldn't remember any of it. He took to sleeping on the floor but neither of them got any rest.

"Come to bed," she coaxed, turning back the covers. He crept in putting his cold feet on her legs. "You're freezing" she said, moving further into the bed. "Come under the blanket."

They often talked or made love under the tented bedclothes so as not to wake Elizabeth or Albert. The night hid his wounds. "Sleep, Tommy" she said drowsily as they lay so close their heads touched.

Margaret woke choking. Tommy's hand was round her throat. He was gabbling menacingly. He squeezed harder. She couldn't make out what he was saying. It sounded like Japanese or Chinese. He came round straddled across her.

"You were dreaming, Tommy."

"Dreaming! I mm . . . might have killed you."

He stumbled out of the bedroom and into his father.

"What's up lad?"

"Dad, s . . . send Margaret to Scotland," was all he could get out of his son.

"Margaret, what's going off?"

"I'm not going anywhere, dad."

"Ow the bloody 'ell can I 'elp if you won't say owt . . .?"

Margaret didn't need help now. She wasn't afraid of the present. It was the future that held her fears.

* * * * *

Doctor Mac said the grenade blast had shaken Tommy's brain so badly that it could be years before his condition improved. Margaret asked about the long term prognosis. The doctor chose his words carefully, "What you see is pretty much what you get. The pioneering surgery used on Tommy is experimental. You see lassie by all rights he should be dead. We don't know much about the treatment of survivors like him."

The doctor wasn't convinced anything could be done to alleviate Tommy's condition but a quiet spell in hospital might help everybody.

Tommy was admitted to The Royal Infirmary at Sheffield. Albert and Florrie suggested sharing the visiting to give Margaret a break but Tommy got upset when they tried it. They could afford the bus fares to Sheffield for hospital appointments, but visiting daily was an extra financial strain. Albert paid the bulk of the cost. Margaret was fighting bureaucracy for a better pension. The form filling and tribunals were endless; the begging for hand outs demeaning.

* * * * *

From December decisions about anything were impossible. Heavy snow transformed the cindered streets. There were snowball fights and sledging. Snowmen guarded the entries to the backs. Men became like the pit ponies out to holiday grass.

There was no let up with the weather. Power lines were down, blizzards blocked roads. Coal was in great demand but transporting it hazardous. Trains and lorries ground to a halt. Areas of the country were cut off for weeks. Albert's coal arrived on schedule. Mineworkers were entitled to free coal. It was part of their wages. He shovelled a path through waist-high snow to the coal house. Margaret kept it clear with hot ash. Black henna-like lines patterned her hands, sore from mending the hungry fire.

In India, Muni had made a mixture of olive oil and sugar to massage and soften Margaret's hands. In Denaby, Margaret used it to get rid of the dirt and prevent the roughened skin from scratching Elizabeth. Albert accused her of gross extravagance. Didn't she know this was England? As if she could forget!

The glistening snow turned slimy grey. The everlasting wet washing drying on the wooden clothes horse round the fire and keeping Elizabeth clean were a dreary depressing background to life. Then there was the cost of everything now she wasn't working.

Margaret spent hours cooking, scraping every scrap of waste food and vegetable peelings into buckets at the bottom of the yard. Albert called them 'slop buckets.' A man came regularly to empty them. Sometimes she was so drained she didn't want to get up in the morning.

Floods followed snow and for a few days the bridge over the River Don was submerged cutting off the pit. Groups of flint-eyed men gathered at the water's edge, testing the depth with sticks. Some miners waded through, swearing as the icy water crept up their legs. There was no room for weakness. Miners fought the elements or the owners when they had to.

Albert said that to go down the pit you had to be strong in the arm and weak in the head but Margaret didn't appreciate his humour. She had come to believe that the circumstances of their birth dictated the miners' future. She admired the risks they took underground and their dogged persistence in fighting for better working conditions. They might not have books but they were clever, resourceful and loyal to each other.

* * * * *

As soon as the water receded Albert went back to work the night shift in the pit time-office. In the morning he was late arriving home. Margaret went out of the back yard gate to look for him and found him leaning blue-lipped against the entry wall. She reached for his pulse.

He tugged at his overcoat, "For Christ's sake woman! Get this bloody thing off mi and I'll be alreet!"

For once Margaret did as she was told. Under the coat, wrapped around Albert's slight frame, was a side of freshly butchered pork encased in newspaper and string.

He hauled himself up the back step and into the kitchen. Margaret cut off the string and unrolled him. "Tha knows nar what slops were for," he said, getting his breath back, "to feed pig int allotment. Its mi 'alf share; slaughtered when bobbies were too busy wi weather to notice owt else."

He sliced thick fatty lumps off the pork and fried them for breakfast. "This'll keep cold out," he said, giving seven months old Elizabeth the crispy rind to bite on. The grease dribbled down the baby's chin. "Gis it 'ere lass," he said wiping Elizabeth's chin with his shirt.

"Dad . . ."

"It'll be reet, Margaret." He gave Elizabeth another piece. "She likes it."

* * * * *

Daisy was a widow whose husband had been killed by a roof fall underground. Small, bird-like, head-bobbing, she was the unofficial bookies runner for Cliff View. Her son Jack had fought in France and recently returned with a shy bride who spoke very little English. Margaret resurrected her rusty French, translating what Claudette said for Daisy.

The two women were refugees, for that was how it felt to Margaret. Claudette told Margaret that she had a son, the result of the German invasion. Her family had stood by her but the boy faced an uncertain future in France. Jack accepted him and they were arranging to bring the child to England. Claudette didn't know if she was doing the right thing. Margaret couldn't confide her own circumstances but said that these days, after the war, a lot of people were escaping from something, especially if they ended up in Denaby. They could only survive by putting aside their past and looking forward. It was easy to advise someone else.

* * * * *

Daisy had taken to occasionally looking after Elizabeth. It made Margaret consider returning to work. Albert was usually up by two o'clock in the afternoon. If Daisy and he agreed, they could share Elizabeth between them. Margaret got a job at The Western Hospital, on the maternity unit, where she'd given birth to Elizabeth. It suited everyone except Tommy.

"I'm useless, Margaret" he said, "I can't look after my own daughter. I don't like her going to Daisy."

"She's kind, Tommy, and only across the road. You can go over . . ."

"It's not the same as having her here, Margaret." He hung his head, "I know you miss your Indian children. They should be with us . . . and Elizabeth."

How could Margaret explain without hurting him or his family? It wasn't that she was ashamed of Denaby. She had experienced nothing but kindness since she arrived, but she wasn't alone in her quest for a better future. Many brave men returned from the war actively seeking something other than the pit for their sons. Jack and Claudette had gone to London with Daisy's blessing and if Tommy hadn't had his accident?

It was no use thinking what might have been but the labour government and trade unions were changing the country. There was a free health service and scholarships for miners' children who passed the Eleven Plus Examination. Bursaries had taken Margaret as far as University. One day, the 'Scholarship' might do the same for Elizabeth. Until then, Margaret must be strong and somehow get them out of Denaby.

* * * * *

Florrie's husband left her. Broken hearted, unable to pay the rent and with no man working at the pit, she was evicted and landed on the doorstep with four young children. At night during the week they slept in Albert's bed. In the morning they got up and he got in. At weekends Albert and Tommy shared a room with Florrie's boys. Margaret and Florrie shared with the girls.

Florrie cooked, cleaned and ran the house. Up at five, she battled boiling water, scrubbing, mangling and rinsing clothes; stringing a line of washing across the backs before seven o' clock in the morning. They were overcrowded but Florrie's good nature, Tommy's affection for his sister and Margaret's willingness to compromise kept relationships steady. The price was the terrible toll on Tommy's health.

* * * * *

The local council had started building houses in Conisbrough, high above the rocky limestone ridge of the Crags, overlooking Denaby. Smog and dense chimney smoke was blown away over the other side of the Don Valley. Margaret added their name to the ever-growing housing waiting list.

* * * * *

The parish priest arranged a pilgrimage to a holy shrine at Walsingham to pray for a house for Tommy and Margaret. Donations from religious denominations, pubs, clubs, and the National Union of Mineworkers financed the venture. The selfless generosity of Denaby people was worth more than the empty words of politicians who so often maligned them.

Four months later Tommy and Margaret walked hand in hand up the Crags to see the progress on their house. Singing skylarks soared from nests in the swaying grass, cream and purple clover burst over variegated grey rocks, buttercups spilled onto the rocky paths dividing the two communities. Men exercising their dogs called out 'All the best Tommy', or stopped and shook his hand. It was almost too good to be true.

CHAPTER 37

Conisbrough 1948-1956

The new house in Conisbrough boasted a bathroom with a door that locked. There was no abrasive coal grit to scratch Margaret's legs in the smooth white bath, no one waiting impatiently for their turn and no shared tepid water. All she had to do was turn on the tap for a constant flow of hot water.

Jean had sent her a round art deco blue and gold tin of talcum with a velvety powder puff and matching Lily of the Valley bath cubes. Margaret crumbled these into the hot water, squashing them with her toes. She stretched out, sinking into the milky scented water. She thought of the luxurious baths prepared by Muni, of girls talk, relaxing massages and idling the day away. One more cherished memory to let go. These days there was scarcely time to wash her face.

Left alone while Margaret was at work Tommy became moody, with no sense of purpose, wandering back to Denaby, taking Elizabeth. The *ad hoc* arrangements with Daisy had worked when they lived in Cliff View but she was seventy seven and Margaret couldn't expect her to step in until Elizabeth started school. It was no use asking Peggy and Michael who lived next door. They were willing to help but couldn't provide the extensive support Tommy required to keep him stable.

The pension's tribunal categorized him as 100% disabled. The findings listed him as having: ' . . . *lost his right eye: sustained gunshot wounds to the wrist: wounds to the head and face: confused: rather simple and childish: obviously mentally deteriorated* . . . '

Margaret couldn't read any more but the facts were daily in front of her. There was nothing mentioned about Tommy's courage. They'd written him off. Well she wouldn't! She hid the letter with the tribunal's findings.

Margaret had longed to have Tommy and Elizabeth to herself, without Albert. She'd felt mean about it. He'd been so kind to them but she genuinely believed Tommy might make more progress without his father always helping him. The last few weeks made her realise she was wrong. It was wishful thinking, made more painful by the acknowledgement that Tommy needed all the help he could get to function normally. If Margaret was to be able to work, she would have to ask Albert to live with them.

Tommy's dad was looking for an excuse to be with his son. He signed over his house in Cliff View to Florrie and Matt, a soft spoken Irish miner, who was courting Florrie.

* * * * *

Tommy was happy to have Albert living with them, a boy chumming up with his dad, who would do anything to please his son. They set to digging and planting potatoes to clean the garden soil. Carrots, onions, leeks, sprouts, French beans, peas, lettuce and radishes were planted according to the season. Rhubarb, raspberries, gooseberries, black and red currants, interlaced with a netting of twisted paper and string to keep off the birds. There were lawns and rose beds, sweet peas, lavender and lilac trees and Elizabeth's patch of garden with a giant scarecrow.

Seeds sprouted on every window ledge. Albert rotated the trays to catch the sun, commandeering the kitchen table for potting up. Compost, plant pots and twine were likely to become the meal of the day. Margaret banished them outside. Albert bought a green house.

* * * * *

Margaret's father came from Scotland to stay. The two old men's pipes sat adjacent in the ashtray on the mantelpiece next to Tommy's cigarettes. There was a stream of visitors, friends of the men. Florrie was seldom away. She had married Matt and flitted to Conisbrough.

Their family had increased to six, too many children for Cliff View.

Tommy attended Doncaster Infirmary for physio-therapy. Albert took him to the hospital and the men made a day of it, having a couple of pints in the town. It wasn't enough for Tommy. He combed the district knocking on doors, searching for a job. The local post master asked Margaret if Tommy could manage to deliver the post in Conisbrough. It would be temporary, for six weeks. Albert offered to carry the post bag.

In uniform, with the peaked hat set jauntily hiding his missing eye, Tommy was a man again. Up at five o'clock whistling his way to work, back home for a cup of tea about eleven. Dinner cooked by Albert at one. Out again for the afternoon collection, calling at Florrie's for home baked buns and tarts.

He took messages; was first with the news of marriages, births and deaths. Handed in the milk off the doorstep and checked on the sick and elderly. Tommy didn't need Albert to help him. The whole of Conisbrough watched out for him.

The annulment of Margaret's marriage to Ben freed her to discreetly marry Tommy in the vestry of Saint Alban's Catholic Church, and make peace with God.

The pension board reduced Tommy's meagre allowance because he was working. Margaret continued saving; enough for a washing machine and a holiday with Jean, Nan and Rosemary, Nan's youngest daughter.

* * * * *

The glittering globe at Blackpool Tower threw coloured lights across the polished ballroom, highlighting Tommy's smile and Margaret's gold satin dress, made from material stored in one of the suitcases. He confidently waltzed her round the floor. They made plans. Perhaps they should buy a house or a car. She'd drive. It looked easy. Tommy teased, "Driving easy . . . like roller skating?"

"Well I can't be much worse at driving."

"Just let me know when you plan to start, so I can get my bike off the road."

Nan, Jean and the girls were fast asleep when Tommy and Margaret got back to the boarding house. "Another day to look forward to tomorrow," Tommy whispered.

The rest of the week the weather was perfect. They reclined in deck chairs on the beach. Tommy built sand castles with the children and buried the women's feet in the sand. He rode beside Elizabeth and Rosemary on the donkeys, making his go faster across the sand. Margaret and her sisters were certain he'd fall off, but he didn't. He bought plaster figurines and heaps of bargains at auction houses on the sea front, too many to fit in the cases. He gave them to the landlady to keep until next year. Stress-free and golden brown, they were sorry when the holiday ended.

* * * * *

Tommy's job, as a postman, was made permanent so Elizabeth spent the school holidays in Scotland with Nan. Margaret put her on the train at Doncaster and she was collected in Edinburgh. Sometimes Margaret wished her daughter wasn't quite so enthusiastic to go, but there were outings to the seaside at Gullane and Portobello and the companionship of her cousins. Elizabeth liked Mary's boys. They were full of bright ideas and things to do.

The year Elizabeth was nine Tommy missed her terribly and kept asking when she was coming back, "I don't like it when Elizabeth's away. She's my little ray of sunshine on bad days."

Margaret agreed. Their daughter was a distraction from the fact that Tommy's condition was rapidly deteriorating. It was as if he was unravelling. His stammering was hardly noticeable unless he was under stress but his unpredictable temper was easily triggered, and innumerable murderous headaches sent him stumbling upstairs to lie down.

He pleaded, "Don't let me lose my mind Margaret! I couldn't stand it." Her heart went out to him as he fought to retain his loving personality, "I don't want you looking after a gibbering wreck and I don't want Elizabeth to see me like that. Promise me you'll put me down first."

"Tommy Waters we'll have no more talk like that. Elizabeth loves you. I love you."

"But it's not going to make me better?" There was nothing she could say.

"I've been lucky to have these years," he said thinking aloud.

"There's lot more to come," she said, trying to focus on the future, "Wait until Elizabeth goes to university."

"Do you think she will?"

"She's your daughter and . . ." Tommy joined in, finishing the sentence "only the best will do." Margaret's lion-hearted husband laughed and kissed her.

Bringing Elizabeth home early was easily remedied but was it right to keep the severity of Tommy's condition from him? Margaret was convinced he was aware of what was happening. It was almost as if he'd read the years of detailed assessments, securely hidden in the tin hat box, each one worse than the last. He had unknowingly defied the experts by leading a worthwhile life, but how long could it last?

CHAPTER 38

Elizabeth raced down the garden path. "Daddy I'm home . . ." but the door was locked. She rattled the handle; "Granddad it's me! Let me in! Let me in," but no one came. "Mum where are they?"

Margaret was fearful of the answer. She put the suitcases in the outside toilet and, fending off more questions from Elizabeth, went to find out. Florrie caught up with her before she reached Peggy's gate.

"Margaret, it's Tommy . . . He's in hospital but they're moving him to Sheffield."

"Whatever for . . ."

"There's been an accident. Dad's with him." Florrie's tense anxious face said it all.

Margaret hesitated, she'd have to go. She'd ask Peggy if she could phone for a taxi but Peggy came out to meet her.

"Margaret I'm so sorry. When you're ready we'll run you to the hospital in the car."

"Go Margaret," Florrie said urgently, "Leave Elizabeth with me. She'll be alright with Aunt Florrie til 'er dad comes home."

* * * * *

Tommy was cocooned in intensive care. How peaceful he looked. Margaret lightly swept his lips with hers; wanting to feel him, let him know she was there. She talked to him, on and on, meaningless words to bring him back to her. She mimicked Elizabeth's reaction to having her hair trimmed in Edinburgh, "Wait 'til my daddy sees this. He said my hair was to grow and grow until I could sit on it like an Indian girl."

Dearest Tommy, he thought they should tell Elizabeth about Pavia and the boys but Margaret wouldn't. Life was complicated enough without adding more problems.

She was grateful that the hospital staff allowed her to nurse him; smooth his bed, nestle his helpless hands against her face, hands that had taken lives, but were equally capable of wiping away tears and gently brushing his daughter's waist-length hair.

Visiting was strictly observed. Dad didn't come but Jean and Florrie brought clean clothes for Margaret who hadn't changed for three days. The women weren't allowed onto the ward. She met them outside. Tommy's father had taken it badly, not sleeping or eating, staring out of the widow. Calvary must have been like this.

Tommy's eyelids flickered. Margaret heard again his cheerful whistling, felt a bristly kiss on her cheek. How many times had she told him he needed a shave? His answer had been to tease her by gently rubbing his whiskery face against hers.

"I love you Tommy. Don't leave me . . . please . . . I'm not ready."

Margaret tried to bargain with God but the doctors said that the accident had dislodged the metal plates in Tommy's head. If he lived, he would be paralysed and they doubted he'd recognise anyone. Tommy, who wasn't afraid of anything, had always been afraid of this.

"Your husband is dying," the nurse said softly.

"I know nurse. I know . . ." Margaret said, "It's just . . ."

But as if choosing the moment, Tommy sighed long and deep and was gone. The swiftness of his death stole their tomorrows.

Matt took Margaret's phone call. He broke down as she spoke. Florrie wept loudly. Her children wailed. Elizabeth shrank into silence.

CHAPTER 39

The coroner gave a measured account of the accident. It was lunch time. Tommy had finished work but volunteered to deliver some urgent letters on his way home. Margaret pictured him crossing Doncaster Road near the XL crisp factory. The turbaned girls sitting on the wall, taking a break, watching the world go by. They'd cheekily call out to him. He'd reply, making them laugh. They'd call out some more. The lorry speeding down the hill, the careless young driver, distracted by the waving girls, Tommy pushing his bike into the road, burning rubber, mangled metal, sickening screams.

The coroner said he was sorry. The accident took place on Tommy's blind side. It would have helped if the driver had shown some remorse but he took his instructions from his solicitor. Margaret's anger burned.

* * * * *

Florrie brought Elizabeth home the night before the funeral. Margaret was barely functioning. She mechanically made cocoa and took her daughter upstairs. It had been over two months since Elizabeth's bed was slept in. She slid between the chilly sheets and burst into tears when her feet touched the cold hot water bottle. "Daddy . . ."

Tommy's last act of love had been to air the bed for his daughter's return from Scotland.

Elizabeth sobbed, "Why . . . ?"

"I don't know," Margaret answered.

"It's not fair" Elizabeth said, reaching for her mother's hand. "Make it go away."

"Oh Elizabeth if only I could . . ." She let her daughter cry on until there were no tears left.

"Sing to me like you did when I was little and frightened of the dark."

The song came slowly, Margaret's voice trembling, *"Golden slumbers kiss your eyes. Smiles awake you when you rise. Sleep pretty baby do not cry and I will sing . . ."* What would she sing now?

* * * * *

Summer was on the turn and autumn tiptoed in with a crisp bright morning, but there was no fire in the grate. Wreaths rested on the piano. Wall hanging photographs were draped in black. In place of parties, Tommy's open coffin filled the front room. The slumberous scent of white lilies and deep purple violets made it difficult for Margaret to breathe. She had taken part in an all night vigil by the coffin. Nan and Jean repetitively chanted the rosary, emptying her mind of everything but the prayerful drone.

The kitchen was filled with women in pressed aprons brewing a constant supply of funeral tea; so many sad eyed figures with not enough chairs to sit down.

A never-ending queue filed past the marbled body that once housed Tommy. Inconsolable, his sisters kissed the corpse wishing their brother goodnight and sweet dreams. They expected Margaret to copy them but she recoiled, her voice breaking, "I can't . . ."

The undertaker screwed down the coffin lid twisting every nerve in Margaret's body. Albert pinned Tommy's medals on the front of Elizabeth's navy blue jacket. They hung like monstrous pendants across her flat chest. Margaret gathered her close and felt the strip of black ribbon someone had sewn on the sleeve.

Tommy's Union flag draped coffin was carried to the flower-laden hearse on the stout shoulders of his brothers-in-law and friends. Their campaign medals flashed in the rays of sunshine. Hunched women leaned on each other, handkerchiefs fluttering like doves. Men self-consciously stamped and blew their nose. No one knew what to do or say.

A tattoo of soldiers' boots and the voice of a sergeant cut through the mourning, "Squad 'shun!" The clasping rasping of rifles dragged Margaret out of her stupor.

Houses with tightly closed curtains marked the processional route. Cars glided behind the parade-polished soldiers, slow marching down the main road, round the castle, past the pit into Denaby. Coal-dusted miners, fresh from the day shift, stood to attention, blinking in the daylight. Old and young in Sunday suits lined the pavements. Trilbies were raised, cloth caps tucked into pockets, bareheaded men saluted. British Legion, regimental flags, and mine union banners dipped in respect as the hearse passed by.

The vicar waited outside All Saints Church to lead the coffin in. Mourners crowded around him. Margaret couldn't make out the faces. There were so many saying their own goodbye. The church bell tolled as the soldiers carried the coffin, taking over the duty from the family. People touched it as it passed. Inside the church eulogies spoke of the decorated soldier and a much loved man who lived courageously with the consequences of war.

The slow-marching soldiers led the hearse past the Miner's Welfare, bowling green and tennis courts, towards the cemetery on the fringes of the Crags. Mother and daughter, straight backed, heads held high walked behind, flanked by the family. A hushed crowd parted sympathetically at the cemetery gate to let them through.

Margaret saw the Catholic priest by the grave, his lips moving in silent prayer. The flag was ceremoniously removed from the coffin. Matt and Albert restrained Florrie from throwing herself on top of it as it was lowered into the gaping earth. Others were on the verge of collapse. Incense and holy water, prayers and pleas, it was as though Margaret was watching some horrific slow motion film.

A crack of rifles tore through the air — a lull — the smell of cordite and the poignant heart rending bugle notes of *The Last Post*, drifted over the gravestones and onto the open Crags.

Handfuls of earth and roses scattered into the grave battered the bereaved. Margaret's heart threatened to burst. If only she could crawl away like some poor wounded animal. If only she could cry.

* * * * *

A month after the funeral Albert said it wasn't proper for him to continue staying with Margaret. He didn't want to be in the way of her remarrying. He left carrying two oversized suitcases. She guessed he was going to Florrie's. It was hard to accept that Tommy's father couldn't be there when she most needed him. Margaret thought he cared, but did anyone?

* * * * *

A tribunal decided Tommy's death was solely due to an industrial accident. Margaret was denied a war widow's pension and the accompanying benefits. The British Legion and Limbless Ex Service Men's Association decided to fight the decision on her behalf, but advised that it could take years.

CHAPTER 40

Jean came to Conisbrough for Christmas. They tried to make something of it for Elizabeth and somehow it passed.

New Year had been party time when Tommy was alive. After tea, Florrie and Matt came with their children. The men went to the Ivanhoe, a working men's club. If you didn't get there at opening time you'd have to stand all night. They saved a seat for Florrie who would join them after she'd put her youngest two children to bed. Elizabeth and the older ones were allowed to stay up.

Every time Margaret turned her back there were high jinks between Florrie's children. "You'll go upstairs," generally calmed things down but she soon had them busy polishing glasses, folding damask table napkins into triangles and setting out knives and forks in a wheel pattern. Then they practised their party pieces, singing and dancing with more gusto than talent.

Tommy, Albert, Matt, Florrie, friends and neighbours streamed into the kitchen, after the club closed. Later, in the front room Matt played the piano, his elbows bent and workman fingers stretched across the keys, moving rhythmically, while his feet pressed the soft and loud pedals. He couldn't read a word of music but, like Margaret's father, heard a song and was able to play it.

Tommy's dad put on a flat cap and sang, "*Pack up your troubles in your old kit bag . . .*" dancing a march across the front room, saluting and winking. He taught Elizabeth to sing, "*My old man said follow the van and don't dilly dally on the way . . .*" Margaret pictured her, holding a small wire bird cage, dancing the music hall routines.

She could still hear Tommy's voice reciting, "*There's a one eyed yellow idol to the north of Kathmandu . . .*" the tale of Carew, a soldier in the East, who for love, steals the eye of the idol and goes mad. By the time Tommy reached the climax, when a knife is buried in the heart of mad Carew, the children were suitably terrified.

Last year, Tommy had locked the doors to keep everyone inside, counting down the seconds to midnight, and then they sang *Auld Lang Syne*. Albert unlocked the doors. In came first foot of the New Year, Michael McCabe, blackened-faced, carrying a lump of coal, shortbread and whiskey, for good luck. The party started again.

At dawn the room went quiet while Margaret sang, "*My love is like a red, red rose . . .*" to Tommy, and he replied by singing, "*If you were the only girl in the world and I was the only boy . . .*" They kissed under the mistletoe. It was time to go. Matt's touching rendering of *Danny Boy* brought an end to the celebrations. The pains in Tommy's head had been dormant for one night.

No one came to see out this dreadful year. At midnight Margaret and Jean drank a glass of sherry to 1956, in front of the television. Elizabeth had fallen asleep on the sofa. Jean said that often people didn't know what to do when someone died but it made Margaret feel abandoned.

* * * * *

Margaret had negotiated with the hospital to start work mid January. She would work five weekdays, from half past eight in the morning, to three in the afternoon. Who would take care of Elizabeth? The sisters discussed the possibilities. Jean couldn't help. She was teaching and would have to return to Scotland for the start of the term. Florrie was ill. Albert had gone to Alice. The obvious solution was to move to Scotland.

Giving up the house would be like giving up Tommy, and his grave was in Denaby. Margaret couldn't bear to go so far away from him. Conisbrough was her home. She belonged here, not in Scotland. A letter from the Postmaster added weight to her decision to stay:

> Dear Mrs Waters,
>
> We were all deeply grieved at the death of your husband in such tragic circumstances. Christmas must have been a painful reminder.
>
> Words are difficult on occasions like this, but it may afford you some comfort to remind

you that your husband was very popular and well thought of, not only by us but by the public generally.

Keep faith in God, with his help you will no doubt find the necessary fortitude to bear your sorrow.

Should you need any help, acquaint us of the facts and we shall be ready to do anything within our power.

The staff join with me in a further expression of sympathy.

Yours sincerely
Harold Wormsley
Postmaster

Margaret didn't feel so confident when Jean returned to Scotland. There was no alternative; Elizabeth would have to come home alone, into an empty house, for the rest of the winter.

Margaret bought a two-bar electric fire to use in the morning and laid the coal fire. Elizabeth put a match to it when she came in from school.

* * * * *

The electric iron broke. Margaret used the two flat irons she'd kept as ornaments, heating them on the gas rings of the cooker, spitting on the iron's flat plate to test for readiness. Permanently tired and melancholic she subsisted from pay day to pay day.

The morning the shovel scraped along the concrete floor of the coal shed without stopping; Margaret closed the door and cried in the dark. There was nothing left, except dusty slack. You couldn't light a fire with that. She sent Elizabeth to school telling her to switch on the electric heater as soon as she came home.

Margaret rushed back from work to find a note on the kitchen table:

> *Margaret, Collected Elizabeth. Given her tea.*
> *Will fetch her home. Matt has got you a half ton*
> *of coal. It will be delivered tomorrow.*
> *Florrie*

That night Elizabeth slept with her mother to keep warm.

* * * * *

The coal was dumped on the road. Matt would lose his job at the pit if it was known the load belonged to him. He certainly couldn't be seen helping to get it into the coal shed.

The streetlamp cast enough light on the garden path for Margaret to see her way. She found Albert's wheelbarrow in the outhouse and some bits of wood to make a ramp. Then she put on the immersion heater for hot water, filled a bucket with coal and made a fire in the little room she used daily.

"Mum, what are you doing?" Elizabeth asked seeing her mother getting into Tommy's gardening trousers.

"Getting ready to get the coal in . . ."

"Can I help?"

"Get changed first . . ."

Margaret filled the barrow too full and couldn't get it up the ramp from the road to the pavement. She worked out that a lot of lighter runs would be easier. Elizabeth picked up the fallen coal and swept the dust into a pile. In two hours they'd done it.

Bathed and warm, Margaret brushed Elizabeth's hair by the fire, told magical stories from pictures in the coals and toasted bread for their supper. It was good news that Florrie was better. Soon it would be the Easter holiday and Margaret reminded Elizabeth they were both going to Nan's. She could do without spending the money but wasn't ready to be without her daughter.

"Do you think Aunt Jean will take me to the ballet?"

"I'm sure she will if you've asked her. We can all go" Margaret said, looking forward to seeing her sisters. She talked about Elizabeth's love of Nan's homemade 'tattie' soup. They could have buns at Crawford's; go to the zoo, to Aunt Mary's, and to Our Lady of Carfin's grotto.

"Not Carfin again" Elizabeth groaned. "Last time my knees ached with praying."

"They'd have ached more if the priest hadn't blessed them."

"Oh mum . . . You are funny."

"Not as funny as you, young lady" Margaret said, trying to stifle her laughter. "Now off to bed."

"I want to finish my library book. It's due back tomorrow."

"Leave it out. I'll hand it in on my way from work. You can get another at the weekend. Night-night . . . I'll switch off your light when I come up."

YORKSHIRE
1985-1986

CHAPTER 41

Yorkshire 1985

The clock struck six . . . Elizabeth . . . the library . . . Margaret sensed it was dark. She must have been dreaming? She didn't want to open her eyes, didn't want to face the reality of today, of Elizabeth grown, of the years gone without Tommy. She'd lie for a few minutes to get her bearings. The empty space beside her in the iron framed bed had grown bigger. It wasn't the original mattress. There'd been several replacements, each put on top of the one shared with Tommy. It reminded her of the story of the princess and the pea which had been one of Elizabeth's favourites. Margaret had read to her every night and she grew up to love books, they both did, often reading side by side in the evening.

Elizabeth was interested in everything. There were copies of *The World of Wonder* and *Mee's Children's Encyclopaedia* in the bookcase in the front room. Margaret had bought them from door to door salesmen, spreading the payment. Now the books were out of date, including an expensive Atlas. Countries had merged, become independent and had different names. You couldn't stop change.

She was shrinking, or so Elizabeth said, getting shorter and more stooped, but to Margaret it was the opposite. There was so much happening, nine grandchildren and two great grandchildren when she didn't expect to have any. She wondered if they resembled her. Would she ever meet them? Elizabeth, Pavia, and the boys exchanged letters. Their regard for each other poured out from every page.

Margaret counted the blessings that had arrived so late in her life. Materially she didn't have much, a few sentimental keepsakes. The council owned the house. There'd be a couple of thousand pounds from the insurance, enough to bury her. She had always saved. Most of it went on educating Elizabeth but she had some put by for a 'rainy day'. She toyed with changing her will to include some of this money for her Indian children. She'd talk to Elizabeth about it. She'd also have a clear-out, get rid of some of the rubbish Elizabeth said she hoarded

* * * * *

Margaret turned out the suitcases, drawers and cupboards. There were photographs of Tommy in India, and one of him outside his quarters in Burma playing with puppies. There were university photographs of Elizabeth and some of her in a ballet dress, taken the year after Tommy died. She must have been ten.

Margaret didn't know why she'd kept the comic seaside postcards, except they still made her smile. They could go but she'd keep Elizabeth's certificates for playing the piano and Tommy's First Aid certificate from the Home Guard.

She came across a papier-mâché box, delicately painted with kingfishers. The lacquer coating had preserved the colours so it seemed like yesterday when she had bought it in Kashmir. It rattled as she moved it. She took off the tight fitting lid. Inside was the heart-shaped box containing the blue sapphire ring, the gift of love from Ben to celebrate Saurabh's birth. Tommy hadn't minded her keeping it, but she buried it out of sight to be forgotten. One day she would give it to Pavia. It didn't belong to Elizabeth.

There was also a glittering sari pin attached to a scrap of turquoise silk, and a brass engraved letter opener from her desk at Aakesh, gifts for Saurabh and Rajeev. Margaret had thought she had nothing tangible from the past to give them. These treasures were mementoes of some of the happiest years they spent as a family. When the pain and bitterness overtook her it was easy to forget how much she had loved their father.

Margaret filled the dustbin with rubbish and put plastic bags in the outhouse ready for the bin men to collect. There were more plastic bags with clothes, handbags, knick knacks; extra table cloths and bedding stored under the stairs. An assortment of paper carrier bags emblazoned with shop logos contained knitting wool for her favourite charity, Mother Teresa. The Albanian nun didn't pass by the destitute and untouchables who Margaret had seen dying on the streets of India's cities. Raising money was the least she could do.

It had taken a week, but past midnight on Saturday the work was completed.

CHAPTER 42

"Scottie where are you! It's James! "

James, what was *he* doing here? Margaret called down stairs, "I'm up here. I'll be down in a tick . . . just let me put a few clothes on."

"It's Sunday" he said, as she joined him at the foot of the stairs.

"So it is. I must have slept in."

James had waited to collect her outside the church until everybody had gone, including the priest. Seriously concerned, he'd broken every speed limit driving to Conisbrough.

Unperturbed, Margaret continued, "I've been packing a few things for Elizabeth. This bag's rather heavy . . . will you lift it down for me?"

"Good God, Scottie! Don't tell me you're coming to stay for good?"

"You should be so lucky. I've been having a clear out."

"I can see that!"

"It's not *all* for Elizabeth! The things under the stairs are for Mother Teresa. They're coming for it on Monday."

"I hope this India business isn't too much for you? You can stop it at any time. Just say the word."

Margaret told him that she hadn't been sleeping properly and had been to see the doctor who had prescribed sleeping tablets. They hadn't worked so she stopped taking them.

The whole situation was worrying James. He'd tell Lizzie but there didn't seem much they could do. He said innocuously, "It'll all come good in the end."

"I expect so, but meantime there are things I have to do."

"Yes, like being where you're supposed to be."

"James, a lady likes to keep a man waiting, even at my time of life."

"You're incorrigible! Lizzie will sort you out."

"Well she's not managed yet." They grinned conspiratorially. Lizzie was always organising something or someone. Margaret said it went with being a head teacher.

* * * * *

"I thought you'd never get here . . ." Elizabeth complained. It looked as if her mother hadn't combed her hair and the ancient lilac cardigan she wore in the house was incorrectly buttoned. James explained that her mother had been unwell.

"Has she been to the doctors?"

"I am here, Elizabeth," Margaret said crossly, "I've told James and I don't want to talk about it now."

Elizabeth made no more reference to her mother's bizarre appearance and served dinner.

Afterwards while Margaret rested, husband and wife shared their worries in the kitchen.

"God James, mum looks awful. She's lost a lot of weight."

"Lizzie, I don't think we appreciate what a toll this has taken . . ."

"I wonder if I should ring and have a word with the doctor."

"Without telling her? She'd be livid."

"Maybe she's just exhausted? Look, we'll talk about it when she's gone. Go in the lounge and see if she's asleep."

James touched Margaret's shoulder, "We can't have you wilting away on us."

"I've no intentions of doing that. I was merely resting my eyes. Elizabeth, pass me my bag, not my handbag, the big one by the door."

"My God, mother, what have you got in this? It weighs a ton."

"That's James' whiskey." Margaret pulled out the bottle.

"A full bottle . . . Scottie you're a miracle worker!"

"It's not from my Lourdes trip. It was on offer at the Co-op, their brand. I hope it's all right."

"Just say the magic word, 'whiskey', mum, and he's happy."

"Don't be horrid Elizabeth. There's Black Magic chocolates for you."

"What's the occasion?"

"My clear out."

Margaret produced a pile of photographs. Ordinarily these would have been skimmed through politely but the past was increasingly more relevant to Elizabeth's present. "Look James, there's one of me balancing on my dad's bike."

"Don't remind me," said her mother. "My heart was in my mouth every time your father got on that wretched thing."

"Dad taught me to ride a bike. He put wooden blocks on the pedals so my feet could reach them. Then he ran alongside of me holding the seat. I was fine until I realised he'd let go. I crashed into the kerb."

"You wouldn't believe it, James. Elizabeth was always a mass of bruises."

"Roller skating down the hill was my best trick, slamming into the gas lamp to stop."

"You looked like a prize fighter with an enormous bump on your head and purple bruised eyes. I gave your dad a hard time when that happened. He was supposed to be looking after you! Not long after they changed the lamp for an electric one."

"I'd learned to stop by then. Mum you're not ill or anything?"

"Don't be silly Elizabeth. The news from India has made me think a great deal and I want to set my life in order." Margaret explained the things she'd found for the

Indian children. Elizabeth agreed that the ring, sari pin and letter opener were rightfully theirs.

"This belongs to you." Margaret said, fishing in her bag and drawing out a slim cardboard box, the size of a paperback book, on which she'd written

> *To Elizabeth with love from mum, your father pinned this on your chest before he pinned it on his own. He wanted you to have it and so do I.*

Elizabeth opened the box. There was a medal, and a letter. The medal had numbers inscribed round the rim and on the back the words, *For Bravery in the Field*.

Margaret said the number was Tommy's army number and the letter was from the King. Elizabeth read the letter.

> *I greatly regret that I am unable to give you personally the award which you have so well earned.*
>
> *I now send it to you with my congratulations and my best wishes for your future happiness.*

James studied it but couldn't find the date. "I think the King must have been ill when this was written. He'd been ill for some time with tuberculosis and lung cancer. He died before your father did."

"Elizabeth, your father named you after his daughter, our present Queen."

"So we both lost our fathers and they both had T.B. I didn't realise the king had the same disease. In fact there's a lot I don't know, especially about my father."

"You only need to know how much he loved you. Nothing else matters." Margaret said, giving Elizabeth a copy of the citation that accompanied Tommy's military medal.

> *This medal was awarded to Thomas Waters for conspicuous gallantry, coolness under enemy fire and devotion to duty during airborne operations in the Ranville area on 6/7 June 1944.*
>
> *On the 6th of June Cpl Waters volunteered to bring in a wounded comrade from an exposed position: in the face of accurate enemy sniping which had already caused casualties he coolly went forward and brought in the wounded man.*
>
> *He then continued his duty of laying a single line along an exposed route under constant enemy sniping and small arms fire. When this line was cut by enemy fire Corporal Waters again went out voluntarily and repaired communications in full view of the enemy.*
>
> *By his gallantry and complete disregard of personal dangers Cpl Waters maintained communications between Brigade H. Q. and a Battalion holding a vital position.*

James said thoughtfully, "I don't think I'm a coward but I've no idea what I'd do if I had to go to war."

Margaret said that no one could possibly know how they'd behave. There were brave deeds that went unrecognised. She thought Tommy was braver after the war, dealing with his injuries.

Elizabeth remembered him cleaning his medals and marching in the Armistice Parade. Gradually, while they talked, more memories returned. Her father's artificial eye was kept on cotton wool, in a red Captain Web match box. Granddad would send her running with it, across the field at the bottom of the garden, to head her father off on the road. He'd stop. Take out the eye. Pop it into its empty socket. Hop on his post bike and ride on. How she wished it could make him see. She began to feel sad, in the way she sometimes had as a child. "I'm sure he'd have got on with you, James."

James winked at her mother, "He could have helped me keep you two in line."

"Oh I don't know about keeping us in line. Tommy and you would have been as bad as one another . . ."

"We couldn't have that, mum! James is bad enough on his own!"

"Maybe so Lizzie, but I'm sorry I didn't get the chance to meet him."

"My dad was quite a character. Once, when we came back from Scotland, mum got a taxi from the station to Conisbrough. We passed dad sitting outside the pub with his leg in plaster. He made the mistake of waving his pint in salute. Mum wouldn't let the taxi driver stop to pick him up!"

"No wonder!" Margaret said, eager to put the record straight, "Instead of coming to Scotland with us he'd stayed behind to go to the Parachute Regiment reunion dinner. Granddad sent a telegram saying there'd been an accident, worrying me to death. When I saw your father large as life I was so cross. He said it was my fault for moving the bedroom furniture before going away. The bed was in a different position. He'd woken up to go to the toilet. Half asleep and with plenty of beer inside him, he must have been dreaming he was in the aeroplane over France. He climbed on the bedroom window ledge, opened the window and jumped out. He caught his foot in a hole that granddad had dug in the rose bed below. Peggy McCabe found him."

"Wasn't his father there?"

Margaret laughed, "He slept through it."

"Slept through it!"

"Oh James, dad was always doing something."

It was true. One thing after another, but somehow Margaret got through it. "We were so poor Elizabeth, I wonder if you missed out."

"Missed out!" Elizabeth said. "I had wonderful holidays with the aunts in Scotland, beach picnics, camping and making concerts with my cousins in the cellars of Aunt Mary's house in Edinburgh. Bike rides and blackberrying with dad at home, singsongs round the piano with Aunt Florrie's lot. I loved every minute of it but the scholarship to Notre Dame changed my life."

Margaret recollected the day the teacher called to inform her that Elizabeth had passed the Eleven Plus. It was a courtesy call. The primary school had assumed Margaret couldn't afford the school uniform and bus fares to either Mexborough Grammar school, or to Notre Dame.

Why had they bothered to take her daughter to Sheffield for the convent school entrance test and interview? They hadn't said anything when Elizabeth passed it. "If I'd had to take in *washing* you'd have gone to Notre Dame!"

Elizabeth hadn't seen her mother look so angry. James thought Margaret was going to cry.

Elizabeth's childhood memories contained no hint of the poverty her mother fought to compensate, or the times when a feather falling from the pillow was too much for her father. After his death there were days when her mother's purse had held only the bus fare to work. They'd made do with second hand clothes and, from autumn to spring, went to bed early to conserve coal and electricity. Yet they were happy. Material things weren't important and there were people worse off. Not having a father was different, that hurt. She squeezed her mother's hand. "Mum, you mustn't think for a minute that I've missed out on anything."

A lump rose in Margaret's throat, "If you don't mind, James, I'd like to go home."

The bright red of Margaret's winter coat clashed with their sombre mood. Elizabeth tried to persuade her to stay but she said she was happier in her own bed.

Margaret travelled in the back of the car. James tried to make conversation. She didn't reply. He used to think she couldn't hear him because of the sound of the engine. He now believed her deafness was selective but today she would have too much to think about to talk.

CHAPTER 43

Monday morning and James was reading the *Guardian* at the kitchen table. Elizabeth flicked at the open pages as she passed.

"Steady on Lizzie, I was reading that" he said, turning out of her way.

"The paper boy's early."

"No, I walked into the village and got it before he left the shop."

"Couldn't you sleep either?"

"I've snatched a few hours but it feels as if I haven't." James yawned and folded the newspaper.

"It's Mum, isn't it? I've absolutely no idea what to do . . ." Elizabeth stuck her porridge in the microwave, switched on the radio, and watered the herbs on the kitchen window ledge.

"Sit down a minute, Lizzie."

"I haven't time."

"Well, make time. This is important!"

She turned the radio off, poured a coffee and sat down to eat her breakfast.

"Scottie's not my mother but I think we need to help draw a line under the past. I don't mean to sound unfeeling but Ben and your dad belong there. Your sister and brothers are alive, in India. We should encourage her to enjoy them." Elizabeth nodded. He buttered his toast. "If your mother met the Indians it might help."

"I've invited them to come here but, when I've mentioned it, she's not keen. They sort of hint it would be easier if we went there."

"We'll go then."

"I'd love to, but Mum won't have it. She thinks something might happen to us."

"I can't see why."

"I know it's ludicrous but we can't go unless she's happy about it."

"Precisely, but the odds of her going to India are slim. She isn't getting any younger. It's foolish to put things off."

"I see what you mean. It's odd that we've not had a letter for ages. On the other hand I've been so busy I've not written to them. I'll drop a line tonight . . . suggest dates." Elizabeth said, finishing her porridge and picking up her car keys.

"Hang on Lizzie. What's the rush? School will wait this might not."

"Five more minutes, then it will have to wait 'til tonight."

"Look there's no need to get annoyed . . . I'm not sure your mum knows what she wants."

"I'm not annoyed. It's just so worrying." Lizzie leant on the table. "If mum would make up her mind we could do something. It seems such a shame they can't be together." She glanced at the clock. "God look at the time! If she'd had the phone . . ."

"Don't rake that up again. We are where we are. I'll find a way to call in."

"If you do, be careful what you say . . ."

* * * * *

Margaret was dressed, her coat, hat and gloves warming on the kitchen storage heater. "Another minute James and you'd have missed me. I'll stick the kettle on,"

"Going somewhere nice?" he asked, warming himself by the fire in the snug sitting room.

"It's my week for Tommy's grave, but there's no hurry."

"If you like Scottie, we can skip the tea and I'll drop you off. I'm on my way to a meeting."

"In Doncaster . . . ?"

"Okay you've got me. I *have* got a meeting this morning but it's in Leeds. We wanted to see if you were all right."

"I won't be if you two don't stop fussing." She drank the tea that neither of them wanted. "James, you get off. I might as well wait for the post. I've not heard from India for weeks."

"Neither have we. We were talking about it this morning. Lizzie thought she'd write and suggest dates they might like to come, if not, we could go there."

"Let's wait and see. There's no rush. "

James wondered if his mother-in-law was deliberately delaying meeting the Indian children. He'd promised Lizzie he wouldn't press but Scottie could be so awkward! He drove to Leeds blasting out a tape of Leonard Cohen's *Hallelujah.*

So like James, Margaret thought fondly, ready to dash off to India, at a moments notice. How could he, with his secure childhood in York, envisage Elizabeth's impoverished growing up, let alone the complexities of Indian families? Margaret had learned to her cost that it was wisest to take things slowly . . . be certain what you were getting into.

* * * * *

The frank exchange of letters renewed Margaret's confidence in the children's affection but not enough to risk Elizabeth visiting them. There could be hundreds of reasons for the present gap in contact, the most logical being the boys' military duties. She couldn't get directly in touch with them except by letter; to suddenly acquire a British mother might compromise their careers. Her heart lifted when the late post came.

Bhopal

Dearest Mama,

I am sorry to tell you that my father is no more. He was admitted to the All India Medical institute on the 6th of October with a stoke resulting in paralysis. On the 7th my son sent telegrams to the family to come to Delhi. On the 8th my father entered a state of coma and had no senses. By the 10th of October all reached Delhi and on the 11th at 15.30 he died.

I took his dead body to the Sacred River Ganges and cremated him as per Vedic rites on the 12th. From the 13th to the 24th daily procedural worship was performed and then I left for Bhopal as I am posted here.

I have been to church to pray for you. The time for regrets and anger is over. One day we will sit together in peace and love and you can bestow your blessings on your unworthy son.

Saurabh

It was forbidden to write letters or socialise during the days of mourning and ritual ceremonies. After that the bereaved could take up their lives again. Margaret was sorry for the unhappiness Ben's death had caused but he'd died peacefully with his children round him. His mother had died a frightening, lonely death from a heart attack while travelling on a train. Hiten too, murdered by acid flung in his face, with no children to avenge him or carry his name. This late settling of scores brought Margaret no satisfaction.

Had Ben ever been truly happy? Maybe in their early days together, they were both so different then, drunk on youth. She didn't regret falling in love with him, going to India, having the children. The regret was in the ending. The unnecessary cruelty . . . the sacrifice of the children — but it was finally over. Saurabh was right. The anger had gone, and with Ben's death everything was in the hands of the next generation.

* * * * *

The cemetery at Denaby was meticulously kept by the relatives of the dead. It was somewhere to stroll through, admire the flowers, read the gravestones or pass the time of day. Margaret kept her gloves on while she emptied the withered chrysanthemums from the vase on Tommy's grave. These nippy winter days stiffened her fingers but she took out the duster and scissors from her black cemetery bag, polished the headstone and trimmed the ragged grass growing over the base.

She talked to Tommy while she worked, telling him she'd been ready to come when James arrived and, that she almost hadn't when she read of Ben's death. The strain of being one person one minute and a half forgotten shadow the next was wearisome. A great burden was lifted. She was indisputably his wife: Mrs Waters: Elizabeth's mother.

There were few people alive who knew the truth, just her sister Jean and their brother John, Nan's daughter Sheila, Florrie and Matt. The rest were all dead. Florrie's eldest son was buried in the plot next to Tommy. At Christmas the grave would be covered with bouquets and holly wreaths. Tommy had been alive when Florrie married Matt. What a party! They had celebrated in the Miner's Welfare.

Over the years Florrie's children increased to seven, united by her generous heart. If Margaret achieved that for Elizabeth and the Indians her life would be complete. Reconciliation between Elizabeth and the boys had been easy. At first there was a little distancing between the girls but they became friends through their innumerable letters.

Elizabeth said that having Indian brothers and a sister enriched her life . . . enriched her life! It was time to get things out in the open. If Tommy were alive he'd say, "Don't be daft woman. Stop shilly shallying around and get on with it." He always said she thought too much, and after his first accident it was true, and more so after his death. Tommy considered himself a lucky man, but she was luckier to have been loved by him.

He wouldn't recognise Denaby now. One of the collieries had closed and the council had replaced the old pit terraces with modern semidetached houses, each with its own garden. However the latest miners' strike had set family against family, fragmenting the tight community. Margaret believed Thatcher's plan to smash the miners' union and close the pits would rebound on the country for years to come.

It began to rain, icy drops. The day was drawing in. Margaret put up a tartan umbrella and pulled the blue woollen shawl Pavia had sent over her heavy coat. Nothing would get through that. She left the cemetery, and Tommy.

* * * * *

Margaret wrote separately to Saurabh, Pavia and Rajeev. The invitation was short and to the point, a plea rather than a polite request, to come as soon as possible. Then she finished sorting the jumble of her hidden life. One suitcase was completely empty, back in the cupboard where it belonged. The other held the precious silk kimono. She took it out. It was soft and smooth in her sun-freckled hands, as beautiful as when she wore it decades ago. She held out a sleeve, twirling gracefully, forever young in Tommy's arms.

CHAPTER 44

* * * * *

There was something about snow that excited Margaret. It had started yesterday, a few flakes dusting the road and gardens. Last night the weather on the television forecasted further snow. Margaret said her bedtime prayers, asking God to keep it at bay until Saurabh, Pavia and Rajeev's plane had landed safely at Heathrow.

This morning she opened the bedroom curtains, pulling them back further than usual, and climbed back into bed. She could see the field at the bottom of the garden, and the wavy lines of black paw prints belonging to a dog that had strayed during the night.

So many things were going through her mind. The first time she heard Saurabh's voice on the telephone he sounded so like his father she couldn't speak, and then she didn't know what to say. She spent the phone call to Pavia crying. Rajeev sounded shy and there was a catch in his voice when he said, "I'm so happy that we found you."

Elizabeth had arranged the calls but Margaret couldn't express her feelings over the phone. In a way it made the distance harder to bear. She had nearly capitulated and caught the first flight out to India. She hadn't flown since James and Elizabeth paid for her to go to Lourdes with Nan and Jean, that was years ago, before she had to wear the surgical collar. A nine hour flight to Delhi would be too much, and out of the question while Ben was alive.

Margaret would rather James had dropped Saurabh, Pavia and Rajeev with her at Conisbrough, after he collected them from Heathrow. Elizabeth wouldn't hear of it. "Come to us, mum. We can look after you all. Take you round, go to York . . ."

Elizabeth always took visitors to York, and Edinburgh. Margaret expected this would be the same, London too. She wouldn't go to London. It was too big and she didn't like the underground. However, she could relax knowing her capable daughter would organise the domestic arrangements. Elizabeth had been experimenting making Indian vegetarian meals which, according to James, were delicious. In his opinion it was worth the Indians coming for the food.

She had sampled a curry but refused anything else. The spicy taste evoked the meals and power games that accompanied them at Aakesh, an India Margaret didn't want to remember. If a simple thing like this upset her how would she cope with the trauma of the visit? Perhaps it was a good idea to use Elizabeth and James's home.

Their comfortable house with six bedrooms would provide privacy and a quiet space for the initial welcome.

Margaret had written to Jean and their brother John in Scotland, to let them know what was happening. They would come to Conisbrough, if things went well. There would be two or three weeks to introduce Pavia, Rajeev and Saurabh to Florrie and Matt, friends and neighbours. She'd have a party. Matt would play the piano. She'd recite *'My Love is like a Red Red Rose.'* She hummed the tune. The high notes were out of reach, not like in the old days.

She'd better get up. In this bad weather Elizabeth wouldn't want to be delayed. Margaret put fresh sheets on the beds, put her suitcase and presents by the door, and left the storage heaters on low.

* * * * *

Elizabeth was late. Something must have cropped up at school. Margaret was annoyed: didn't her daughter realise how important today was? What if the plane was diverted or her children didn't come? What if she didn't measure up to their memories? What if she did? Margaret had hung on to the notion that they would know each other anywhere. Maybe it was all foolish. *She had left them.* They hadn't seen her weep, but she hadn't wiped their tears. She knew from their letters the damage she had done. Could they really forgive her?

Margaret put her coat and hat on. If the plane from Delhi was on schedule, it would have already have landed at Heathrow by the time Elizabeth got here. At last . . . !

"Thank goodness you're ready, mum. I want to get home before dark and in case James phones. I don't know how long it will take him to drive up from Heathrow. On a good day it takes anything from three and a half to five hours, depending on the traffic, but with this weather . . ." She packed the car and drove speedily to the motorway.

This section of the A1 north was clear but the trees and fields on either side of the carriageway were covered with snow, and the wind was getting up. Her mother was quiet. Elizabeth wondered if she was excited or apprehensive, probably both. It was always difficult to tell what she was thinking.

"Elizabeth . . . ! Slow down!"

"Sorry, I hadn't noticed." She slowed to a more sensible speed.

There was so much riding on this visit. Maybe she should have swapped cars with James. This one was made for rough weather. She'd come off the A1 at Junction 44. The gritters should be out on the road towards Bramham but if the weather carried on like this they'd have to use snow ploughs. She'd take it steady. The lane to their house would be the tricky bit.

The snow was falling heavily, drifting across the road in flurries like Margaret's memories. She tapped on the Range Rover window "Snow, snow, go away . . ." Would the presents she'd chosen with such care be suitable? Rajeev had a sweet tooth. She'd wrapped bars of nougat for him, the nearest thing she could find to the nutty treats she'd bought to send him from Kohat. She had given them to the servants before leaving for Bombay.

Security lights flashed on as they pulled into the drive. Elizabeth switched off the engine. "Stay in the car, mum . . . I'm going to get a shovel and clear a path to the door." Margaret watched her stamp a track to the stable block.

The garden dazzled silently, a peaceful English wonderland, outshining the showy mountain majesty of Kohat and Nainital. It was so long ago. Margaret had loved India and Ben but, like moths in the lamplight, they were destined to burn out. Was it really God's will or part of a primitive, spiritual universality that bound life together, a sort of cosmic dance? She thought of the statue of the dancing Shiva. Margaret wouldn't let superstition rule her but if the separation from Ben hadn't taken place, then Elizabeth couldn't have existed. And without Elizabeth where would she be?

Irrepressible Elizabeth, hair corkscrewed with snow, pushed an enormous snow-shovel towards the four by four. Margaret prayed that when they met the children would like each other. It would be the end of her if they didn't. She couldn't give any of them up. She wound down the window. The cold air brought her to her senses. They'd all been writing for ages. It couldn't happen?

Elizabeth panted, "I'm going to let Rory out." She grunted and shovelled, every now and then turning and grinning at her mother until a rudimentary path led to the front door. The dog was released. It raced round the garden, leaping higher and higher, twisting and snapping at snowflakes, rolling madly on the white blanketed lawn. Elizabeth tried to coax the crazy animal indoors but it made a game of it, coming close, and then dodging out of reach. She grabbed its collar as it tried to sneak in through the open door and was dragged into the hall calling, "Won't be a minute . . ."

Margaret wound up the window to shut out the cold. Elizabeth's eyes were sparkling when she returned. Margaret could hear the dog howling as soon as she got out of the car.

"What a noise!"

"Just concentrate on where you're walking, mum. I don't want you to fall. I've shut Rory in the drying room."

"You're not going to leave the poor animal shut in there?"

"No, just while I get you in safely. He'll quieten down in a minute."

Elizabeth lit the log fire, checked the answering machine — there were no messages and switched on the lights decorating a pine tree by the french windows. The crystal star at the top skimmed the high ceiling.

But it was a tiny Christmas tree taking centre stage on the Georgian mantelpiece that drew Margaret's attention. No more than eighteen inches high, glass baubles drooped down from its spindly faded branches. She smiled with recognition, "I remember buying this with your father for your first Christmas . . . but Elizabeth, we've had Christmas."

"Mum, I'm not going batty . . . that was when the Indians were *supposed* to be coming, but Rajeev couldn't get leave. It's a good job we hadn't told you. We'd bought all the presents so we decided to have a surprise Christmas when they arrived, even though it's February. The snow is a bonus."

"It's a daft idea Elizabeth, but I love it."

Elizabeth ferried Margaret's luggage and the rest of the presents from the car. Then she hung her coat in the drying room and let the dog out.

"Down Rory, down" Margaret said, tapping him on the nose to stop him nibbling at a parcel.

"Everybody's got their own spot, mum. Be sure to put them in the right place."

"I wish I could put this dog in his rightful place."

"I know. It's hopeless. One word and Rory does as he likes . . . I don't have many failures but he's one big one. Aren't you, fella?" The dog barked.

"Don't set it off, Elizabeth. What about the neighbours?"

"We haven't got any near enough to bother."

Margaret turned over the neatly-written tags on the three piles of gifts under the enormous tree. "There should be a parcel in the gold wrapping paper . . . with your name on?"

Elizabeth said she hadn't been sure what to do with it and brought it in from the hall table.

"It's something special that your father gave me from China. I wanted to remind you of how much we loved each other, before and after his accident. *No one could take his place.* Open it now before the others come."

Elizabeth beavered at the sellotape but the parcel was so soft it changed shape under her hands. "It's got to be the kimono! I haven't seen it since the day I asked you about the bracelet and the Atrey name . . ."

"You were nine or ten . . ."

Elizabeth tore open the paper. The silk kimono blossomed out like an exotic flower. "It's even more beautiful than I remember." She rubbed the fabric against her face then slipped her arms in the sleeves.

"Oh Elizabeth, it fits you perfectly. You could almost be me."

"I'll treasure it forever. You know I will . . ." The phone rang. Elizabeth went to answer it. Margaret held her breath.

"Everything's fine" Elizabeth reported. "They're about an hour away, the snow ploughs are out . . . I'd better put the food on but first I'll go upstairs and take this off." She gave a final twirl in front of her mother. "I'm so happy. I can't wait . . ."

Margaret sat in her favourite armchair. The dog licked her hand and curled up by her feet. It would be the longest hour of her life.

* * * * *

Elizabeth woke her. "I thought I'd let you sleep. Pavia, Saurabh and Rajeev are here. The car's on the drive."

Margaret nimbly avoided the dog in a joyful race for the door.

"Mum you're not going out? It's freezing . . . At least get your coat!" But Margaret didn't stop.

They were there under the light. Saurabh, in his dark overcoat, hat and scarf, was the image of his handsome father in the winter of Nainital. Rajeev, tall and straight, hatless, his mop of dark hair tamed in manhood, a blue woollen scarf wound round his neck. And her beloved

Pavia, a beautiful woman, her magnificent plait tucked inside a heavy camel coat, crying out "Mama . . . Mama . . ." while Rajeev steadied her on the icy path.

Saurabh was the first to touch Margaret's feet. "My son . . . Oh my son . . ." She wept, blessing him. He rose to stand at her side. Margaret drew strength from his presence. Her love blazed out at him and his smile healed her broken heart.

Rajeev came next. Margaret rested her hands on his head, "Can you forgive me?" she asked this once sickly boy whose dark eyes and likely death had haunted her.

He stood up and took her in his arms, bending to bury his head in her shoulder as he'd done as a boy.

Pavia was the last to pay homage, laughing and crying; tears streamed down her cheeks. The boys tenderly raised her up.

Saurabh tried to speak for all of them, "We three are here, and Elizabeth . . . Continents may separate us, but Mama your loving children will be united in their hearts for ever."

Together for ever, after so many broken dreams Margaret didn't feel the cold.